For the Folkes and De Lisser Families.
Family First.

We etched out our own path. We did it without manipulation. We've proven that what we have is not infatuation. We equal two squared like math.

Our thing holds vital STATS. And even though they dropped us in a chaotic maze like rats— we solved the puzzle. Thought there was no coming back but we did so determined, wiser... more experienced. We recognized the difference. We've survived.

So keep your box while we reshape a reality that fits our program. Instead of trying to catch up we're already there refusing to be boxed. Who said what we share couldn't withstand the test of time? This thing we own it, it's ours. Keep your box society while we reshape reality that fits our program. No need to play catch- up because...poof, we're gone—surpassed you. Box that!

TERI WOODS

Rectangle of Sins

BY NURIT FOLKES

For information on how individual consumers can place orders, please write to Teri Woods Publishing, P.O. Box 20069, New York, NY 10001-0005.

For orders other than individual consumers, Teri Woods Publishing grants a discount on the purchase of 10 or more copies of a single title order for special markets or premium use.

For orders purchased through the P.O. Box, Teri Woods Publishing offers a 25% discount off the sale price for orders shipped to prisons including but not limited to federal, state and county.

TERI WOODS

Rectangle of Sins

BY NURIT FOLKES

Teri Woods Presents, Rectangle of Sins

This novel is a work of fiction. Any resemblance to real people, living or dead, actual events, establishments, organizations, and/or locales are intended to give the fiction a sense of reality and authenticity. Other names, characters, places and incidents are either products of the author's imagination or are used fictitiously, as are those fictionalized events & incidents that involve real persons and did not occur or are set in the future.

Published by:
TERI WOODS PUBLISHING
P.O. Box 20069
New York, NY 10001-0005
www.teriwoodspublishing.com

Library of Congress Catalog Card No: 2005908136
ISBN: 0-9672249-9-3
Copyright: To Be Supplied

Rectangle of Sins Credits
Story by Nurit Folkes
Written by Nurit Folkes
Edited by Teri Woods
Text formation by Teri Woods
Cover concept by Teri Woods and Lucas Riggins

Printed by Teri Woods Publishing

Printed in the USA.

Chapter One

"**O**h, hell no! You being here will only make her condition worse," Andre screamed.

Mark's eyes glossed over with a coat of hurt and his usually masculine voice weakened as he replied, "Junior was my baby too...I really need to see her. Maybe my apology will help her."

"She watched her baby die and now she's catatonic and locked up in here all because of you! Get the fuck out!" Mark had no choice but to leave. He knew that although Andre was flamboyantly gay he was still a man. Mark languidly walked out of the hospital room into the hallway. He looked down the hall at orderlies and nurses scrambling. *How did it come to this?*

Natalia wasn't responding to external stimuli and her pulse weakened frequently. The doctors told him that it was as if Natalia were sabotaging her own recovery. Her body had become frail and emaciated. Her eyes did an occasional jump or roll then returned to its glazed state and she had been that way for weeks.

Mark knew that he was lucky to be alive let alone sane. The wound he ended up with from that fateful day with the intruder in his Cobble Hill brownstone wasn't serious. The knife didn't sever or damage any major organs or blood vessels. He looked down at his torso and sighed. He thought about his ex-wife, Natalia and how he had caused the death of their child. Both his children died in one year. The baby that he had wanted so badly with Natalia was gone all because of revenge. The baby he'd had with her best friend, Tracy died months after Tracy was murdered. It was almost as if he were forsaken by God because of the lies, cheating—the sinning. *How will I live with it all?* The thought hit a nerve and he sniffled, trying to hold back tears. He wiped his face with his handkerchief and stuck it back into his jacket pocket, folded his arms and waited for the elevator. The doors opened and a man, woman and toddler got off. The man's arm was around the woman's neck and the little girl held on to the mother's hand tightly. They looked picture perfect. A range of emotions engulfed him. Mark couldn't do it. He couldn't leave. He knew now that to get Natalia back from oblivion and into the real world again he'd have to aggravate the hell out of her and force her to fight her way back. He rushed back to her room. Andre was whimpering with his head on her stomach. Mark tried not to make any noise when he slipped into the room. Natalia's eyes were still vacant and lifeless and Andre's whimpering reminded him of a wounded dog. Mark inched closer to the bed and stopped right behind Andre.

"Nat, you better come back here and get your revenge. You need to face me. What's wrong with you, huh? Aren't you strong enough? Don't you want to tell me what a dick head I am?"

Mark's voice was steadying, loud and taunting all at the same time. Andre was shocked speechless. He slowly turned around, shaking and pointing his finger disapprovingly at Mark. Mark ignored Andre and continued.

"I said get up woman! It's just like you to be stubborn. You're so selfish. You just check out when it's convenient for you. What about everybody else? I need help with this too. You're not the only one who lost Junior. WAKE UP BITCH!!!"

Andre regained his senses, sprang to his feet and grabbed Mark's shirt and began forcing Mark out of the room.

"Calm down, I'm doing this to help her. It's the only way she'll wake up. Trust me," Mark said, fixing his crumpled shirt.

"You ignorant bastard! I don't give a fuck what you think you're doing. All I know is I don't want you around her. Now get out!" Andre forcefully pushed Mark one last time for

2

the road. Mark reluctantly conceded but half way down the hall he heard Andre scream like a banshee. He ran back down the hall and into the room. Andre's body was draped over Natalia. When Mark got closer he could see Natalia's eyes struggle to adjust to the brightly lit room. She was back. *It actually worked!* Mark breathed a sigh of relief. "I knew you'd be alright."

But, Natalia wasn't. Not only was she traumatized by seeing the death of her child but she also witnessed the man she loved being gunned down by the police. She was overwrought with guilt. She believed that she had caused all this death. It was her curse. Everyone she loved dropped like flies. Even though she was alive she looked dead. Her eyes were sunken in, her lips pale and dry. Her cheekbones stuck out as if she were sucking on a lollipop. Her skin's healthy glow was replaced with dour dullness. She looked up and saw the tears sliding down Mark's cheeks. She attempted to speak but her throat hurt too much.

"I know you want me to go. I'm just glad that you're back. I know you don't believe me but I am. I'm very glad," Mark said, wiping away streaks of tear water from his cheek.

She lifted her frail hand slowly, waved her bony forefinger and pointed to the pitcher on the table. Andre poured out some of the shaved ice chips into the matching mustard yellow cup. He tilted the cup to her lips as she slurped some of the slush, cleared her throat and whispered. "Stay."

Andre looked at Mark then at her. Mark smiled hesitantly. "Thank you," he said, unsure that his response befitted the situation. She smiled at Andre and spoke a tad louder than a whisper. "You look so handsome as usual. I missed you." Andre fought back the urge to blubber and kissed her hand.

"I missed you too. Please don't do this to me anymore."

She caressed his cheek. "I won't." She looked at Mark and in an emotionally strained voice said, "I'm sorry."

"Why are you sorry?"

"F...for... Junior," she couldn't finish as she began crying. Mark wanted to hold her but he wasn't sure if it was his place. Andre gently squeezed her hand in his arms.

"No, it wasn't your fault. Please don't think that." Mark began crying also. Andre realized they both needed consoling and motioned for Mark to come over. Mark hesitantly sat at her side. One look at her sad, wet face and all the old feelings came rushing back. *How could I have hurt her like this?* He hugged her as she slid her hand up his arm and squeezed with what little strength she had. They cried loud, hard and long as Andre watched in amazement. It was ironic how thin the line between love and hate could be. Even more amazing was that death could revive life. A smile crept onto Andre's face as he remembered why he used to prod Natalia to marry Mark. He wasn't such a bad man after all.

"I'm going to get a doctor. I'll be right back," Andre said and left the room. Natalia and Mark awkwardly smiled at each other. Their tear ducts were empty now.

"I-I'm sorry I did this to you. Please forgive me. I never meant for any of this to happen. I'm so sorry Nat."

"I'm sorry too. Oh God...he's gone. I can't believe he's gone."

"I know..." he squeezed her tighter.

Mark had seen to it that Junior's funeral was postponed until Natalia was well enough to attend. He paid a swanky funeral home thousands of dollars just to maintain Junior's corpse, keeping it in the best condition possible the entire time.

The funeral home wasn't gloomy or cast in dim light. In fact it was brightly decorated in a colorful circus theme. There were blue, green, red and yellow elephants, monkeys, lions and bears everywhere. Natalia had specifically ordered happy colors. She wanted it to be like a party. Her baby was gone but he was going to heaven and that was something to celebrate. She pictured Junior sitting on an angel's lap getting his wings and halo. He was smiling his little shiny, gummy, smile. Everyone was instructed to wear white. No black for her baby's funeral. There were bouquets with balloon animals and fuzzy teddy bears. Natalia requested a closed casket service because she couldn't bear to look at Junior's lifeless pale little body. She was sure that she would've lost all of her composure. The pallbearers were all color coordinated with cerulean ties that added a splash of color to their white suits. Walking down to the pulpit she admired all the variations of white outfits in each pew and it gave her the feeling that she had anticipated. The feeling that she had entered the pearly gates and was on her way to junior's heavenly nursery. She knew it was Hollywood's rendition of heaven but it was all she knew so it suited her just fine. She needed to believe that it was okay that Junior was gone. She needed to accept her loss. She knew she had to move forward.

Andre winked at her and unbuttoned his suit jacket as he took a seat next to her attorney, Susan who wore a cream pants suit. Natalia's assistant Renee strolled down the aisle to join them at the pew. Renee's snow white wrap dress flattered her tall lean figure. Mark's sister and her sons showed up in beige and white. His brother flew in from Austria with his wife and four children. Most of the pews were filled with Mark's family, colleagues and their families. Mark looked especially handsome in an off white cashmere blazer and slacks with a white knit tunic underneath. Natalia's eyes were glued to him as he approached the podium. He looked good. Even though they were on speaking terms, even on their way to becoming friends— there was no reconciliation, no love rekindled. Natalia still longed for Shawn. No matter how much Mark insisted that Shawn was the one who stabbed him, she wouldn't co-sign his claim. There wasn't enough proof in her book and thankfully so since she was in on the whole kidnapping ploy. All Mark had were his suspicions since he admitted he didn't see the intruder's face. Natalia knew Mark was still filled with hatred and jealousy for Shawn and she couldn't allow him to sully Shawn's already tarnished record regardless of his death.

She completely dismissed Mark when he informed her about the accomplice that confessed to helping Shawn kidnap Junior from his brownstone in Cobble Hill. The old woman was tracked down by the police after one of Mark's neighbors seen suspicious black people running into Mark's yard. They gave the police the old woman's license plate. An officer who desperately wanted to join the FBI knew Shawn's older brother's wanted status and thought that he'd definitely get in with this newfound information. So he squealed to the Bureau and the FBI swooped in once they found out Shawn was involved and quickly acted on the information that the older woman reluctantly gave the police. They called the airport security and headed Shawn and Natalia off at the airport. But what the FBI didn't count on was the old woman's death. With all the commotion and the threat of prison and fear of Shawn's revenge, she had a heart attack right after her confession, which the local precinct failed to record on tape. So, Shawn refuted the old woman's confession, citing senility.

The pastor whispered to Natalia as she neared the pulpit. The pastor smiled at her and placed his hand on her shoulder.

"I think this service is the sweetest one yet. It's nice to have someone who truly respects the journey to God's kingdom. I believe God would agree with you that it is to be celebrated," he said and patted her shoulder. "Which one of you will give the eulogy?" he asked as Mark joined them at the pulpit.

Mark looked at Natalia. "Well I think you should, Nat."

"Mark, don't you think we should both be able to have our say. Is that okay, Pastor?"

"Yes dear, it's perfectly fine. Now who will go first?"

"Mark, you go first." Natalia took his hand, squeezed gently and smiled at him.

"Thank you." He looked at her lovingly. For him just being able to stand that close to her and hold a conversation with her without feeling as though she wanted to slit his throat was more than enough for him. He was still in love. He knew he'd be kidding himself to think that their child's death would reunite them romantically but he couldn't help but hope that somewhere down the line it would. He stepped up onto the stage and went behind the podium and leaned close to the microphone.

"My wife...uh, pardon me, uh, Natalia and I would like to thank you for coming and we appreciate your support throughout this time of sorrow." He looked down at the casket, took a deep breath and while holding back tears, he continued. "My son, Junior, was the most beautiful little boy I've ever seen. His smile made me smile and he touched my heart. Although his stay on earth was a short one, I'm grateful to have had the time with him that I did. I'm grateful to Natalia for giving birth to such a wondrous miracle." He wiped his eyes with the back of his hand and looked into Natalia's saddened eyes. Her eyes were glossy but she maintained her composure. He looked at the casket again.

"Junior, my son...you will always be in my heart. I know that you are in heaven and you're okay now. We all love you and send prayers. My beautiful little boy...I'll always love you." He sniffled and rubbed his forefinger under his nose quickly and stepped down from the pulpit. His sister mumbled some words in Italian and began whimpering loudly. Andre turned around and handed her a tissue. She practically snatched it and started blubbering even louder.

"Oh, shut the hell up, bitch," Andre mumbled under his breath. Renee covered her mouth to stifle what she knew was an inappropriate giggle.

Mark and Natalia embraced briefly before she took her place behind the podium. "I'm usually good at this...I mean it's my job," she said nervously. "But... under the circumstances I can't even think straight let alone put two sentences together." She began wringing her hands together, her eyes went from the casket to Mark before relenting to the top of the podium. "Junior was my angel. He was so perfect. I don't pretend to understand this. But I know that God works in mysterious ways. He doesn't set out to hurt his children so I know that Junior is safe and now he'll be an angel watching over all of us. He'll never, ever be forgotten. He is part of me and I will carry that part with me forever and..."

Her jaw dropped. Her eyes grew big and she looked as if she had seen a ghost. Mark watched her, confused along with everyone else. Mark followed her gaze straight to the source of her astonishment. There stood Shawn in a snazzy ecru colored suit that complemented his creamy beige skin. His almond shaped eyes twinkled under the church track lighting then slanted even more as his mouth formed a sly grin. Mark jumped up and stormed over to him.

"You're like the fucking energizer bunny!" he growled under his breath.

"I didn't come to start trouble. I just need to speak to Natalia," Shawn said ignoring Mark as he limped right past him straight toward the pulpit. "Nay-nay."

"Oh, Shawn," she gushed. She reached out her hand and he grabbed it as she stepped down. "H-how?" she asked in amazement.

"You should know they can't keep this man down." He smiled sheepishly. "It's a long story but we can talk about it later. Look, I'm sorry to interrupt...I'm so sorry for all of this... Just tell me you don't hate me."

"I could never hate you." She squeezed his hand in hers.

Mark had just about enough of all the mushiness. "Excuse me this is a funeral. Nat, this is very inappropriate not to mention disrespectful."

"I-I'm sorry Mark, you're right. Come on Shawn." She led Shawn to the row of seats where Renee, Susan and Andre sat. Andre grinned at Shawn.

"You've got more lives than a cat. But I'm glad to see that you're okay." Andre winked knowingly. He was the one who found out that Shawn was very much alive and well. He told Shawn of the service and even what to wear.

"Thanks, man...for everything," Shawn said respectfully and sincerely.

After the crystallized baby blue casket descended into the ground, all the stuffed animals and flowers were thrown in along with it.

"Let's bow our heads in silent prayer," said the pastor.

The sun was blazing and it bothered Natalia even with her eyes closed. She reached into her purse and pulled out a pair of shades. She knew that her son was definitely being inducted into heaven by God himself. That was her explanation for the clear blue sky, the sun shining brightly and the comfortable refreshing breeze accompanying the sixty-four degree weather.

Mark occasionally opened his eyes just to be nosey and watch Shawn's every move. With Shawn back in the picture he was sure that he didn't stand a chance in hell with his ex-wife. As the pastor preached, Shawn whispered one of his own. "I love you Junior. I miss you my little quarterback. I know God is taking good care of you. I promise I'll take good care of your mom. I ask you to watch over her too."

"And we ask for all of this O' Lord in Jesus' name," said the pastor finishing his prayer.

"Amen," everyone said in unison.

"Look." Shawn pointed to a unique colorful bird on Junior's casket. It pecked at the flowers and flew away.

"See that was a message sent by Junior that everything is gonna be okay...my wife." He smiled and continued, "You didn't forget the vows we both said at the Justice of the Peace did you?" He slipped his arm around Natalia's waist pulling her closer.

"But, of course not, that day is forever etched in my

memory, my husband." She smiled sweetly at him, rested the side of her face on his arm and sighed. A lone tear formed and slid down her cheek as the happy memory of her nuptials with Shawn was eclipsed by that of Junior's demise.

"It's alright baby girl, Junior will always be with us. That's why he sent that beautiful bird to put you at ease. We'll get through this my wife."

Shawn gently squeezed her while kissing her temple. Shawn purposefully said wife knowing that Mark was eavesdropping the entire time. He wanted to rub it in Mark's face. Mark scoffed at Shawn's words and the thought of his ex-wife actually marrying an ex-drug dealer and murderer, not to mention the man that he believed caused his son's death. But, Natalia beamed. Her unconditional love for Shawn clouded her rationale. She snuggled up closer to Shawn and a slight smile formed on her face. *Yes, Junior everything will be alright.*

CHAPTER TWO

All of Natalia's assets, including her businesses, except for the McDonald's that she signed over to Andre had been seized by the FBI. They were in the process of auditing her to make sure that she hadn't laundered money for Shawn or his fugitive brother, Tymeek. Her house in Manorville was sold along with the condominiums that she had owned in Brooklyn. Even though she had a wrongful death lawsuit against New York City for Junior, she knew that the case would drag on for years before she saw a penny of the seventy-nine million dollars her attorneys sued for. All she had left was her clothes, shoes, jewelry and seven thousand dollars in cash that she stashed in Andre's safe in his co-op as emergency cash.

Natalia's financial problems were beginning to change her as a person. She moped around Shawn's condo leaving trails of potato chips. She desperately wanted to re-gain the rest of the weight she lost because Shawn kept saying that she looked like a crack head. Even though he was joking, she took the comment to heart. She'd barely leave the house and she watched TV all day long. Andre constantly called her to invite her out, but she would decline every time. It was as if her not being rich anymore had brought about the end of the world as she knew it.

Shawn managed to keep his condo since it was in his cousin, Gerald's name. Luckily for him, Gerald was an entrepreneur with a real estate agency so he was able to open up another Bubblin' Brite Laundromat using his name. Shawn's money wasn't as long as it use to be, but he was on the come up. He was doing a lot better than he expected for a guy out of the game. The only thing that bothered him was the fact that Tymeek was living like a king in Amsterdam. That instigated Shawn's mission to get enough money to move to Amsterdam and buy his own kingdom.

Shawn was grateful to have his life and freedom. He took solace knowing that he wasn't on the run like Tymeek. Once again, he escaped death and imprisonment. He knew that he was one lucky son of a bitch. Natalia nagged him repeatedly for the story of how he managed to survive and remain free. He told her that when he hit the floor at the airport he knew that he was dying. He told her that he felt cold and tired, yet he was still conscious for a few minutes before he blacked out. The next thing he remembered was waking up in a hospital handcuffed to a gurney.

But the Feds seemed more interested in Tymeek than Natalia and Junior's kidnapping. They pumped Shawn for information on Tymeek's whereabouts and his suppliers. Shawn pretended not to know anything. But then the Feds threatened him with life imprisonment. Shawn wasn't sure if that charge was plausible but he damn sure didn't want to find out. Thankfully, he still had one trick up his sleeve. He remembered a widely feared dealer named Monstar who used to be his brother's enemy back from his early hustling days. Monstar was wanted for the death of two FBI agents and had a twenty-five million dollar bounty on his head. As luck would have it, Shawn knew the location of Monstar's hideaway. One of his workers had a baby with Monstar's daughter. The worker had told Shawn how he had to take his baby's mama to the airport because she was headed to San Pedro Town in Belize to bring Monstar the rest of his hidden fortune. Shawn knew this information could earn him his freedom and maybe the twenty-five million dollar reward. So he snitched for the first time in his life. The Feds granted him his freedom, but refused him the bounty of course. Shawn didn't care about the money, he was more than happy to accept immunity. After three and a half weeks in the hospital, the doctors gave him a clean bill of health, even though he was shot four times. Fortunately, three of the bullets exited his body and left his major organs in tact. But one bullet was still lodged in his torso right above his pelvic bone. He could walk and function normally and that was all that mattered to him.

Shawn came home to find cracked potato chip pieces scattered on the floor in the living room. After following the trail with a piece of tissue in his hand scooping them up as he went along, he stopped at Natalia's feet. She looked up at him. The light in her eyes that he was used to returned. She seemed to come alive.

"Hi daddy."

She licked her fingers and dropped the bag of potato chips on the couch. She braced herself with her hands on the couch and sat up straight. Shawn looked down at the greasy spot her fingers made in the leather and then at her.

"Aiight now, I don't know how you can look this damn good, but be so damn nasty."

She looked at him innocently and snatched up the bag of chips. "I'll clean up. I'm sorry daddy, I'm just not used to menial labor." She batted her eyelashes, looking up at him innocently.

"Yeah, whatever just clean up after yourself."

"Well, you should have a maid."

"And you should give me the money to get one. I don't need a maid. I've got you."

"Whatever." She brushed past him and went into the kitchen. Shawn followed her and smacked her on the ass with a folded newspaper.

"I bought you this paper so you can find your ass a job."

"Oh please, first of all who'd want to have anything to do with me since the whole FBI fiasco? Secondly, I'm not working in some useless position because I'm boss material," she sighed.

He shook his head, "So if we ass out tomorrow you wouldn't be gully enough to help a brother out by getting a job?"

"I'm not work material." She threw the chips in the garbage. Shawn sucked his teeth and walked out of the kitchen.

Lately, she wasn't the same woman he fell in love with. He tried to chalk it up to her many losses but then he started to believe that she was defined by her wealth. Without it, she appeared less personable. He often left her in the house alone during the week while he managed his laundromats but on the weekends he tried to spend quality time with her. But, this weekend he had plans and she would have to fend for herself.

He pulled up in front of a white house, beeped his horn and within minutes a shapely young woman stepped out. Shawn looked at her and smiled to himself.

"Wassup?" she said as she shifted all the junk in her trunk into his passenger seat.

"You, that's wassup," he chuckled.

She grinned and reached up and pulled down the mirror and fixed her bang. "So where are we going?"

"Out," he said, as he pulled off.

"Oh, now you can't talk? You had a lot to say the other night," she giggled.

"Just shut up and look pretty." She was gorgeous, yet young. So young, that listening to her inexperienced banter annoyed the hell out of him at times. But, Natalia wasn't herself and she also had him on a sex diet because she felt self-conscious about her weight loss. For some strange reason getting head from young girls was his new past time. Seventeen had become his magical number. It was an still young enough to be easily manipulated, yet old enough not to bring charges.

"Shawn, I'm tired of you just taking me to the motel. I wanna go out somewhere nice. Shit, you owe me."

"Tammy, shut the fuck up aiight."

Shawn shot her another icy glare. She sucked her

14

teeth and folded her arms. Despite her whining they still ended up at the motel and she hit him off with her usual head game and he fed her Chinese food from the corner take out spot. He knew if Natalia didn't up some sex soon he would have no choice but to go all the way.

When he got in the house he could hear Natalia sobbing. *Here we go again,* he thought. It seemed that all she did was cry and eat. He understood in the beginning about her loss. Hell, he missed Junior too even though he wasn't his biological father. But, now time had passed and he felt that she really needed to get over it and buck up! He walked over to her and sat down next to her.

"What's wrong with you now?"

"I have nothing."

"What are you talking about?"

"They've ordered the McDonald's I signed over to Andy to be shut down while they audit the books. Now, I have no income. I'm broke!"

Shawn thought about it for a moment and realized that it was inevitable. She should have seen it coming. Besides, he was basically taking care of her now anyway so nothing was going to change. "Look, you know you gonna get all your shit back. The FEDS are just fucking with your money to piss you off that's all. They have to give it back when they realize that your money is clean. Don't worry about it I'm going to take care of you. But just for your own sake you should get into something else, you know like giving speeches again or something like that."

She looked at him as if she smelled a foul odor.

"What?" he asked hoping she was willing to do something for herself.

"You know damn well nobody wants me after everything that has happened. I've practically been blacklisted. Didn't you hear what I said? I'm broke! I've never had to deal with being...poor."

"BG you're not poor. You got me and I'm not poor. What's mine is yours...until death do us part, remember?"

She looked at him again, this time with a smile in her eyes. She didn't particularly care for her newly abbreviated nickname which stood for baby girl but she loved that he was still there for her as always. No wonder she loved him. He smiled his irresistible smile and grabbed her. She wrapped her arms around him and they passionately kissed with open mouths and eager tongues. Having been deprived of actual intercourse, Shawn didn't waste any time getting her naked.

He plunged into her tightness with such force that she screamed in delicious pain. He started out with slow, drawn out strokes. But, after a short while his pace quickened and he rammed into her until he couldn't hold back any longer and exploded inside her.

"No, daddy not yet," Natalia whimpered.

"Sorry baby girl...but it's been too long and it was so good." Shawn exhaled and rolled off of her.

"Two minute motherfucker," Natalia giggled.

"I'ma make you eat those words. Give me ten minutes," he grinned.

She made it a point to put her expensive NYU sociological degree to good use. She became a supervisor for a privately owned center for the mentally challenged. It was owned by a philanthropist but run like a prison. She hated how structured it was. She was so used to being her own boss that punching a time clock and reporting to higher-ups was pissing her off. Although it was sad to see people whose lives had gone awry, she managed to bring a little sunshine in their life with special programs she specifically named 'Sunshine Steps' which she headed up herself. Most of the patients loved her and called her mommy angel because of her long crisp white overcoat. In the upper right corner, right above her heart she wore a pin of a baby angel boy, which was her keepsake for Junior.

The sudsy water and papers scattered all over the

floor were a telltale sign that Mr. Davis was up to his usual menacing antics. He was swinging a mop around in the air and babbling. She got as close as she could without him being able to gorge out her eyes with the mop handle.

"Okay now Super Dave, I think you've saved the day already. It's time to put that villain in jail. I've already called the police."

Mr. Davis thought he was a super hero and he was constantly trying to save inanimate objects from peril. Just three days ago it was the vacuum cleaner. After hearing Natalia's voice he slowly lowered the mop. He carefully smoothed out the strands of cotton from the mop's head.

"You'll be okay now, madam. The authorities will be here to dispose of that incorrigible villainous vermin."

Natalia took the mop from him and he patted her on the shoulder. "We work well together winged angel."

She walked with him down the hall to his room. Everyone was amazed at the way she could get the most challenging patients in the center to behave without panicking or breaking a sweat.

"Give him a sedative, Lucy. He'll be alright. Oh, and please turn his television to the TV land channel, he loves it."

"Okay, but if he tries to save me again, I'm going to hurt him," Lucy chuckled.

Natalia laughed and took the mop down the hall to the porter's closet. One of the office assistants ran up to her.

"Mrs. Wilson the man from the computer company is here to set up the new system for the center. But he has a problem with the contract, something about the numbers being incorrect."

"Alright, calm down. You act like the sky is falling." She followed her to the front desk where she saw a blast from her past. "Wow!" she exclaimed.

"Double wow," Seth said with a smile. It was Seth Williamson. Natalia remembered the day they met. She was in a delicatessen in Brooklyn near her condominium and was on line for the cashier. A tan colored man with a clean-shaven head stepped in line behind her. His cologne overpowered her dainty perfume. He inched closer to her. The sweet smell of her freshly shampooed hair tangoed with his nose. "You smell delicious!" He exclaimed.

"Thanks," she said dryly without turning around. Her soft voice made him want to see her face but all he could see was the back of her head. After she paid the cashier, she sauntered out of the deli with an air of grace and he finally caught a glimpse of her profile. He hurried outside to catch up to her.

"You're a very beautiful woman. What's your name, sexy?" He sounded cocky to her so she was all set to dismiss him. She stopped her stride and turned to look at him. Surprisingly he was attractive. She couldn't help but stare. His bald head was smooth and round. There were no bumps or lopsided lumps. His goatee was neatly groomed, his skin impeccable and devoid of a single razor bump. *He must be a yuppie*, she thought to herself. Her assumption was based on the beige, Brooks Brothers suit adorning his athletic frame. He looked so sharp in his suit that it was hard for her to remember what she was supposed to be doing.

"Come on tell me your name."

"Nuh-tal-yah," she pronounced slowly. He smiled and took her hand gently shaking it.

"I'm Seth. It's nice to meet you Natalia."

"Hi." She smiled meekly.

"Do you live around here?" He asked, still holding her hand. He appeared to be caressing it, making her uncomfortable. She gently pulled it from him.

"I'm briefly staying here."

"I live over there," he pointed to a huge co-op building across from the delicatessen.

"Oh, that's nice," she said.

He smiled at her, showing his sparkling white, straight teeth. "Can I walk you to your destination?" He licked his lips after the question. It didn't seem intentional

18

yet it was seductive. For a moment she wondered what he was like behind closed doors.

"No thanks. I'm fine. But it was nice meeting you." He didn't let her brush him off. He followed her as she walked.

"Can you stop walking for a minute? I want to give you something." He stopped and opened his briefcase. He pulled out a gold plated card dispenser. He handed her a gold and black card. "I don't want to seem pushy, but I just wanted to make sure that I gave it my best shot. So, please take this and call me...don't shatter my ego." He insisted with a sexy smile. She gracefully thanked him and nearly tripped as she began walking off. Embarrassed, she turned to see if he caught her clumsiness but he was already across the street.

"Thank God," she said to herself and glanced down at the card. It read: S.W. *Compuanalys Inc. Universal Computer Specialists, Seth Williamson, Owner/President.* The title was impressive. His polished good looks didn't hurt either. She ran into him three weeks later in the neighborhood and they jogged together at the promenade she even called him once. She remembered thinking back then that if she weren't juggling two men already, he would've gotten more than the phone call.

"What are you doing here?" she asked ignorant to the fact that he owned a computer company.

"The question is what are you doing here?"

"Well I work here."

"Work here?"

"Well it's a long story and we don't have that kind of time right now."

"Who says?"

"I say. Read my tag. It says administrator, that means I'm the boss... well sort of," she sighed.

"So you're doing community service here?"

"What?"

"I saw the whole ordeal in the papers. I know about you and the drug dealer and the...um...the death of your baby. I'm so sorry about that. Please accept my condolences."

"Thank you, Seth."

"Wow, I'm honored that you remembered my name."

Natalia flashed a troubled smile. She wasn't comfortable with the fact that her life was now an open book. Oddly enough she managed to forget how the news reporters hounded her and followed her around for months, in and out of court. She had become their fixation. Now, she wished that she was invisible. She wondered what Seth thought of her.

"Seth, I'm not performing community service. I haven't committed any crimes. I took on this position because they need me." She spoke indignantly. Seth was too busy checking her out to notice her agitation. *Apparently everything she's been through hasn't taken a complete toll on her. Hmmm, she's lost a bit of weight but she still looks good.* To him, she was still beautiful and still a class act. She grew nervous under his gaze.

"So what's this about a problem with the contract? Should I retrieve our copy?"

"Uh, yes please," Seth answered, barely snapping out of the trance she had put him in. She asked the desk clerk to get the contract and escorted him back to her office. "Have a seat."

"Thank you." Seth sat down then continued, "Look, Natalia I want you to know that I really understand your loss because... well you remember what I told you about my child right?"

"Yes I do," she said remembering the story Seth had told her of how he moved to New York from Minnesota seven years ago because his ex-girlfriend was pregnant. He asked her to marry him. But she had an abortion and pretended to still be pregnant. She didn't plan on telling him about the abortion. She planned to fake a miscarriage weeks after they got married. She knew Seth didn't love her enough to marry her but she also knew that he would do it just to be a part of his child's life. He explained to Natalia how badly he wanted children but the women he would get involved with usually didn't want children so soon. She could see that it still pained him.

"I'm really sorry about what that girl did to you."

Just then the clerk came in and dropped off a folder. Natalia pulled out the contract.

"Thank you, Natalia. What I was trying to say is if you ever need someone to talk to or whatever...you know I'm here for you."

"Seth, I haven't seen you in such a long time and I barely even know you. Why are you offering me you're shoulder? I have a husband for that."

"This is true...but I still feel that you're a special person. We're going through the same emotions dealing with loss and I want you to know I can just be a person that helps you figure it all out or at least come to terms with it."

At first she was annoyed. He was openly hitting on her and using her son's death to slide his way in. Then she remembered how he opened up to her about his ordeal. She knew that was serious to him and she felt bad about her assumption. *Maybe he's really just trying to be supportive.*

"I will take that into consideration, Seth. My husband has been a bit pre-occupied with his businesses lately." She seemed to be feeling sorry for herself and she caught herself and tried to clean it up. "But, he certainly does make up for it when he is home," she snickered. *Why the hell did I say all of that?* Feeling a bit embarrassed she directed her eyes toward the contract and began reading, mouthing the words under her breath.

"I'm sure he does," Seth replied, feeling awkward. That was too much information for him. He already hated her phantom husband for being her husband. He was a lucky bastard in his eyes and if he could persuade her to test his greener grass he would. In fact, the more he watched her lips move he decided to put that plan in motion.

"Well, I have here that we're supposed to have twenty-one new systems, including towers, monitors, keyboards and the Gold accessories package."

"Hmmm, okay because our copy states that the Basic package was purchased, which is why I came with the basic package equipment. I guess I'm obligated to go by your copy. The customer is always right," he smiled.

"You damn right," she laughed. He laughed too and the flirting had officially begun.

"Gimme a minute, Maleek," Shawn said into his cell phone and looked over at his wife who was undressing. She was still slimmer than he was used to but her soft skin and curves she didn't lose still made his dick salute. "Mmn, baby," he licked his lips. She grinned at him.

"I'm going in the shower. You're welcome to join me."

"You ain't got to tell me twice. Yo, Maleek I'ma holla at you later," he hung up, jumped up and followed her into the shower. He massaged her with his hands first, then his penis massaged her juicy center in every position they could manage in the cramped shower stall. Afterwards he stumbled his way to the bed still wet. "Girl, you can wear a brother out. Shit, how am I gonna get to New Jersey now? I can't feel my legs," he chuckled.

Natalia burst out laughing. "You know something Shawn? I don't think you're human. You were shot so many times and you're still here. You're like Wolverine from the X-Men. You just regenerate and come back stronger than before."

"Hey that's how it is. I'm the real Superman, stronger than steel baby, all over." They both laughed hard.

He was dressed now and ready to go. She was in her nightie laying in the bed feeling very satisfied. Her man was leaving and he looked like a million bucks but she didn't mind. She just finished putting it on him so she believed that he was set for the night. Besides, he was always forcing her to watch CNN when he stayed home on the weekends. He had become a news and sports buff all of a sudden. While he was gone she would watch whatever she wanted to watch, stretch out, pig out and just let it all hang out. "Aiight baby girl I'm out. I'll call you later."

"Okay daddy. Drive safely and you and your hoodlum friends behave so y'all don't get arrested," she giggled.

"You got jokes, huh? Well, you just be a good girl and don't eat everything in the refrigerator. Shit, I think you got a tape worm in your ass or you must be smoking crack on the low cuz you eat everything in sight and still ain't gaining no weight."

"Whatever. You keep it up and I'm gonna get fat just to spite you then what?"

"Then I'ma leave your fat ass!" he laughed loud. She mimicked his boisterous laugh and threw the TV remote at him.

The Black Tie Baller's Ball in Atlantic City was all everybody in the game talked about for the past month. Shawn bought his Armani suit weeks in advance. He was grateful that he was doing well enough to splurge and look as if he were still 'Lord of the Streets'. He was driving a Cadillac Escalade now, riding on 23" dubs and turning heads with the unique pearled money green color, 7" TVs in the headrests.

"Sup PB."

A dark skinned man stepped up to his truck as he pulled into the Casino parking lot.

"Sup niggah. You look like you fuckin' wit' Trump cash," Shawn chuckled.

"Look who's talking. This Escalade is sick. This shit must be bullet proof. Oh, I forgot you don't need that shit. You're already made out of Kevlar," he laughed. The boys in the hood called Shawn Jason from Friday the 13th because even after all the murder attempts he kept coming back—again and again.

"Whatever nigga," Shawn laughed then said, "So what you doing out here?"

"Waiting on this bitch. She got this package for me and she got a nigga mad heated right now."

"You need to stop trusting them ho's with them X pills. She probably popped all them shits for dolo," Shawn laughed.

"That bitch knows better. I'll fuckin' kill her ass. She knows better than to play wit a nigga's money!" he laughed.

"You seen Maleek?"

"He's inside."

"Aiight, I'm going in. I hope she show up soon before your ass freeze out this bitch!"

Inside the ball there was a smorgasbord of women. There were every types of women imaginable; model types, around the way girls and exotic women. He tried to ignore their advances, but some of them just looked too delicious to pass up. His woman was still gorgeous but she lost some of the feminine fat that he loved so much. He swaggered into the banquet hall, his sex appeal commanding adoration. The women swooned and the men either hated or respected.

"Whut up?" Maleek approached him then slapped his hand into Shawn's then turned it into a tricky gang-like handshake. "I see you made it after all."

"Yeah and I'm definitely glad I did," Shawn grinned, mischievously.

"That's wassup, fam. I told you it was gonna be off the chain. But before we get to the pleasure let me holler at you about some serious business. You remember what I've been telling you all this time and you know how I do so fuck all that other bullshit and let's just say it's a done deal."

"Man after all the shit I done been through I don't know if I wanna start up some new illegal shit."

"Listen, PB that X shit is everywhere. It's bigger than crack and coke put together right now. It's easy money PB trust me. You get in and out when you're ready. I'm about to get out in like another few months cuz I'm almost at that millionaire status where I wanna be."

"I'm trying to keep my nose clean nahmean. The laundry mats and the new restaurant are doing good and I damn sure don't want to go back to square one, nahmean?"

"Aiight, well it could be a plan B for you if you need one. Just remember I got you when you ready aiight?"

"Yeah."

The two men went about their rounds inside the ballroom greeting other big time ballers, patting fat asses and sipping Armadale. It didn't take long before Shawn was in the mix, rubbing his growing bulge on a sexy woman's voluptuous buttocks. She wore a scent that intoxicated him. The more she gyrated the more he became aroused. He didn't expect to stray, but at this very moment he was being tested and was about to fail miserably. He downed his fourth shot of Hennessy and that was all she wrote. The dark cognac took a hold of his sensibilities. All he wanted was to make a major sperm deposit in this woman whose body seemed to be plumping up right before his eyes like a Ball Park frank.

She, on the other hand, knew exactly what she was doing. She knew all about Shawn and his reputation. It wasn't every day that a girl of her undeserving caliber could mingle with ghetto royalty such as Shawn. She was a real dirty birdy, a high school drop out with three kids at the tender age of nineteen and her picture was next to the word chicken head in Webster's dictionary, the ghetto edition. She lived in a filthy broken down house with a dysfunctional family of eleven. But looking at her tonight you would have never guessed any of that about her. She looked like a super model in her best friends' clothes. The dress she wore complimented her brick house body. Her jet black hair was relaxed bone straight with weave tracks sewn in so tight and so flat that Shawn thought all that European hair was really hers. She had snagged her a prince tonight and was willing to do whatever she had to do to keep him. She squeezed his crotch as they danced close on the dance floor and Shawn responded just as she expected.

"Come on." He put his empty glass on a speaker and left the ballroom with her tagging along.

Shawn had become a cheapskate. He wasn't frivolous anymore. So, if she expected him to get them a suite inside the Trump Casino she was out of luck. He was even wary of doing her in his Escalade. "You got a room?"

"No. Do you?" she answered with a confused look.

"Nah," he replied, deep in thought trying to figure out where to take her. He came up with a scheme to test her integrity. He grabbed her ass and pulled her close to whisper in her ear.

"I'm saying, Ma I can't wait. Let's just go over there right in that supply room." He was giving her the benefit of the doubt. If she refused then she wasn't a bird and he'd actually consider getting a room.

"Let's go," she said grinning. Needless to say she failed his test.

In the middle of the sexual act, the condom broke and Shawn was so hyped up on alcohol that he kept right on going until his sperm blasted off inside her. It wasn't until he pulled out and saw his dick without its rubber slicker that he realized what he'd done and he panicked. Without saying thank you or anything he rushed out of the supply room to the bathroom. He didn't care who saw him as he scrubbed Max with paper towels soaked with water and overflowing with soap. The thought of AIDS scared the hell out of him and it was then for the first time in his life that he prayed to God. *I will go to church God every Sunday for the rest of my life if you bless me right now. Please don't make me have AIDS Pleassse God.*

CHAPTER THREE

It wasn't a bad day at the office that pissed Natalia off it was the ride home. She was stuck in traffic that seemed to halt to a stand still. She honked and honked but it made no difference. When she finally got to Shawn's condo, road rage had already gripped her. She stormed in the house with an attitude. Shawn wasn't home yet so she called his cell.

"Where are you?"

"I'm at the restaurant picking up some food for us. Hold on." After a brief pause he came back on the phone. "Aunt Free says hi, baby." He tried imitating his Aunt's southern strained voice. He made her smile and her attitude changed.

"Tell her hi. Daddy, I need a massage when you get home, okay?"

"Aiight, BG I got you." Natalia laughed as she always did whenever he called her BG.

"Aiight, PB." She giggled at saying his longtime nickname which was short for Pretty Boy. As soon as she put the phone down it rang.

"Yes, daddy?" she answered immediately with a smile.

"Can I talk to PB?"

"Who's this?" Natalia's heart skipped so many beats it sounded like Doug E. Fresh himself was beat boxing in her chest.

"Don't worry about it. As a matter of fact, who are you? Fuck it, I don't even care who you are. Just tell that nigga I need to talk to him right now!"

"Bitch, you're calling my house so don't fucking

disrespect me. Why do you want my husband?"

"Husband?"

There was loud, thunderous laughter in the background then there was a click followed by a dial tone. Natalia's heart was still thumping, pumping Kool Aid. She didn't know what to think. *Is Shawn cheating on me? After all we've been through?* She started to call him but something told her to just be patient and wait until he got home. She needed to see his facial expressions when she grilled him for answers.

The doorbell rang and Natalia wasn't expecting anyone so she didn't get up. She assumed it was someone ringing the wrong bell. But, whoever it was didn't care what she expected or didn't expect and kept right on ringing the bell. Natalia ripped off the covers, put on her robe and shoved her feet into her slippers.

"If it isn't the Publisher's Clearinghouse people at the door I'm gonna kick some ass," she grumbled. She looked out the peephole and didn't see anyone. Now, she was really pissed. She started walking away from the door when the doorbell rang again. She flung open the door and was face to face with what looked like a 12th grader in drag.

"Do you have the right address?" Natalia asked, suspiciously.

"Yeah, I'm looking for PB."

"Um, he's not here but I'm his wife. Can I help you?"

"Yeah, you can just tell your husband that Peaches, his baby's mama, says he better start coming up with some cash!"

"Baby's mama?" Natalia laughed hard.

"Yeah, bitch I didn't st-stutter did I?"

"Bitch? First of all you stupid ghetto looking Furby my name is Mrs. Wilson not bitch. Secondly, my man would never fuck anything as hideous as you; ringing my damn bell looking like a troll on steroids."

"Oh, no, you didn't bitch."

Peaches grabbed at Natalia's robe trying to pull her

outside. Then out of nowhere she whipped out a razor and slashed at Natalia's face. Natalia's cat-like reflexes saved her face from twenty stitches but got her hand ten instead. The razor sliced through her palm and blood gushed out. As angry as Natalia was she didn't feel pain but she was ready to dish some out. She chopped the girl in the neck then kicked her down the front steps. Then she jumped down on her and began wildly beating her with closed fists and kneeing her in the stomach. She was in such a crazed frenzy pulverizing Peaches that she didn't even notice the crowd of onlookers nor did she see the police running up on her. With all the blood all over both of them the police were reluctant to touch her or Peaches who was laid out unconscious. When the haze of anger passed, Natalia was shocked at all the blood and even more shocked at her behavior. One of the policemen walked over with rubber gloves on his hands and an EMT followed behind him and they both escorted her to the back of an ambulance. After she was treated for her cut, she was handcuffed and hauled off to central booking.

"Susan give me the short version." Natalia said nonchalantly to her long time attorney.

"There is no short version to this. That woman was pregnant and miscarried from your violent attack. She also has a ruptured spleen and damaged eye socket. My God, Nat what drove you to do that?" Natalia looked down in shame. She didn't know she had it in her. She took an innocent life all in the name of love.

"I'm sorry about the baby. I had no idea she was pregnant. But she came to my house and instigated this. She claimed she was Shawn's baby's mother. I thought she was saying she already had a baby."

"Nat they're charging you with manslaughter for the baby and aggravated assault for the mother. Since it's your first offense I managed to get the prosecutors to offer a deal for three to five years which means you can get out early with good behavior. Now, I know the last thing you need is to end up serving a jail sentence, but sweetie I don't think we have a choice and it's the best offer we have so far under the circumstances."

"Jail? Jail? Susan I can't go to jail."

"You can and you will. You will be a good girl while you're in there and I will do damage control out here as far as possibly getting you only 18 months based on this being you're first offense and of course the fact of provocation. But, that's the least I can get you if I can even convince them to do that."

Susan could see that Natalia was coming apart, again. She reached over gently rubbed her arm.

"Nat I'm sorry you're going through all of this. But you keep letting your love for Shawn override you're common sense and it's really taking a toll on you. I'm not a relationship expert but it just doesn't seem like you guys have a healthy relationship."

Natalia couldn't rebut that statement. She had come to feel that way as well. How could he do such a thing to her knowing all she had gone through just to be with him? She looked at Susan with puppy dog eyes and instantly Susan hugged her. She cried in Susan's arms. She cried for Shawn's dead baby, she cried for her deceased son and she cried for herself.

She huddled in one corner of the holding pen in Central Booking. She was sure that the smell alone would kill her. That is if the disturbed burly woman standing across from her didn't do it first. All the women looked rough and didn't seem the least bit out of place. They were laughing and giggling and talking as if they were at a sorority reunion. Some, actually lay out on the corroded cell floor. Natalia kept her mind on her dead son to sustain her. Thinking of him made her realize how precious life really was and as soon as she got out, she planned on kicking Shawn to the curb and really getting her act together.

It came time for them to be transferred to Rikers' Island and she couldn't wait to get out of the pen even if it was for a brief moment or just until she was safe, in another rat infested hole.

She refused to eat for the first few days. Gradually she drank milk and ate a little bit of food each day. She only made calls to Andre who was ready to murder Shawn for his foul indiscretions. She walked around with her guard up at all times. It wasn't long before her strength was tested. One day in the library a woman came over and sat down beside her. She looked like a dyke, but Natalia tried not to stereotype her. The woman definitely wanted some of Natalia. Natalia didn't notice.

"Hey princess, I know you don't belong in here. So who framed you?" The woman whispered with a wide grin. Natalia laughed lightly.

"I guess the Devil himself," she continued reading her book entitled, *Lament Law*.

The woman stuck out her hand and said, "I'm Frankie. What's your name?"

"Natalia," she replied and shook the woman's hand. The woman looked down at the book Natalia was reading.

"Are you trying to appeal your case?"

"Actually, I'm reading up on seizure and audits."

The woman looked confused and she rubbed her chin slightly and said.

"Now, you done lost me. What the hell...?"

"It's pretty complicated to get into, but I'm sort of researching the subject...for a friend."

Natalia wasn't about to explain to this convict that she was really rich and was just waiting for the FEDS to release her money. It had been almost a full year and she was tired of their claims of implementing an extensive auditing process. They were just trying to bullshit her and make her life difficult all because of Shawn. They played this game with her where. Her attorney would inquire about the aud and people in charge would mysteriously be indisposed. d read up on it so that the next time that she called she in be prepared to give ultimatums and get answers. The

31

sized Natalia up. She assumed she had to be a stuck up Oreo type that caught a bad rap. With this assumption she figured she stood a good chance of making this sexy trophy her bitch. Not only would the other prisoners envy her but Natalia would be good for negotiating services and products. Natalia was reading a paragraph that she found quite helpful when Frankie extended her services.

"Natalia, that's real different...and pretty."

"Thanks," Natalia said, without looking up. If she had, she would've noticed the lust in Frankie's eyes.

"So, Natalia I know you're new to this shit and it's not your thang and all that. Shit, I can tell you're too sophisticated for this place. You shouldn't be in here. But, while you are here I wanna offer you my protection. Anything you need just ask and I'll see what I can do. Anybody come at you the wrong way tell em' to see me, ya feel me?" Natalia finally looked up from the book and looked her square in the eyes.

"Why do you want to help me? You don't know me."

"Trust me princess in here you're the type that will need help."

"My type?"

"Come on Ma, I can tell what you're about. You're not from the streets. This place will eat you up," she chortled.

Natalia took offense to this remark. She had been through hell and back and survived it all. This woman must've taken her for a fool and she was no fool. And with her being the sarcastic, independent, stubborn person that she was she threw caution to the wind.

"Look, I don't need your protection. You shouldn't jump to conclusions about people because sometimes you end up jumping right out of a window." She slammed the book closed and got up. This fire not only enticed Frankie but pissed her off at the same time. She thought she had this one pegged and it would be easy to recruit her onto her ん. She grabbed a hold of Natalia's arm.

"Listen princess, I'm tryna do you a favor. Don't catch

a beat down with all that fake hard shit. I guess you need time to see what's what. Just watch yourself." She let her arm go and watched Natalia walk away, licking her lips.

Shawn tried to get his explanation out to Andre so that he could relay it to Natalia. But, it was all to no avail. He waited patiently for the day that he could visit her without her turning him away as she'd done repeatedly. As angry as Andre was he managed to slip up one day and divulge more information than Natalia would've wanted him to. He told Shawn how Natalia kept to herself and hadn't run into any trouble. He told him that she wasn't eating so she would probably be a stick figure when she got out. He also told him to give her some time then go back to visit.

In the early hours of the morning he found himself clutching a bottle of Hennessy, the very thing that got him in trouble in the first place. He was now colliding with another one of the things he tried avoiding his entire life, alcoholism. He didn't want to drink, but with his wife in jail and the chance of him becoming a father squashed by a miscarriage caused by the woman he loved had the Hennessy talking to him, dictating nothing but destructive behavior. To make matters worse, his money was getting low. He was actually counting every dollar, something he had never done before. He didn't want to go back to hustle and bustle of the street game, but things were getting too hectic. So, without pause he jumped back into the drug game. This time he dealt with X pills more so than cocaine. Just as Maleek had promised the money rolled in fast. He'd only been doing it for a couple of months and he had more than enough money to start living it up again. The fast life welcomed him back with open arms. Contacts that he thought wouldn't want to touch him now reached out to him. Maleek introduced him to new contacts that seemed to respect him and his past tribulations with the law. They took good care of him and even hit him off with extras. It wasn't long before the need of pussy overpowered him and made him move mountains to set up a conjugal visit with his wife. He contacted his hook up on Riker's Island who set it all up for him. He planned everything out all without his wife's knowledge.

"Am I in trouble?" Natalia asked innocently. The correction officer looked at her pensively.

"Why would you ask that? Did you do something wrong?" he chuckled.

"Well, I don't know where you're taking me but it can't be out of this hell hole." She replied sarcastically.

"Actually sweetheart you're going to heaven."

"Um, are you taking me to bible study or something because I'm not a religious fanatic and I'd rather not go."

"Don't worry, I think you'll be happy to see where you end up."

"Huh?" she asked, dumbfounded. The correction officer just chuckled and shook his head. He led her out through the gates into a yard where they walked across and ended up at yet another building. Finally he took off her handcuffs and opened the door to a small, musty room. The room had a cot with rose petals all over it. A bowl of strawberries and a bottle of apple cider sat on the middle of a small table. Natalia not only scratched her head in confusion but she turned to walk right back out of the room. She grabbed the doorknob but it wouldn't turn. A flash of panic hit her. She'd seen news reports a while back about correction officers taking advantage of female prisoners, even prostituting them. Her nerves were shot and she anxiously shifted back and forth. She looked at the bottle on the table. She could use it as a weapon but then she realized that a CO was God in jail. He could shoot her and claim self-defense. She was defenseless. She sat at the edge of the cot and wrapped her arms around herself.

The door opened slowly and when the tall figure stepped into the room she tensed up then exhaled.

"What in the world...?"

"Shhh, don't start screaming at me or trying to hit

me." Shawn put his hands up to block his face just in case she ignored his request.

"Excuse me? Are you insane?" she asked. He ignored her remark, walked over and forced her to stand up by grabbing her armpits with his strong hands and tugging. She didn't resist. In fact, she had missed his handsome face and sexy smell. She was still angry but if she could get some dick to last her for the next eight months, she would cherish this moment like no other. He kissed her and she kissed back.

"You know that I love you right?" he asked after gently pushing her away. She refused to answer him. This was no time to explain himself or ask for forgiveness. It was time for sex and that's all she wanted from him right then. "Right?" he asked again.

She sighed and walked over to the table. She grabbed a strawberry and ate it. She took the bottle of cider and began opening it. Shawn grabbed the bottle and put it back on the table. "I said you know I still love you right?"

"No, I don't know. I can't believe you fucked some ashy, project reject and without a condom."

"Listen, I was drunk and the condom broke. BG, I know that's no reason to give away your dick, but baby I'm only human. I'm prone to mistakes. You know there was no way in hell I would've fucked anybody else unless I was ripped. You know what we've been through. I would never fuck up this marriage over a bitch. I'm waiting for you out there. I'm gonna be there when you get out and I'm gonna do what I have to do to get your trust back."

"No amount of sorry sorries will convince me that you're trustworthy. Our whole relationship has been a whirlwind of disasters. All you do is lie and deceive me. And you know what? I'm tired of it." She rolled her eyes at him.

"I know what I've done to your life. I understand all of that but I'm still in love with you...you're my wife. Now, you can either get over it and we can rebuild or you can dwell on the past and stay mad at me forever."

"I choose the latter."

"There you go with the big ass words. Just cuz you went to a University and got a degree and shit don't mean I can't use a dictionary and figure out what the fuck you talkin' about." He laughed.

Natalia couldn't help but laugh. Shawn took advantage of that laugh and he kissed her long and hard. She didn't protest. She practically ripped off her county issued jumpsuit. He threw her down on the bed and devoured her all to her delight. It had been so long and her overflowing fountain of horniness turned him on so much that he came instantly. But, she saw to it that he delivered more of what she craved minutes later.

Afterwards she couldn't remember why she was mad at him. Somehow the great sex that transpired pushed the anger so deep down she couldn't remember where to find it. They lay there in each other's arms, cramped on the small cot. Natalia almost forgot that she was still a prisoner. However, the annoying knock on the door reminded her.

"Baby Girl, I'm out here waiting on you so don't worry. I'll visit you again real soon. I love you." Shawn kissed her forehead, nose then her lips.

"I love you to, way too much." She sighed as she watched him leave and she was led back to her cell.

"Hey, sexy! I like those slippers. I wonder if they're my size."

Natalia sucked her teeth, knowing this was the prelude to an ass beating for the scrawny rat of a woman who stood in front of her with folded arms. She looked up and saw what looked like a twisted African version of the Hulk standing right behind the scrawny woman. She knew that not only was she risking her release that was coming up in just three weeks but she was going to be hurt if they both jumped her. But she also knew if she didn't stand up for herself she'd be munching carpets and tossing salads from here on end. She didn't stop sipping her milk.

"Bitch you hard of hearing?" the scrawny woman spat.

"Bitch? Hmmm the last person that called me a bitch

woke up in intensive care," Natalia said unmoved by the two women inching closer.

The monster-like woman smacked the milk carton from Natalia's hand. Just when Natalia jumped up and was ready to take her beating like a man, out of nowhere Frankie butted in and punched the monstrous creature in the face with her big thick fist and she stumbled backwards. The scrawny woman backed away like Frankie was God or something. Frankie grabbed a milk carton from another woman's tray at the table and handed it to Natalia.

"Thank you," Natalia murmured. She couldn't believe how happy she was to see Frankie. Frankie just smiled and walked away as if nothing happened. Everyone else quieted down and went back to eating their food. Natalia couldn't wait to tell Shawn what transpired in the cafeteria. When she called him the line kept breaking up and all she managed to hear was that he was in Atlanta.

"Atlanta?" she asked the air. *What the hell is he doing out there?*

CHAPTER FIVE

Shawn had done what his older brother Tymeek couldn't and didn't. He started a construction company then built his own townhouse complex in Atlanta. After selling all of the other sites in his complex he renovated the model townhome for his friend Maleek. He had another townhome specially designed on the largest plot in the complex for himself. He named the complex The Rowen Estates after his dead father. He couldn't wait for Natalia to get out of jail so that he could surprise her with his newfound success. He knew she'd be disappointed that he returned to his old life, but eventually she'd get over it. He walked around his brand new house and inspected every nook.

"So far so good," he told the foreman.

"That's good. When the boss is happy everyone's happy."

The tiles for the patio are being delivered later today along with the artificial waterfall pipes, so by the time you come back next week everything will be done," his foreman advised.

"Good cause I'm moving out here in a couple of weeks."

"It looks real good PB. You make me wanna take this one now. I know mine is cool but this one looks better," Maleek chuckled.

"Hey they're all fine pieces of work," the foreman smirked.

"True, true." Shawn nodded.

"Let's go check out mine again," Maleek said, sounding like a child with a new toy. Maleek had become Shawn's new sidekick. Unlike Shawn's old sidekick Nut,

Maleek was rolling in cash too and was his own boss. They weren't in competition but on the same level. They got along so well the two adopted one another as brothers. At times though Shawn found himself jealous of one thing that Maleek had and he didn't, children. Maleek had two daughters and one son. They were all adorable and whenever Shawn saw Maleek with his children a pain struck his heart. He wished he could have known the joy that he saw in Maleek's face when he was with his children. That made him resent Natalia and even angry at times for what she'd done.

They went to Maleek's house. They looked around and Maleek pleasantly inspected each of his children's bedrooms and beamed as he told Shawn how he couldn't wait to see his son play basketball on the court in the backyard. Shawn smiled through it all but secretly wished Maleek would shut up about his kids. Before they left for the airport they made a few drop offs and picked up some money that was owed to them. While at the airport, the call came in that would rock Shawn's world.

"Sup bro?" Tymeek's voice was still rough and raspier than ever.

"Sup nigga." Shawn was surprised, but elated to hear from his brother.

"I'm not gonna stay long but I've got some bad news. Some crazy shit done went down out here."

"What happened?"

"Nut fell into a canal out here and he's dead."

"What? Get the fuck—"

"Listen, I can't stay long but you know what's up so just come. I need to talk to you about the shit I hear that's going on out there so I want you to do what you have to do and make this trip aiight?"

"Yeah," Shawn replied, solemnly and slowly closed his clam shell cell phone.

Maleek noticed the wave of sadness alter Shawn's expression.

"What happened?"

39

"My man from New York is dead. He drowned or some crazy shit like that."

"Drowned?"

"Yeah, I gotta make this trip."

"I got you if you need me."

"I'ma need you to hold me down while I'm gone. I don't trust that nigga Vic with my shit. So you do that for me aiight?"

"Done."

Shawn had never seen so many white faces in all his life. They looked at him funny and he thought maybe they were plotting against him. He was on the look out for Tymeek's Milk Dud looking head. *It won't be too hard to spot this nigga out this bitch,* Shawn thought to himself. No sooner did Shawn's thought dissolve from his brain when he began to see all kinds of people mixed into the pale faced crowds. There were Asians, Indians, Africans all the colors of the Rainbow Coalition. Now he noticed a lot of Americans were about because after hearing the funny sounding Dutch the pale faces were sputtering he noticed he could actually understand a lot of the passersby. He even saw black people speaking Dutch. As he became immersed in the culture of Amsterdam the time slipped by. It wasn't until his stomach growled angrily because he was hungry that he realized that he was still waiting. He called Tymeek's cell phone.

"Nigga, where you at?"

"Turn around dickhead," Tymeek laughed hard into the phone. Shawn did as he was told and was never so happy to see his brother in all his life. It had been over two years and they hadn't spoken much via telephone, so this was a reunion of importance. "Damn nigga what you done got prettier and shit." Tymeek laughed heartily.

"What about you? Look at those guns, nigga. All you do is lift weights out this bitch?"

"Man, I gotta do that cuz these bitches out here love a big black nigga!"

"So what's good nigga?"

"Ain't shit good no more. I'm going through some changes but I'ma be aiight."

"So, explain this drowning shit to me."

"You know Nut is a crazy muthafuckah right?"

"Yeah and?"

"Well we was out by the canal chilling, smoking, drinking and shit. Cause out here that's all you got to keep sane. I miss the hell outta my hood bitches though. Shit I miss the hood period. Life out here is so different than what I'm used to. Man, I was thankful to have Nut in the beginning. When Big Stew agreed to come out here I was mad grateful. He brought some more of New York wit em' and shit. We have our own little piece of Queens out here now, we eight deep." Tymeek's smile faded as he paused before continuing, "Anyway we was all buggin' out and talking about home and shit...we were twisted. That shit we smoked had us fucked up. So Nut started doing some ol' Jackie Chan type stunt on the ledge then he..." Tymeek started out telling the story fine but choked up to finish. Shawn did it for him.

"He fell over into the canal?"

"Yeah." Tymeek rubbed his head then shook it apathetically. Shawn was hurt but didn't show it. His best friend from childhood was gone. The one man he trusted with his life besides his brother. He missed Nut ever since he left New York. He started reminiscing about his many adventures with Nut. Memories of his crazy friend made him laugh out loud. Tymeek watched him with a look of confusion.

"I was just thinking of all the crazy shit me and Nut been through. That nigga earned that name." They both laughed then hugged each other. "I'm ready to get out of this airport." Shawn sighed and grabbed his bag.

"Listen, we gon' stop off at this restaurant that serves Indian food. It's real good."

"Don't have me eating no nasty shit."

41

"Hey, if you can eat pussy then you can eat this food."
Tymeek laughed.

Shawn didn't like the narrow cobbled streets. He didn't like how the small houses were joined together either. Tymeek's house seemed bigger on the inside than it looked on the outside. It was definitely more feminine than Shawn expected. He knew that a woman decorated it.

"So it's not too expensive out here, huh?"

"Hell yeah it is nigga. Shit you don't know what I went through to get this piece of shit right here. This place is worse than New York when it comes to finding a place to live. It's crowded out here. Too many people, not enough space or jobs, but still niggas stay happy," he chuckled.

"Shit, I'd be happy too if I could walk down the street smoking a blunt," Shawn laughed.

"That's what's up." Tymeek laughed. Big Stew came running into the room.

"Where's that pretty muthafuckah at?" Big Stew shouted. Some other familiar faces wandered in behind Big Stew.

"Sup niggaz?" Shawn shouted with a hearty laugh. After making rounds of giving pounds and brotherly pats, they all sat down and reminisced. Night fell and Shawn became tired after seeing the darkness cover the quaint buildings outside the window. Everyone else left and Shawn and Tymeek were finally by themselves in Tymeek's overly feminine bedroom. Shawn tasted some new Dutch liquor that Tymeek raved about as Tymeek smoked a blunt. It smelled so fresh Shawn could've sworn that it was just grown and picked right before Tymeek rolled it up. Tymeek took a long draw from his blunt.

"Listen...my shit is suffering out here. I need some money to build it back up." Small clouds of smoke escaped his lips with each word.

"I knew that was coming. I came prepared for that," Shawn smiled and went into his bag and pulled out another bag. He threw it at Tymeek.

"So, you the man out there now, huh?"

"You know how I do." Shawn drank some more of the putrid liquid and coughed. He could feel it creeping up on him though. He knew that any minute now he was going to be inebriated. Tymeek opened the bag and peeked inside, reached in and flipped his fingers through the stacks of bills and grinned.

"Good lookin' out, baby. Now know this...I hear shit. I'ma always have eyes and ears on you. When you went clean I was proud of you even though I know how it is and I knew you were gonna fall back in. But that X shit is risky. Plus, you need to be careful of who you're dealing with. I hear those X dealers are usually rich white kids with chemistry sets in their basements." He chuckled then became serious as he continued, "Me and you are gonna do this on a different level. We'll do this long distance and Svel will be my pigeon cause she's trustworthy. That bitch goes to the US all the time for me. She brings me all types of shit and never gets busted cause them white muthafuckaz be mesmerized. I love that bitch for that."

"So, you're saying that you're in? Because I'm getting so much paper that I need to bring in a partner. I got this gully nigga down wit me out there but he got his own thing. He put me on but he's dealing with his own load so this works out good for me. I can get you the X and you can rack up out here."

"That's why I'm trying to set shit up in Paris, too. I got some connects but they can't get that X shit easy." Tymeek took another draw of his marijuana packed cigarette.

"You rolling like that? You are a true international hustler...I like that." Shawn chuckled then became solemn. "So I guess you waiting on me to call Ms. Braithewaite to tell her that her son is gone, huh?"

"I think it'll be better coming from you, nahmean? She knows you more than she knows me."

"Yeah...damn my niggah is fuckin' dead. I can't believe

43

this shit. I don't even have anybody to get at behind that... that's some weird shit how he died. I need to get blitzed right now. So, wassup with that dutch dro that I keep hearing about?"

"You ain't said nothing but a word, bro," Tymeek laughed and pulled out a big glass jar from under his pillow. "See, now the only reason I smoke this shit is cause it's pure. See, the shit in the States is mixed and ain't no good for you. This shit right here is medicinal nahmean? No preservatives." He laughed.

Natalia picked up some towels that fell on the floor from the laundry bin she had to lug around the laundry room. As she bent over and picked up the towels she felt a hard slap on her ass, which caused her to drop the towels back onto the floor. She picked them up again and turned around. Frankie stood with her arms folded and was grinning from ear to ear.

"You owe me and I came to collect," she sneered. It amazed Natalia how just minutes before the laundry room was bustling with fellow inmates pulling laundry duty but now it was empty. Although her back ached from all the hard labor she was forced to do while in jail and her strength was drained from barely eating she prepared herself for a fight by raising her fists and planting her feet in a firm stance. Frankie's friends popped out of nowhere and for the first time in her life Natalia gave up. "I'm so tired of this shit. Just go ahead and beat me up. I don't care anymore," she sighed, dropping her hands.

Frankie just chuckled. "Naw, I don't wanna do that. I just want payment for saving your ass earlier. And oh, what a pretty ass it is." Frankie licked her lips, leaning to the side to peek at Natalia's jumpsuit covered rump.

"Payment? Oh, hold on while I go to the ATM and get you a few crisp twenty dollar bills," Natalia said with a boat load of sarcasm saturating each word then sucked her teeth.

"See?" Frankie turned to her goons. "Now that's how I know her pussy is gonna be sweet." She turned her attention back to her soon to be victim. "It's that rebel in you that makes me want it so bad. You got a little heart so I know you gon' fight hard."

"What?"

At first Natalia wasn't sure about what she'd just heard. Then after noticing the way Frankies' eyes hungrily undressed her, she finally figured it out. Then her instincts kicked in and she took off running like a bat outta hell. Frankie ran right up on her and yanked her long hair so hard that she stumbled back into Frankie's arms. Frankie yoked her. "See, now this is the sweetness I'm talking about. Slow down princess cause you gonna love it." She laughed hard. "I'ma make you love me, bitch."

"Get off of me you fuckin' dyke!" Natalia screamed. Her screams only turned Frankie on more. Frankie threw her into the maintenance closet while one of the other women held Natalia's arms down and the other closed the door. After closing the closet door the two women came over and grabbed Natalia's legs and held them down. Frankie went to work on Natalia with her tongue, savoring Natalia's essence because she couldn't taste Natalia's juices since there wasn't any flowing. At that moment Natalia was drier than the Sahara Desert. But, as disgusted as Natalia was she still couldn't vomit as she hoped. Her plan was to think of every nasty vile thought that would make her want to hurl. Then she could repel Frankie by vomiting right on her. It didn't work. The amount of time she took thinking up more disgusting thoughts was the same amount of time it took Frankie to pull out a makeshift dildo made from plastic wrap and a paper towel cardboard tube. Natalia caught a glimpse of the monstrous makeshift dildo and shrieked. This excited Frankie and she took pleasure in shoving it into Natalia as if she were stuffing a Thanksgiving turkey! Frankie put one hand over Natalia's mouth and finished her off with the dildo until they all heard a strategic code banged onto the door. Frankie yanked the dildo out of Natalia and shoved it back in her sock. The other women let Natalia's arms and legs go. Frankie put her finger to her lips and whispered.

"Shhh, don't say shit. If you say anything to anybody I'll fuckin' kill you! You hear me?"

Natalia was too stunned and in too much pain to answer.

"I said do you hear me?"

Natalia still couldn't answer. Her mind was drawing a blank. The next sound she heard was, WHACK! Everything faded to black.

When she woke up she was on a cot in Riker's infirmary. A woman in civilian clothes walked in with one paper cup filled with water and a little white pill in another.

"Sit up and take this." She offered both to Natalia.

"What happened?"

The woman sighed and shook her head. "My dear I don't know how to put this to you," she urged Natalia to take the pill by tipping the cup with her finger. "Go ahead trust me I'm a doctor. See my ID?" she pointed to her laminated picture ID that was clipped onto her shirt. Natalia popped the pill and drank the water. She crumpled up both paper cups and waited for the doctor to enlighten her. The doctor busied herself with tidying up the infirmary as she spoke.

"I did some checking and I found out that you're getting released soon. That's something to look forward to." Natalia started to have flashbacks of Frankie violating her and her eyes welled up from anger. The doctor inhaled then exhaled. "You were found in a closet and you were sexually assaulted. I found abrasions on the left and right labia. And to make matters worse your cultures came back positive for vaginitis. The vaginitis was incubating. So, I believe you may have had it prior to coming here. Males don't really notice symptoms, so it could lay dormant for long periods of time in both partners. Usually women assume it's a yeast infection. It's improbable that you contracted it from what took place here. The pill I gave you is part of the treatment but you'll have to take one daily for four more days."

At first Natalia was ready to tell the doctor she was sadly mistaken because she never had to worry about any vaginal infections before in her life. Then she remembered that Shawn cheated on her and didn't use a condom. She felt so humiliated and it was almost as if the doctor picked up on it because she immediately changed the subject.

"So, are you all ready to bust out of this joint?"

Natalia sighed as she tried painfully to smile.

"Definitely."

CHAPTER FIVE

It wasn't until the night before he was to leave Amsterdam that Shawn met Svelanka. She was almost a double for Pamela Anderson Lee except with more of a black woman's body. She had hips and a heart shaped ass.

"Is your father black?"

"No," she giggled.

"Oh, you're English is much better now, I see."

"Yes, Ty make me learn every day. He teach me all the slang, u know I mean, Shun?"

Shawn had to laugh even though her accent sounded cute to him. He watched Svelanka glide around the kitchen with her natural blonde tresses idling in the breeze from the kitchen window. She was extremely appealing and that made Shawn imagine having sex with a white woman. He teased Tymeek all the time about him fucking a cracker and sniffing their baloney smell. But, the more he checked Svelanka out while she fixed dinner, he could see why Tymeek was fucking her.

"So you take care of my brother real good out here, huh?" Svelanka laughed as she passed him a fork.

"He takes good care of me, too."

They both looked at each other knowingly and tittered. She sat down with him and they discussed business arrangements about her coming out to New York and Atlanta to make pick ups and drop offs. He told her the rules and she actually took notes. Tymeek walked in as Shawn finished off his food.

"Svel call Milla and tell her to come meet my brother."

"Oh, that's good idea. Milla will love Shawn."

"Oh, yeah? How you know?" Shawn stood up and

emptied out his plate in the trash.

"I know." Svelanka grinned and left them in the kitchen.

"Shit if I didn't know any better I'd say she talkin' about herself," Tymeek said jokingly but seriously wondered if Svelanka was *feeling* his brother a little too much. Shawn laughed at him.

"Niggah she done told me that you be hittin' her off lovely."

"She ain't have to tell you that shit cause you know what's really good. I taught your ass how to fuck!" Tymeek laughed.

"Yeah, whatever nigga! So, I'ma need a wake up call tomorrow cause this time zone shit got me all fucked up. I don't know when to be sleeping and when to wake up."

"Svel will wake us up."

Tymeek took Shawn to the Red Light District where they watched live sex acts performed on a stage as if it were a Broadway musical. Shawn laughed at the show at first but ended up aroused after a while. Svelanka's girlfriend Milla wasn't equally beautiful as Svelanka, but she was fresh meat, fresh white meat that he never sampled before. Before leaving the house Tymeek supplied him with a pack of Dutch condoms that were especially thin for that raw feel. Milla let Shawn fuck her in the Red Light District where sex was a passing fancy or just a regular nine to five. He couldn't get into it too much because the attraction really wasn't there. He wasn't enjoying it as much as he thought until Milla sucked him like he'd never been sucked before. Then he hit her off with a major dose of nine and a half inches. Milla damn near fell in love with him and his dick. He couldn't help but love the freak in Milla. She let him enter every hole on her body that was big enough for his dick to fit in. And after they got back to Tymeek's house, Shawn could hear Svelanka's moans through the wall and it turned him on again. Tymeek was drilling her in his bedroom, which was right next door to the one Shawn was in. Milla was knocked out from the rigorous sex-a-thon Shawn put her through earlier. He rubbed his penis on her thigh hoping to wake her up. Svelanka's scintillating moans ascended until Shawn wished he were banging her instead of Tymeek. He looked down at Milla whose legs were open just enough for him to nudge them even further apart with his knee. He eased her torso down to him and put on a condom. When he slid his dick into her she awoke, pleasantly surprised of course. But Shawn was so turned on from fantasizing about Svelanka that he only needed a few strokes to Milla's dismay. All she could do was witness his climax. Shawn pulled out of her and sprinted to the bathroom. She sighed and went back to sleep.

"Bye." Svelanka kissed Shawn's cheek.

"Aiight bro. Call me as soon as your feet touch U.S. soil."

"I will."

Shawn and Tymeek patted each other's back and as their lingering embrace ended, Shawn winked then headed down the airport corridor.

When Natalia stepped out of the gates and turned back to look at the hellhole she was leaving behind. She shook her head in a mix of disbelief and respite at the stoned container of depravity. It never ceased to amaze her how many times she asked herself. *How in the hell did I get into this mess?* Every time she asked the question the answer was always...Shawn!

Natalia squealed in delight. She ran to him and jumped into his arms. He squeezed her so tight she thought she would pass out.

"Ma, I'm sorry you had to be up in here."

He held her small face in his large hands and planted a delicate kiss on her eager lips. "Damn, I'm so glad to see you my little convict."

Natalia kissed his face all over. She had never been so

happy to touch a man. Her body ached all over but her loins were on fire for her sexy man. That is until she remembered that she had contracted an STD from him. She slid down him until her feet touched the ground. She pulled her arms from around his neck, stepped back and gave him a condescending glare. She knew that forgiving him was going to be hard but forgetting would be even harder. All the wrong he'd done flooded her memory. The STD was more than embarrassing, it was demeaning and she resented him for exposing her to it. He looked down at her with a smile. He had no idea what was going through her mind.

"Aiight BG I got a surprise for you."

"I've got one for you too."

"Oh, yeah? What is it?"

"You better go see the doctor to get rid of the surprise you gave me, courtesy of you're baby's mama."

She folded her arms and looked him straight in the face awaiting his explanation or at least an apology. He appeared confused.

"What are you talking about?"

"Well after those girls assaulted me and beat me..."

"What?"

"Oh Shawn...had you been around for the past three weeks you would've known all of this."

"Wait, wait...girls assaulted you?"

"Yes. They sexually assaulted me and beat me unconscious. Then when I woke up in the infirmary the doctor told me I had a sexually transmitted disease."

"From the girls?" he asked, taken aback.

"No, nigga from you!" Natalia truly sounded ghetto at that moment but returned to her usual proper speaking self when she elaborated on the subject further. "The doctor explained that I didn't acquire it from the girls."

"How she know it wasn't from the girls?"

"She determined it was incubating, which means I had it well before I got in that place. Plus, the girls don't have sperm to shoot up in me, okay?"

51

"Look I didn't know...fuck.

"Yeah...fuck," she sucked her teeth. "Look, I don't want to argue it's just that I want some sex now that I'm free and now I've gotta wait until you get rid of your disease."

Shawn shook his head and a smile crept onto his face. "I know that you must be ready to fuck me up, huh?"

"Amongst other things." She twisted her mouth to the side and said. "Now where's my surprise?"

"Well, one is right outside that gate. The other is far away from New York."

Natalia looked at him suspiciously as he motioned for her to follow him. She did until she saw a platinum hard top convertible Lexus. Her jaw dropped. She knew that Shawn wasn't broke, but she didn't think he had enough to afford that type of car.

"Shawn how did you?"

"Don't look a gift horse in the mouth BG. Just be happy."

"Shawn how did you get this? Please don't tell me that you're doing that again."

"Listen, everything is aiight. Trust me."

"No, we're not alright. I can't do this. I can't live through this again."

"Live through what again?"

"After all it has cost me...us...you went back to selling drugs?"

Shawn ignored what she said and just opened the passenger's door and got in. Natalia stood there staring at the tinted glass. The passenger window descended revealing Shawn's annoyed expression. "So are we leaving or what?"

"What?"

"Get your ass in the car and drive. We'll talk later." For some strange reason his harsh words sent a tingling sensation through her like a lightning rod. It brought her back to the beginning of their relationship. The way he was with her when he had kidnapped her. His dominance was what drew her in, as it was doing now. "Get in," he said interrupting her thoughts.

She sighed and did as she was told. She looked around and smiled. Inside, the car was gorgeous. She couldn't help but love it. She smiled at him.

"God I hate this Voo-Doo spell you have over me." Shawn just smirked knowingly.

Maleek threw an elegant New Year's Eve get together at one of his nightclubs in Buckhead. Every time he saw Natalia he wished he were blind. He always felt as though he was a man of honor. He would never go after any of his friends' women, especially their wife. But Natalia was his first real temptation. He wanted to know what it was like fucking her. He knew that curiosity killed the cat but he couldn't help but want to find out.

The New Year rang in and everyone shouted HAPPY NEW YEAR! Maleek planted a huge kiss on Natalia's cheek inadvertently catching the corner of her mouth. "Happy New Year, Natalia."

"Happy New Year," she smiled nervously. She wondered if he could tell that she was blushing. The kiss would've been innocent had they not been flirting ever since Shawn introduced them when he brought Natalia to see their new home in Atlanta. Shawn's complex was complete, every lot purchased with houses built and furnished. Natalia loved the new house but hated that it was in Atlanta.

"Are you enjoying yourself?" Maleek asked.

"Yes. The club is gorgeous."

"Thanks. Faye helped me pick out the design." He was glad to mention his wife's name. It put a damper on the fire brewing in his pants. He tore his eyes away from Natalia's cleavage to look around the faces of partygoers to find his right hand man, her husband, who was a distance away. He wanted to dance with Natalia, but felt a bit self-conscious about asking her while Shawn was close by. Then, he figured it would be innocent since the music playing was fast and they wouldn't be too close. "Can I get a dance?"

Natalia didn't think anything of it.

"Sure. Just don't laugh at me if I can't do all the latest dance moves."

Maleek laughed and they began dancing. He was doing the cool rock and she tried to do the cool girl bounce, rock and slide. They both seemed to awkwardly keep their distance. It looked painful the way Maleek would reach for her to pull her closer, then remember where he was and display restraint. She, on the other hand, giggled and gently placed her hand on his arm and chest from time to time when she would step on his feet or miss a step. The song was over and Maleek seemed regretful.

"You can dance so why you lie to me?"

"Yeah, right, you just don't want to hurt my feelings."

"You want a drink?"

"Oh...ginger ale please."

"I'll be right back." Natalia watched him walk away. Mmn mmn mmn, she heard herself murmur. She couldn't help it when she looked at him. He was just as handsome as Shawn except he had long soft hair that his wife braided into unique designs. His smooth skin was a tad bit darker than Shawn's and he was tall enough to be a basketball player, in fact he was one not more than a year earlier. Maleek's career ended after he tore his fair share of ligaments then pulled a hamstring and the Atlanta Hawks cut their losses by terminating his three year contract.

Every time Natalia saw him she couldn't help but wonder how big his dick was. She stood there day dreaming, fantasizing with a silly smirk on her face trying to imagine Maleek on top of her. Someone came up from behind and slid their hand around her finally resting their hand on her bosom. In her daydream it was Maleek and his big hands went further south and she didn't stop him. But when the person kissed her neck she snapped to attention and instantly knew that it was her husband. His hot breath was tainted by the sour odor of alcohol.

"Ewww, Shawn. Your breath wreaks."

"So? You're my wife and that means you still gotta kiss me," he slurred.

"You think?" she replied sarcastically and turned to look for Maleek. She was sure that he wouldn't approach her now.

"So, you having fun?" Shawn asked with a goofy smile.

"No thanks to you."

"No thanks to me? Fuck you talking about?"

"Ugh! Now you're so drunk that you're cursing at me?"

"Why you tryna start a fight? I was having a good fuckin' time and shit. And I'm not drunk. Fuck this," he swaggered away from her leaving her standing there with her mouth open in awe. Since moving to Atlanta, his drinking had sparked many an argument between them. Especially since his drinking turned into a sport. He did it so often Natalia jokingly dialed AA once and passed him the phone.

"Here you go pretty lady," Maleek said, handing her a fluted glass of ginger ale overwhelmed by beads of condensation.

"Thank you."

Maleek was careful not to say what he was thinking out loud as he watched lustfully while she sipped from the slim red straw. Her lips looked luscious as they puckered in order to suck in the liquid and he wished his dick was the straw stuck between them. He came out of his trance.

"I can't believe that I'm bored at my own party," he laughed.

"I'm glad you said it because I kind of feel the same way. But, it is late and Shawn is drunk and I am ready to leave. I'm sorry to be rude Maleek but his drinking is getting out of hand and it's scaring me."

"I know he gets to trippin' now and then from the Henny but don't take it personal. Trust me he's not an alcoholic, yet." He winked then chuckled. Natalia smiled a weak smile knowing that the word yet was what scared her even more. He could very well become one the way he was going. "You know what? It is late. I'll drive y'all home. Let me go find him."

"Okay."

After searching for more than ten minutes, Maleek was about to give up. Then he saw scraggly Paul whose mouth leaked spit as he directed Maleek to the men's room where he said he last saw Shawn. Maleek walked in as Shawn was coming out.

"Sup, Big Mal?" Shawn slurred with a grin.

"Nigga, where you been?"

"Doing me, nah actually she did me." He laughed then turned around to acknowledge the sexy young girl sneaking out of the men's room behind him.

"What's wrong with you? You're wife is here. What the fuck are you thinking?"

"Nigga, I ain't fuck the broad aiight. What? You my father now?"

"Just come on. I'm taking y'all home."

"I ain't leaving."

"See, now if you gon' act like a child I'ma treat you like one."

"Whateva," Shawn slurred some more then chuckled.

"Come on cause I'm ready to bounce from my own shit. It's getting weak now."

"How you leaving and you gotta lock up?"

"Ray and em' will do it for me. Now lemme get your high ass home before you throw up in my club," Maleek laughed.

"Aiight, aiight I'm comin' damn. Hold on...I think... I'ma... throw up... right...blaagggggh," Shawn jokingly said then straightened himself out and said, "I'm ready now."

"You know you are one crazy muhfuckah right?"

"Why?" Shawn grinned.

"Cause you got a beautiful wife here and instead you fucking with some jail bait in a bathroom. You on some high

56

school shit." Maleek shook his head. He was mad at Shawn for being so rude to Natalia. How could he mess with skanks when he had a beautiful, classy woman who truly cared about him? Shawn just blew hard and sucked his teeth.

It didn't take long before the snoring began. As most drunks do, Shawn fell into a deep sleep in the car. Maleek practically had to hold him up to walk into the house. Once inside the house he collapsed on the floor in the game room.

"Just leave him there. Let him sleep it off," Maleek told Natalia. He took Shawn's jacket and dropped it on the arm of the couch.

"Thanks for your help Maleek. I don't know how I would've managed." She smiled appreciatively.

"He can be a dick at times but that's my nigga, you know."

"Yeah, I know. Need anything before you go?"

You butt ass naked right now! "Um no thanks, I'm straight."

"Okay, we'll see you tomorrow then."

"See you tomorrow." He smiled and left. On his way to the car he kept thinking that she deserved better than what Shawn was giving. It wasn't his place, but he would talk to Shawn about his drinking for her sake.

Natalia walked over to where Shawn lay and looked down at him. He looked so peaceful. He didn't look like the drunken idiot that she had to help get out of his clothes. She wanted to burn them because of the smell. His drinking was getting worse and she wondered how he got to this point. She tried to remember the way things were. It wasn't the same and she knew things would have to change or some drastic measures would be taken.

CHAPTER SIX

Maleek's wife Faye was back from visiting her mother in California and Natalia wanted to get her hair done so she called Faye. She had never been to Faye's hair salon but the way Faye's hair looked so soft and shiny she couldn't wait to see what wonders Faye could perform on her hair. Faye drove them in her brand new Christmas present from Maleek; her canary yellow Hummer. It looked like a monster school bus. Natalia laughed every time she saw it screech into their driveway. Faye's hair salon looked like a million bucks. It was even snazzier and bigger than Andre's salons in New York. Natalia was impressed with the fact that it was more than a beauty parlor. It was a full service salon boasting full body herbal wraps, water massage therapy, mint mask facials and paraffin waxing. When Natalia strolled in people looked at her as though they'd seen a ghost. Natalia ignored their stares. Faye didn't ordinarily do hair, but she told Natalia she'd been dying to get her hands in all of her thick, silky hair. At the time Natalia didn't pay it any mind, but now as she looked around at all the hair stations, she realized they were full of huge hook needles, bundles of thick black thread and loads of weave pieces. It was as if everyone in the salon was getting a weave.

"What is there a discount on weaves today?" Natalia whispered to Faye. Faye's neck jerked as she kindly put Natalia in her place.

"No there isn't. We all don't have long thick hair like you Natalia. Some of us have to accentuate with a weave, hellooo!" she snapped and ran her fingers through her own china doll bang.

Natalia's jaw dropped, displaying her embarrassment. She had no idea that Faye's silky tresses hadn't grown from her own head, but were actually secured with thread. She figured since Faye was so piss colored she had to be mixed with white blood too leading her to foolishly assume that Faye's smooth dark hair was a result of mixed breeding.

"Yes it's all mine...sheeiiit I paid an arm and a leg for this blend of European," Faye laughed.

"Oh...it's so real...I mean it's so pretty..."

"Natalia you will find that a weave ain't a dirty word anymore. It's just like the clothes on our backs, a necessity. Girl don't nobody out here care if you got one or not."

An hour later, Natalia was sitting under the dryer reading a magazine when she noticed Faye laughing it up with a woman that looked familiar to her. She stared intently trying to place the face. Her cell phone went off and she looked at the caller ID and sighed with relief as she answered, "Oh Andy I miss you like crazy."

"I know you do so let's make up for lost time princess. I've booked a flight for Saturday."

"Yaaay!" she beamed.

"I just hope your ass don't plan on staying out there for too long."

"Hell no! I told Shawn I was going back to New York at the end of the month. Susan told me that the FBI claims that next month they'll release my funds. I can't wait."

"Now don't go believing those lying bastards just yet after seeing how they yanked your chain before about that."

"I know, I know...I just need to do something with myself you know. I feel useless."

"Yeah, you miss being the head bitch in charge don't you?" Andre laughed.

"And you know it," Natalia giggled and noticed some girls were watching her. She hoped this wouldn't end up to be another violent incident over her husband's gallivanting. Faye came over and lifted the dryer helmet.

"Girl you are so lucky I bought these high powered

dryers cause you'd have to be sitting here all damn day! Look at all this damn hair. I know you tired of sitting on your ass right?"

"Yes please tell me I'm dry now," she said, her eyes pleading. Andre screamed into the phone.

"I know you ain't got some rookie all up in my hair. You better tell that bitch to get her hands out of there!"

Natalia couldn't help but laugh.

"Who's that? Shawn?" Faye asked.

"No, it's my best friend."

"Oh, hi best friend," Faye bent over and said close to the cell phone.

"Oh, shut up bitch," Andre mumbled.

"He says hi."

Natalia smiled a phony smile. She was dying to burst out laughing but she dared not do it.

"Come over to my throne," Faye giggled.

"Look, you go ahead and let that wanna be finish your hair. Don't worry when I get there I'll undo whatever she does to you."

"Andy you're so crazy. I'll see you Saturday. So you have to call me before then to give me your flight details okay?"

"Yes darling, will do. Love you."

"Love you too."

"Now Natalia I know that ain't no real friend cause I'm sure Shawn would have a fit before he let you have a man as your best friend."

"Shawn knows him well. He's my sweetie pie. Oh and he's very gay," she chuckled.

"Ohhh, I knew it was something like that because Maleek wouldn't allow me to have no man as my best friend." Natalia just smiled, thinking to herself how she would never allow a man to dictate her life. But then again wasn't that just what Shawn was doing?

Her hair was done and although she begged Faye not to put anything other then hair sheen in her hair, she still ended up with a boatload of sticky hair spritz and big doobie pins decorating her entire head. Before she could get out of the chair, the same woman she'd noticed before and thought looked familiar passed her a flyer.

"Hi, I'm Talea and I've got a boutique next door. I design clothing."

"Oh," Natalia looked at all the pictures of models dressed in sexy, yet sophisticated clothing on the flyer. Natalia looked up at Talea and the familiarity hit her like a ton of bricks.

"Do I know you from somewhere? Your face is so familiar to me."

Talea smiled went over to a magazine rack, grabbed a hair magazine and brought it over to Natalia. Natalia looked at the cover and saw Talea with her face adorned with flashy make-up.

"I'm a model slash actress. I've been in a few music videos and on a couple of sitcoms."

"Oh that explains it." Natalia laughed. Talea looked Natalia up and down and said, "You're a model too right?"

"No," Natalia blushed.

"You should be. Look, I'd like to hire you to work the runway for my fashion show coming up this weekend and you can do some print work. Say yes please..."

"Girl, you should do it. I wish I could," pushed Faye.

Natalia wasn't sure what she'd be saying yes to, but it sounded like a plan since she didn't have a job anymore and still didn't have access to her money. It would be a fun way to make a little extra money. "Okay I'll do it."

"Great! Let me give you all numbers and get yours." Talea pulled out her cell phone and they exchanged all their information.

"Okay, so Faye can tell you how to get to the photo studio on Friday this way I can do your measurements and get a fitting in before Saturday. I'm so glad I met you today," Talea smiled.

"Same here and thanks for the job."

Shawn was convinced that Natalia's new job was going to bring too much attention to her. One might call it jealousy but it ran deeper. Shawn was enjoying being the sole provider, keeping Natalia under lock and key basically since she didn't have her own money. She had to ask his permission to go certain places and do certain things since she needed money to do them.

He watched her as she rummaged through the closets looking for an outfit to wear. Talea told her that clothes were waiting for her at the photo studio, but she still wanted to show up in style. Shawn finally spoke after watching her slip into a sexy dress.

"Don't go tempting muthafuckaz cause I don't wanna have to go to jail. Seriously though ma, you look real nice."

"Thank You daddy," she simpered.

He gave her a wink, walked over to her and squeezed her in his arms.

"Daddy needs some snookie right quick."

"Get off of me! You would wait until I'm dressed and ready to go to pull a stunt like that."

"That's some bullshit right there. I can't fuck my wife?"

"Not right now you can't," she grabbed her purse and left with Shawn on her heels cursing her out. She slammed the door so hard a picture on the wall in the game room fell into Shawn's oval ten-foot long fish tank. He cursed her some more as he pulled the picture out.

She walked over to Faye's house quickly. Maleek answered the door and nearly swallowed the gum he was chewing when he saw her.

"Hi, Faye was supposed to take me to the photo studio to meet Talea."

Maleek's eyes narrowed at the sound of Talea's name. He couldn't stand her. In his opinion she was a grimey sneak who would do anything to get what she wanted. He remembered when she was just a lowly stripper who engaged in extracurricular activities for extra cash. She had a checkered past, but she did do a good job of cleaning it up to the point where she actually got respect now.

"Oh damn, I don't think Faye remembered that cause she left last night to go to California. She took the kids to see her moms. She's got cancer you know, so Faye goes to see her a lot while she gets chemotherapy."

"Oh, no...I'm sorry to hear that. I guess I'll call Talea and ask her for directions. I'm just scared that I'll get lost. I've only driven out here like two times and it's so confusing."

"Don't worry I'll just drop you off and pick you up when you're done."

"Oh Maleek I couldn't ask you to do that. Besides I'm sure you're going to be too busy later."

"No, it's okay. Besides if I can't pick you up I'll find another way to get you home."

He looked so good in his wife beater. His muscular arms looked good enough to lick. She wanted so badly to jump his bones right then and there. Although his basketball shorts were extremely baggy, she could almost imagine why he needed all that room.

"Hold on right quick I'm going to throw on some sneakers."

Maleek steered his Escalade EXT truck into the mini mall parking lot. Natalia looked at her watch and saw that she was a few minutes late.

"Thank you so much, Maleek."

"No problem. Look when you're done just holla at your boy and I'll come back for you."

"Okay, thanks again."

She spotted the photo studio sign and hurried in. An attractive woman with burgundy streaks in her hair greeted Natalia with a warm smile from behind the front desk.

"Good afternoon, may I help you?" Her southern drawl befitted the Georgia peach stereotype she was accustomed to.

"I'm here to meet with Talea Gibbens."

"Okay, you can go down the hall to the door on your

right."

"Thank you." Natalia walked into the room and saw two thin models with skimpy dresses huddling close to one another on a bear skin rug. Talea came out from behind a silk screen backdrop with two outfits on hangers.

"Hey, Natalia try these on."

Natalia took the outfits and followed Talea to the dressing room. A woman was waiting to spruce up her face with neon bright make-up and add blonde extensions to her hair to give her a funky punk look. When the woman was done coifing her hair she whisked Natalia off to a floor length mirror. Natalia stood there with a blank stare. She wasn't too fond of the look. Hey it's a job, she told herself. The photo shoot went off without a hitch and it lasted longer than Natalia imagined it would. She got there during daylight and her job as a model didn't end until well after it got dark. She sat out in the reception area and pulled out her cell phone. She felt bad about bothering Maleek to pick her up. He wasn't her man and it was Shawn's duty to see that she was okay. She knew they had argued earlier but usually they made up by Shawn or her breaking the tension with silly jokes. Then they sealed the deal with hot rough sex. She figured she'd call her husband joke about her pussy needing dusting off and he'd come running. She called his cell phone and he didn't answer. It rang and rang until the voicemail came on. She didn't leave a message instead she hung up and called back. But this time the voicemail came on instantly. Just to make sure that she wasn't imagining things she called again. The same thing happened. She knew that meant he must've turned his phone off. She could feel her face get hot as anger and confusion consumed her. Shawn was changing so much. He'd become so argumentative and dare she think it, distant. She was stuck now and she didn't want to call Maleek, but she had no choice. She started to dial his cell phone when Talea walked out.

"Hey girl you still here?"

64

"Well, I'm going to call my ride now."

"Ride? Don't worry I'll take you home or maybe you'd like to hang out with me. I've got an album release party to go to. You should come. You look like you should be in at a party or in a video right now."

Natalia took all but five seconds to decide. She would fix her husband by partying and make him worry about her whereabouts.

"I'm ready to party."

"Haaay," Talea laughed.

Talea was like royalty in the party. She knew practically everyone in there. She networked and managed to introduce Natalia to everyone who was anyone at the same time. She made Natalia feel special. She treated her like she was her long lost friend. They were invited into the VIP lounge and chilled out with the guest of honor who happened to be a famous rapper whose videos featured Talea. Natalia took phone numbers and had so much fun being the center of attention that she totally forgot that she was a married woman. When she did remember she called Shawn's cell phone again and again but he let it ring out until the voicemail picked up. She grew angrier and made it a point to dance with a lot of different men. She even drank champagne just to spite Shawn. Something she shouldn't have done because it made her head soar and she felt as though she could walk on air. She tried it and ended up in a stranger's arms until Talea rescued her.

"Girl it's time for you to go home and sleep it off."

"Nooo! I don't wanna."

"Oh, yes it's time for you to go. You're tore up," Talea laughed and she recruited a couple of willing men to help get Natalia out to the car.

"Shit, I have to fill this tank before I hit that highway." Talea said and looked over at Natalia who just flashed a ridiculous smile. "Girl you are so gone. I hope you'll be alright. You live with your man right?"

"No, my stupid husband," Natalia answered, sounding

agitated.

"Oh. Well I hope he doesn't hate me after this," she chuckled.

"Who cares what he thinks."

"Uh-oh, sounds like y'all aren't on speaking terms right now."

Natalia's cell phone went off and she checked the caller ID. When she recognized Maleek's cell number she answered quickly.

"Hiiieee," she slurred ridiculously.

"Ma, I told you to call me when you were done. I got a message from PB asking me if I knew where you and Faye went. I called him just now and told him Faye wasn't here and that I dropped you off at the photo studio."

"Oh, really? Well PB would've known all of that if he answered his cell. He even turned it off. So fuck him," she growled.

"Um, Natalia you don't sound like yourself. You aiight?"

"Nope, yup...I'm fiiine." She was high as a kite. Now Maleek was really worried. "Where are you Natalia?"

"I'm in good hands. We're pulling up in the gas station right now on...on...where are we?" she asked Talea.

"Bank road."

"We on Bank road, Vrrooooom," she giggled then blurted. "It's the big green gas station! Pump it up gas man!" Talea laughed heartily. Natalia was drunk and it was a funny sight.

"You drunk or high?" Maleek asked.

"And the difference would be...?" Natalia giggled.

"Who are you with?"

"I'm with my good friend Talea. Right Talea, you're my goodest friend right? Good, gooder, goodest."

"Yes, Natalia...now give me the phone," Talea was cracking up with laughter now. Natalia could barely pass the phone to her. Talea put the car in park next to a self-serve pump. She put the phone to her ear.

"Hello."

"Yo, what did you do to her? Why is she all fucked up?"

"I didn't do anything to her and who are you anyway?"

"Don't worry about it. She ain't no trifling ho like you yo, so why you got her out there gettin' high and shit."

"Wait a minute who the fuck are you calling a ho? Who is this? You don't know me," Talea shouted, with her head going in circles. Her ghetto side started coming out even though she vowed to never let it out ever again.

"Just bring her to me at Club Twisted right now."

"Who the fuck are you?"

"Ay, don't fuckin' talk to me like that bitch cause I'm not your child. This is Big Mal. Now you know where the club is so just bring her to me."

"Oh, it's you..." Talea's tone changed to that of a vixen. It was Maleek AKA Big Mal. He was the sexy ex-basketball player turned dealer who wasn't just fine, but rich. She remembered how she sucked him off and he still refused to have sex with her. He acted like she was just another whore. She regretted not getting with him and hated that he chose Faye over her. She still harbored resentment towards Faye because of that night. Now she wondered what he was doing calling Natalia at three o'clock in the morning. She thought she had something on him. She thought she could finally trap him into having sex with her now.

"Why are you calling her?"

"That's my partner's wife and I was supposed to get her home after she was done with the photo shoot so now nosey you can go tell my wife all of that."

"Why are you always so hostile towards me Maleek? Be nice with your sexy self."

"Just bring her to me at the club aiight?"

"Whatever." She quickly hung up visibly disturbed by the way he ignored her childish crush. When she looked up Natalia was stumbling towards the twenty-four hour convenience store at the station.

"Natalia! Come back here." Natalia turned back around and stumbled back to the convertible.

"Just sit here and wait for me okay?" Talea helped her back into the car and shut the door.

"Uh- huh, kaaay," Natalia giggled.

"Girl please don't ever drink again, ever," Talea shook her head. She pumped gas into her tank then went inside the store.

"Natalia?"

"Who?" Natalia looked up in the direction of the familiar male voice.

"Oh God, it is you. What in the world?"

"I know you..."

"It's me Seth."

"Seth? What are you doing out here? Are you stalking me?" she giggled.

Seth laughed loud, "Are you okay?"

"Um...uh nope...maybe."

"You're drunk!"

"No shit, Sherlock!" She said visibly chagrined. Seth couldn't believe running into her in Atlanta of all places.

"Natalia what is your cell number?" he prayed even in her drunken state that she'd be able to give it to him.

"Ummm..."

"Come on tell me your cell number so that I can call you later I need to know you got home safely okay?"

"Okay..." she said and actually rattled off her cell number in slurred gibberish. He made her repeat it and he put it in his cell phone.

"Now who are you here with? Why are you in Atlanta?"

"What are you doing? Leave her alone," Talea rushed over.

"Oh, Miss it's not like that. I know her from New York."

"Natalia you know him?"

"Yep. It's Seth...sexy Seth...he's got hair now. He used

68

to be bald and sexy...SEXUAL CHOCOLATE!" she screamed.

"She's been drinking huh? She doesn't drink I wonder what made her start." Seth observed, looking at Talea as if she were a bad influence.

"I don't know but I've got to get her outta here so good night...good morning whateva," she sighed and put the car in drive and drove out of the Gas station. Seth looked at Natalia's cell number staring up at him from the screen of his cell and smiled to himself.

"Come on Natalia...come on drink this. It will help you sober up. Come on sit up." Maleek desperately tried to get some of his homemade anti-hangover elixir into Natalia's system before he took her home. She spit out the spearmint gum Talea gave her to chew on earlier. When Talea dropped her off at the club she told Maleek how Natalia threw up on the highway. Afterwards Talea not only tried to hug him but kiss his cheek as well. He pulled back abruptly, having known where her lips had been and told her to get out. He didn't like Talea one bit and he let her know it every chance he got. She left frustrated and scorned. He took Natalia into his office and tried to get her to sit up in his chair. She kept slumping downward and laughing. He switched from the elixir in the foam cup to a small plastic cup filled with plain old tomato juice. She sipped it and spit it out. He wiped her mouth and caressed her face. She was still adorable even though she was pissy drunk.

"Maleek?"

"Yes?"

"I'm sleepy."

"Okay I'll take you home. Can you walk for me?"

"Uh-huh. But Maleek?"

"Yes Natalia?"

"Can you carry me?"

Maleek laughed. "Yes I'll carry you."

He carried her out to his car and drove her home. He hoped that Shawn would be home and he could unload her on him. During the drive home she went in and out of a conscious state. She finally became alert right before they pulled into the complex. She seemed more coherent. She looked over at Maleek.

"My head is pounding."

"I bet. Well be prepared for the worse. Why did you drink tonight?"

Natalia looked away embarrassed. "I was being spiteful but in the end I guess I did myself in if anything. It was stupid," she spoke in a hushed tone.

"Ma, don't let nobody make you do anything stupid that will hurt you. If anything you hurt them!" he chuckled. Natalia smiled weakly and opened the car door to get out.

"You need me to carry you to the door?" he laughed.

She didn't find it funny and just hurried to the front door. She opened the door with her keys. All the lights were off and she assumed Shawn was in bed asleep. Maleek came inside to make sure she was okay.

"Is he sleeping?" he asked her as she descended slowly downstairs. "He's not here."

"Oh." Maleek had no clue where Shawn was. In fact, he hoped Shawn was on his way home. Natalia kicked off her shoes and ran her fingers through her hair. Her nails snagged on the blonde extension pieces. She sucked her teeth and flopped down on the couch in the living room. Maleek flopped down next to her.

"Now don't go jumping to conclusions."

"I wasn't, but now...you're making me think things," she jokingly accused. She smiled at him and he at her.

"You know for a first time drunk you handled yourself pretty well."

"Really?"

"Hell, yeah! Shit I've acted worse and I can handle my liquor," he laughed.

"Honestly I can't remember much but I know that I will never do that again."

"Be thankful you can't remember. You'd probably wanna forget anyway."

"True."

"Listen to you. And you cursed up a storm when I talked to you on the phone. You sounded like a real ghetto girl."

"Oh you and Shawn are always making fun of the way I speak. Y'all are so wrong for that."

"Oh see you tryna get ghetto again," he jokingly pushed her. She playfully punched his arm.

"Well, thanks again Maleek. It seems like you're my babysitter...always looking out for me."

"I know. But I don't mind. Somebody has to when PB ain't on his job."

"Lately he's been neglecting that job a lot."

"Don't worry he'll come to his senses soon enough."

"We'll see," she sighed. She started slouching again, which let Maleek know she needed to sleep off the rest of the liquor in her system.

"Aiight Ma I'm out. You need some sleep. Sleep it off and you'll be okay."

"I hope so." They stood up and hugged each other. She put all her weight on the tips of her toes in order to reach up and kiss his cheek. Her lips caught part of his and she couldn't help herself. He couldn't restrain himself any longer and they kissed. He fell back into the couch and she straddled him and they kissed like there was no tomorrow. His tongue tasted every corner of her mouth. She sucked on his tongue until his dick was rock hard beneath her, poking her. She wanted it so bad but he squeezed her so tight and sucked on her tongue with such gentleness that she was frozen. She didn't want him to take his tongue out. She didn't want him to let her go either. She moaned with each delicate suck of her tongue and he breathed loudly and his cock felt swollen under her, as if it were going to burst through his pants and drill its way right through her panties. Something she would've begged for had they not heard the slam of a car door. It was reflex alone that made Natalia jump up from Maleek's lap, otherwise she would've stayed

71

there creating friction between her thinly veiled panty crotch and his pulsating mound of man meat.

Maleek took time getting himself together. He exhaled regretfully and stood up. Natalia looked down at the huge bulge in his pants. If Shawn walked in he would definitely know what went down. She yanked until Maleek's jersey came out of the top of his jeans and covered up the evidence. Maleek looked at her longingly. She gave him her sorrowful puppy dog look. She casually walked to the window to see if Shawn was on his way in and noticed a car leaving the complex. It wasn't Shawn's car door they heard. She ran back into the living room where Maleek stood with his cell phone to his ear.

"It wasn't—," she stopped short because Maleek put his finger to his lips. She waited until he was done on the phone. "It wasn't him."

"I know because that was him on the phone."

"Where is he?"

"He didn't say. He just um, told me about one of my workers and hung up." Natalia looked at Maleek suspiciously. At that moment it struck her. Her man wasn't home and it was in the wee hours of the morning. Revenge grabbed a hold of her, forced her over to Maleek and made her grab his denim covered crotch.

"Finish what you started," she purred like a sex kitten.

He slid his hands down to her tight heart shaped ass and squeezed. Then he looked into her spiteful face and saw the contempt. He knew that before their passion was purely straight chemistry, but now she was just angry and in revenge mode. He would rather it be more than that especially since he would be crossing a line that he'd never crossed before. It was the very same line that he himself condemned others for.

"You're just mad right now and I don't want it like this."

"Huh?" she asked dumbfounded.

"We can't do this," he caressed the side of her face sweetly. "I can't do that to my man and I won't mess up our friendship. If things were different..."

Now she was perplexed and as she reached for him he restrained himself.

"I'll see you tomorrow," then he left the house and her feeling rejected.

Shawn woke up in his Escalade. He looked over at his worker whose head was up against the passenger window. Empty bottles of Hypnotic and Hennessy lay atop of his dashboard. He moved the bottles to the floor behind his seat. He looked down at himself then at his reflection in the mirror. He was a mess. Then he heard a low moan. He looked behind him and remembered the girl that pleasured both of them for a bottle of Hypno the night before. She'd done things that he couldn't resist participating in since his wife never freaked him like that. Now, looking at the girl's young, angelic-like face he wished he'd never left his house yesterday. He drove to where his worker's grandmother lived and nudged his worker's shoulder to wake him.

"Wha-what's good?"

"You home nigga. Take her with you," he gestured toward the young girl still knocked out in the back. He reached in the back seat and slapped the underage sleeping beauty on her ass, hard, waking her up.

"Damn!" she jumped up.

"Get out," Shawn's worker announced.

She looked over at Shawn then slyly grinned, batted her eyelashes and said, "Bye Shawn. Nice meeting you." Shawn just turned around and put the car in drive. As soon as they were both out of the car he sped off.

He reached his complex and eased up to the gate. After pressing in the security code the gates opened and he felt nervous. He'd been out all night and all morning. Hell, it was well into the afternoon and he knew Natalia would yap his ear off with her bitching. He turned the key in the lock and he slowly pushed the door open. He could hear music playing. The music was coming from upstairs so he slipped into one of the guest bathrooms to shower. He quickly washed every part of his body, brushed his teeth and gargled. He dried off quickly and was relieved to find a robe hanging on the towel rack behind the door. He went into the kitchen and poured himself a glass of orange juice. He sat in the dining room trying to figure out an alibi. He left his cell in the bathroom and it went off until it fell right off the sink, bounced off the plush shag rug and slid across the marble floor. Natalia picked it up and brought it to him in the dining room. She threw the phone at him.

"Answer your fucking phone!" It hit him in his chest and if he wasn't so much in the wrong he would've jumped up and smacked the shit out of her.

"Don't throw shit at me aiight?"

"Fuck you, you stupid motherfucker! You were too busy fucking some bitch out there to answer you're fucking phone for me, huh? I could've been dying but you just couldn't tear your dick away from her cunt could you?"

"Shut the fuck up and go back in the room. I don't wanna hear this shit," Shawn retorted, dismissing her, shook his head and went back to drinking his orange juice.

She reached her boiling point. "Fuck you!" she screamed then did something out of character. She hauled off and smashed him right in the face with a porcelain cup she grabbed from the dish drainer. He didn't or better yet couldn't react on the account that he nearly fell out of the chair from shock alone, never mind the hard blow.

Now, that she realized what she'd done it was a little too late to take it back so she hauled ass. He pushed himself up from the chair, took only a few outstretched steps to catch up to her then grabbed her by the hair before she could get away.

"What the fuck is wrong wit you, huh?" he shouted in her face. "Bitch are you fuckin' crazy?"

She'd never seen this look of insanity in his eyes before. Not even when the cops captured them at the airport. It was scary and she truly regretted her actions now. *What the hell was I thinking?* She tried unsuccessfully to get her hair untangled from his fist. He slapped her so hard that she fell into the dining room table and bounced to the floor. Her nose started bleeding. She was so scared that she curled up into a ball to protect herself from his wrath. Shawn grabbed her in a rage and dragged her to the bedroom. He pulled her hands away from her face. Then he put his knee in her chest and slapped her in the face hard—repeatedly. It wasn't until he saw the fear in her face and the blood smeared all over her that he stopped. He instantly became remorseful not to mention nervous. He couldn't believe what he'd done. He eased off of her and scooped her up in his arms. He brought her into the bathroom and gently lowered her into the huge diamond shaped tub. He grabbed tissue from a tissue box dispenser and carefully wiped away blood from her face. Her face was frozen in horror like a deer in headlights. She didn't speak or move. She remained still, very still. He undressed her with care and began filling the tub with warm water. He poured some of the spa salt bubble bath he bought her into the water. Instantly, bubbly foam appeared as water filled the tub. He dropped his robe and stepped into the spa with her. He washed her with his bare hands and massaged and gently rubbed her body, concentrating on her chest where a bruise had formed. He washed her face and bloody nose until there was no more blood. He kissed her nose and pulled her onto his lap in the tub. He didn't notice the blood dripping from the gash in his head that she made with the cup. He didn't even care when a little blood got on his eyelid. He was more concerned about his wife. It was like she'd stopped breathing. He put his ear to her chest and heard her heartbeat. She was alive so why wouldn't she speak?

"I'm sorry baby girl."

He held her in his arms, pulling her into him gently. He could hear her faint breathing and pulled her face in close to his and kissed her lips ever-so-gently.

"I'm so sorry BG. I'm sorry..." he squeezed her gently and it was then that she exhaled and slid her arms around his neck. He stroked her hair and continued apologizing, over and over. She felt something wet on her cheek. It wasn't the bath water. It was a tear from Shawn's own eye. They did not speak. They did not move from the tub for a while. They just huddled there until they realized that their bodies were going to look like prunes if they didn't get out of the water. Shawn never regretted anything as much as he did beating her. He doted over her like an infant. He dried her off and helped her into her robe. He lay her down in their bed and went back into the bathroom to put a bandage on his own wound. He returned to the bedroom and Natalia was crying.

"Baby girl, don't cry."

"What's wrong with us Shawn? When did it turn into this?" she asked incredulously. Shawn couldn't answer. All he knew was that they'd both been through so much together and some days he wondered how they made it thus far.

"We've weathered many storms and yet it's like we're sabotaging our happiness now. Are you tired of me? Am I not enough for you?"

He'd never seen this side of her before. She was not the insecure type. But, now she actually looked the part.

"No, Nay. I love you like no other on this planet. I'm just going through some shit right now. I just need you to bear with me."

"Why are you cheating on me, Shawn?"

"How you figure?"

"You're always disappearing."

"You know what I'm out there doing. I'm taking care of business for us. I don't have time for bitches. You're my wife BG. I married you cause you're the only one that can handle me...and Max." He smirked while grabbing his crotch knowing that maybe his conscious would have felt better if he just admitted the truth.

She smiled and even though she didn't buy his denial, it was enough at that moment. She reached for him and he for her. He made love to her and that sealed the deal.

CHAPTER SEVEN

"Andy, Andy, Andy!" Natalia jumped up and down. Andre dropped his bag and they ran to each other in pretend slow motion playfully emulating characters in a soap opera. He swung her around and she kissed his face all over.

"I missed you sooo much."

"My little honey bunny." He looked at her lovingly then screeched. "Girl you look like a damn toothpick. I gotta get some pasta into you."

Talea walked over and covered her mouth as she laughed.

"And who might this be?" Andre asked suspiciously.

"This is Talea. She's my boss while I'm out here doing that modeling thing."

"Oh, I should've guessed. Well aren't you beautiful? I'm guessing you started out as a model yourself?"

"Yes...and an actress," Talea grinned. "So you're the infamous Andy. All she does is talk about you."

"Oh, really? I can't call it. Mmm, you wouldn't know it from the amount of times she calls me." He gave Natalia the evil eye. They led Andre to Natalia's car and Andre's mouth fell open. "Damn girl, this vehicle is on fire! Lemme drive."

"Go ahead."

Natalia threw Andre the keys. Andre knew Atlanta well. He had family all over Georgia. He pulled into Natalia's garage with confidence.

"Girl, look at y'all living like Bill Gates. So, are you a Stepford wife now?"

"No, Andy."

She laughed. Talea laughed too and added her two cents.

"You should have seen your girl when she was drunk from a couple of glasses of champagne."

"Whaaat? My honey bunny was drinking?"

"Yes she was. Oh, I see she ain't tell you about that huh?"

"Damn Talea are you a reporter?"

"Don't hate cause you're busted Miss Thang. I wondered when you were going to join us grown-ups and have a drink," Andre cackled.

"Well I guess I won't be a grown-up for long. That won't happen again," Natalia said with confidance.

They went shopping together and they took Andre to the photo studio and Talea showed off her creations. Andre agreed to hook up the model's hair for her the fashion show.

Natalia called Shawn and asked him to come see her prowl the catwalk and he agreed to be there. He showed up late, but got to see his wife rule the runway like a professional. She looked poised and confident. He liked the way she vogued down the catwalk. He enjoyed how she looked up there sashaying her hips to the amative beats ricocheting from the speakers to his ear drum. Talea came out on stage after the show was over and thanked everyone and announced the after party.

The after party was at a bourgeoisie club. It was just as fashionable as the patrons shaking their asses, drinking Cristal and Belvedere. Shawn sulked at a corner table with one of his friends waiting for a spare moment with his otherwise indisposed wife. She was in the middle of a crowd of fake industry insiders fawning over her. Andre was attached to her hip and that also bothered him. Now that Andre was here he was sure that she wouldn't have time for him and he was annoyed with having to be mindful of what he wore in his own home because flaming Andre was there. He feared Andre might spy on him just to get a glimpse of his bare ass.

Talea strolled over to Shawn and flirtatiously placed her hands on his shoulders.

"Finally I have time to say hi to you. Thanks for coming out."

"You're welcome." Shawn wasn't too sure who this chick was but she certainly was sexy.

"I'm Talea Gibbens the designer." She smiled graciously.

"Congratulations! I was really feeling you're designs."

"I'm sorry but you are...?

"I'm Shawn and this is Keith."

"Oh are you guys from Da Streetz magazine?"

"Nah." Shawn chuckled looking over at Keith. Keith just grinned. Talea was drawn to their table by Shawn's magnetism. She liked his nonchalant style and his look. He looked like a model but when he opened his mouth he sounded like a thug, she automatically detected his accent, he was a New Yorker. It turned her on even more and she decided that she had dibs on him tonight. She invited herself to sit with them and sat across from Shawn and engaged him in a boring conversation about New York.

Andre left Natalia's side to converse with a debonair Argentinean and Natalia finally realized that she hadn't seen her husband the whole night. She went searching for him.

"I lived in Manhattan and Brooklyn and I have an aunt that lives in Jamaica Estates in Queens," Talea said in one breath and sipped her drink while admiring Shawn. When she was certain that she had his attention she seductively sucked the cherry off the toothpick.

"Yeah? That's where I'm from." Shawn pretended to be interested in the conversation and not her overt flirting. All he could do was stare at her cleavage that begged for attention since she wore an open v-neck dress that made him wonder how those bad boys stayed hidden behind the flimsy material. He kept waiting for one of them to pop out. He watched her lips move as she flirted with him some more.

"I like the way you talk. I've always had a thing for New York men," she grinned mischievously.

"Is that right?" Shawn had his mack on and nearly

forgot that his wife was somewhere in the vicinity. Keith interrupted their mutual flirtation with.

"I'ma be right back."

"Aiight," Shawn replied, returning his attention to Talea. She was still grinning. Then Natalia came over and slung her arms around her husband's neck.

"Hi Daddy. What'd you think?" Talea was stunned. Her heart sank and she tried to cover up her disappointment by praising Natalia's performance.

"You're a natural. You looked good up there tonight."

"Thank you. Well, I had a good teacher."

Natalia rested her palm on Talea's shoulder and asked, "So, you've met my husband already?"

"Well, yes. We were talking about New York." She smiled a phony smile. Shawn's heart pounded a bit faster than usual for some reason. It was like he'd been busted yet he didn't do anything. Then he realized why he felt that way. If it were possible, he would've taken up Talea on her flirting. She could definitely get it, he had thought to himself right before his wife showed up.

"Well Daddy?"

"You looked professional BG and real sexy." He grinned at her. She kissed his cheek. Talea excused herself from the table and sashayed away. "So when are we gonna leave?" Shawn asked anxiously.

"Well, I think Andy's having a little too much fun to leave. Come dance with me."

"Yeah, aiight." Shawn got up and actually danced with her. They had fun and before they knew it Andre was begging them to leave.

Thereafter, Talea kept volunteering to pick up Natalia when there were photo shoots. She'd come over so many times that Maleek swore that she was stalking *him*. But, she had moved on to greener pastures and neither Shawn nor Natalia were the wiser. Shawn was barely home at the times Talea came so she got a little creative and started hanging out with Natalia every chance she got since she knew that

Faye was too busy to play best friend to Natalia. Although she didn't have any problems with hanging out with Natalia, she still had a hidden agenda.

Natalia planned on going back to New York with Andre to find out about her seized assets. So, of course Talea volunteered to take them to the airport. The day before Natalia left Seth called her cell phone and told her that he had left Atlanta but planned on coming back. They caught up on what each other was up to and even planned to meet up when Natalia got into New York.

"Thanks for the ride Talea."

"Don't mention it. Bye Andre it was so nice to meet you. You are every bit of fun Natalia said you were." She hugged Andre and kissed his cheek.

"Ditto, girl, you're a real sweetie."

"Well y'all have a safe flight and Natalia call me as soon as you get into New York and call me before you leave so I can know when to pick you up. Okay?" Talea reached in to hug Natalia.

"Okay," Natalia replied and returned the hug. They kissed each other's cheek and waved good bye. Natalia and Andre rushed to the ticket and baggage check-in leaving Talea standing there grinning to herself like the Grinch Who Stole Christmas. She had a lot of web spinning to do. She rushed back out to her car and as she sat in her car she called Faye's shop to alert them that she needed her hair done. Faye was still in California and Talea wondered how she held onto Maleek when she stayed gone all the time. She knew Maleek had to be getting pussy from somewhere. She stopped wishing it was from her and concentrated on getting Shawn to cash in on one of her coochie coupons.

Shawn and Maleek left Maleek's gym after a vigorous workout. They got into Maleek's truck and he started it up.

"Listen I'm not fucking with Pablo no more. So, it's up to you if you wanna stay with him or if you wanna use this next connect that I got."

"Man, I was doing aiight with Pablo. What happened?"

"He ain't giving me no breaks. I'm tired of his penny-anti shit. I'm trying to make this big cake right quick and get out and he's trying to keep a niggah locked in."

"Well, I got Ty in this shit so his girl gon' be coming out here in like a week and I gotta hit him off wit a heavy load so I can't afford to fuck up the flow right now. So, if you think your new connect is solid I'm switching. Fuck Pablo."

"Aiight well I'm gonna cut ties with him this week so we can go up there together."

"Sounds good to me," Shawn agreed.

"So, will Ty ever be able to come back over here?"

"Nah. Not anytime soon anyway."

"That's fucked up."

"It's aiight out there though. He's having the time of his life out there, living like a fuckin' king."

Maleek pulled into the complex and agreed to go with Shawn later on in the night to pick up money from his workers that came down from New York. They both went into their houses bound for the showers.

Shawn came out of the shower refreshed and plopped down into the bed butt ass naked, eventually falling asleep. The sun was still out but he felt guilty after he woke up and realized how long he'd been asleep. He felt as if he should've been doing something with the couple of hours he let slip away. Bored and hungry he went into the kitchen and started cooking spaghetti and meat sauce. Just as he was about to help himself to a helping fork full of spaghetti the doorbell rang. He thought it was Maleek and checked the time.

"It's too early to go get that shit now," he mumbled on his way to answer the door. He tied his robe closed and opened the door.

"Hi, I'm sorry to bug you, but I forgot to tell Natalia to give me the dress from the other night. It was a sample dress I altered to fit her and the manufacturers need it to make a new pattern."

"Oh, I'm sorry Talea but I don't know where it's at."

"Damn... I'm on a tight schedule with the manufacturers. Do you think I can just check her closet for it? I'd really appreciate it. You'd be saving my ass," she looked at him piteously.

And what a nice ass I'd be saving, Shawn thought and a smile appeared on his face instantly. He opened the door wider to let her in. "Aiight. You know where it is right?"

"Not really," she lied. She couldn't wait to spring her trap on him. She watched his robe as he walked. It flapped open just enough to tease her. She couldn't help but smile to herself at the convenience of him being in a robe.

"Here you go. She got this whole wall. It's all walk-in so good luck," he spread out his hands.

"Maybe if you help me I could find it faster," she said innocently. They were in his bedroom and Shawn was naked under his robe and he was sure that this was a no-no but he still agreed to help her.

"Aiight, so which one from the fashion show is it?"

"The yellow and melon colored one." They were inside the closet taking turns on Natalia's motorized racks to find the dress. Talea hung her purse on one of the racks.

"I'm so hot. Who knew this was gonna be such a job." Talea conveniently kicked off her shoes and began fanning herself. Shawn looked at her pretty feet then his eyes evaluated the rest of her, following her long shapely legs up to the short jean mini skirt with Christian Dior emblems dangling from a denim belt. The strategically ripped T-shirt she wore showed her hard nipples underneath and her long, crinkled chestnut hair shined without illumination. Her pretty face glowed when she caught him staring. "You found it?" she asked, knowing damn well he didn't.

"Not yet," he unconsciously licked his lips just thinking about sucking her perky nipples.

"Damn," she sighed and walked out of the closet and sat on the edge of the bed.

"What's wrong? You tired already?" he chuckled.

"I'm just trying to figure out what I can do if I don't find the dress. I wonder if she brought it to the studio," she said, pretending to be deep in thought.

"Why didn't you ask her when you dropped her off at the airport?"

"I forgot. Now I regret it," she moved strands of crinkled hair from her face. "You got anything to drink?"

"What would you like? Water? OJ? Cranberry juice?"

"Water," she answered and watched him leave the bedroom. His broad shoulders filled out the robe nicely. His calves looked so strong and she noticed that he didn't have ugly feet like most of the men she encountered. She waited until she heard the refrigerator open then she quickly ran into the closet slipped off her thongs and stuck them in her purse. She ran back to the bed and sat down. Shawn came in right after her buttocks hit the down-filled, fluffy duvet cover. He handed her the glass and she sipped sensuously, watching him, hoping he would attack her and rip the clothes right from her body. He walked away from her and went back in the closet.

"Maybe she brought it back to you," Shawn called out from inside the closet.

"I'm so sorry I've got you up and about when clearly you were ready to relax."

"It's okay. But I don't see it. Maybe you're eyes can find it better than mine with you being the designer and all."

"Maybe...but I'm just taking a break right now," she giggled. Shawn came out and stood in front of her. He now knew what she was up to. The first thing that came to mind was that Natalia was setting him up and he wasn't about to take the bait.

"Yeah, well do me a favor and hurry up and find it cause I'm about to go eat." He walked out of the room and got his food. Talea was crushed. She didn't know how to handle this part. She thought for sure that it would be easy to persuade Shawn since she knew he was attracted to her.

She pretended to look around in the closet some more.

The doorbell rang again and Shawn was starting to think there was a conspiracy going on and someone didn't want him to eat his spaghetti in peace. He opened the door and Maleek was standing there on his cell phone.

"Damn, welcome to Grand Central muhfuckah," Shawn laughed.

"Why you say that?" Maleek asked and closed his flip phone.

"A nigga been tryna eat for the past hour and can't cause people keep ringing the bell and disturbing me."

"What people?" Maleek asked then Talea came strolling downstairs.

"Did you find it?" Shawn asked sarcastically thinking he passed one of Natalia's tests.

"Nope," Talea was shocked to see Maleek. She knew he would put Shawn onto her, ruining everything. Maleek expressed disgust as he watched her saunter downstairs. Then he looked at Shawn suspiciously then diverted his eyes to conniving Talea.

"What you doing here?" he asked her accusingly. She approached him hesitantly.

"I was looking for a sample dress Natalia wore at the fashion show. I need it for the manufacturers."

She hoped that Maleek would buy into her lie. He obviously didn't and told Shawn to come with him into the game room.

"I'm just going to use the bathroom," Talea announced, nervously before sprinting back upstairs.

In the game room Maleek spoke in a voice close to a whisper as he filled Shawn in on what a trifling, sex fiend Talea was. Shawn listened intently and was relieved to hear it. Now, this put a spin on things. She was just a slut. There was no covert operation to trap him into cheating. The more Maleek exposed Talea the more interested Shawn became. Now, he wished Maleek would go so that he could take Talea up on her offer. He checked the time and still felt it was too early to make the pick up so to buy himself time with Talea he told Maleek to wait while he called his workers. He pretended to go get his cell phone but he was really going to check on Talea, he hoped she wasn't gone.

Talea lingered in the bathroom trying to figure out how she would explain to Natalia why she came over knowing that she had the dress already. She wondered if Maleek would really tell Natalia. Shawn tapped on the door gently.

"You alright?"

"Yes," Talea answered after quickly putting her thongs back on and opened the door.

"Listen, why don't you take your time and check the closets thoroughly. I'ma be back to help you in a few okay?"

"Okay," she smiled a wide mile, unaware of how eager she looked.

Shawn grabbed his cell phone and ran downstairs.

"Yo, they ain't ready for me. So I'ma go later on. You gon' be busy?"

"I just gotta do something right quick that's why I came by. I wanted to tell you that I'll be back to go with you like after ten, aiight?"

"Yeah aiight that's good. So, I'll call you when I'm ready to go."

"Aiight and watch that ho. Don't get caught up," Maleek warned again.

"Damn nigga why you hatin' on her like that?"

"Cause she's a grimey ass bitch." Maleek shook his head. "I can't stand gold diggin' bitches like that."

"Aiight nigga damn," Shawn laughed.

After hearing the door slam, Talea moved from the hallway back to the closet and started the motorized rack. Shawn walked in.

"Any luck?"

"No and I'm starting to think that she took it with her. Either that or I've lost my damn mind." She looked up at the rack and pretended to see something familiar and grabbed it.

She looked it over quickly then cleverly dropped the dress and bent over to pick it up with her ass facing Shawn. Her ass cheeks spread ever so slightly and the view was just enough to get Shawn aroused. She turned around and saw exactly what she wanted to see, a glimpse of Shawn adjusting himself under his robe. Their eyes met and his signaled what he wanted. She looked at him coyly and hung the dress back on the rack.

"Shawn, I can't find it so I'm giving up," she said and grabbed her purse. Shawn just stood there looking oh, so sexy that she knew she couldn't play the game any longer. She had to go for what she knew. She conveniently brushed past him on her way out. Shawn followed her out. She turned around suddenly bumping into him and dropping her purse.

"I'm sorry," she said, her breathing accelerated.

"I'm not." Shawn grinned as his swollen tip poked Talea right through the robe. She looked up into his brown eyes and saw the lust and melted right on the spot. She fished for his thickness and stroked it with both hands. Shawn palmed the top of her head, applied slight pressure and directed her to his dick with his eyes. She got the message, knelt down and devoured him. She was so turned on that she drenched her thongs with vaginal secretions. After slurping him nearly unconscious, she pulled out a condom from her purse and slipped it on him. Shawn could tell from that move that not only was she every bit the professional Maleek told him she was but he didn't have to dip into his own hidden stash of condoms. Shawn pulled her up by her arms and yanked up her mini skirt. She quickly turned around and slid off her thongs, making a special effort to bend over in an enticing manner. Shawn couldn't wait to plunge deep into her. He grabbed her tiny waist from behind, slid into her and drilled away. They did every and anything that Talea could think of to convince Shawn that he was missing out by being with Natalia. She kept trying to get him on the bed but Shawn would deter her and wouldn't even let her get close to it. He had no problems with any other location though, he did her on the floor, up against the wall, atop his dresser, in his corner chair, in his walk-in closet and in the master bath's steam room. They spent so much time prolonging their pleasure that night came and Shawn forgot about his pick up and about calling Maleek.

"**A**ndy when are you going to buy a house and get rid of the condos?" Natalia asked.

Andre raised a brow and looked at her as if she had two heads. "Now why would I buy a house? I don't have time to mow no damn lawn. Besides, my condo in L.A. makes me money all year round and you know how I feel about this place. There's no place like home." He continued chucking dirty clothes from his travel bag into his hamper.

"I missed New York so much." Natalia searched her bag for her cell phone. "You know I totally forgot to call Talea with my return flight info."

"You know I really like her. She seems like a real nice girl you know," Andre said and zipped up his bag.

"Yeah I know. It feels even more genuine than the little friendship I've established with Faye. But, man do I envy Faye for her husband. Andy did you see how sexy he is?"

"Yes girl. Whoa, I see why you almost gave him some. I don't know about you though Miss Thang. You are getting from bad to worse. But you better be careful because Shawn ain't nothing like Mark."

"Speaking of Mark I should see him while I'm here."

"Oh here we go. You plan on giving him some too?"

"Oh, hell no! I just want to see how he's doing and what's going on in his life that's all. Besides, if anyone would get some it would be Seth." She giggled mischieviously.

"You know you've changed. You've done a complete 360 ever since you got involved with Shawn. All this fucking around is not like you."

"Andy I'm tired of being the prude. I'm going to *live* life to the fullest from now on. Have you forgotten all the shit

89

that man has done? Remember what I told you? Plus, look at how many messages I've left to tell him that I've arrived safely and he still hasn't returned my calls. It's like he doesn't even care about me sometimes. He's got to be cheating."

"If he is, that doesn't give you the right to try and match him at it. Two wrongs don't make a right."

"Yeah, yeah whatever. Two wrongs don't make it right but it sure does make it even!" She laughed. Andre laughed and popped her in the head with the dirty jeans he yanked from his suitcase.

"Eeew! Get those nasty things away from me."

"Call that girl and tell her when you're getting in." Andre shook his head and laughed.

"Yes mother." Natalia dialed Talea's cell phone.

The phone rang four times before Talea answered panting. "Hi Talea, it's Natalia."

"Oh, hi." Talea sounded winded and had a case of the giggles which seemed weird to Natalia but she continued on anyway. "Do you have a pen?"

"Um...sssahhh, oooh... not with me. I'm uh, um riding...Unngh...ohhh...I-I'm in my carrr..."

"Uh, okay...well call me later and I'll give you my return flight information." Natalia could tell that Talea wasn't really paying her any mind so she hurriedly finished with.

"Actually, I'm thinking of staying a bit longer than I originally planned to so I'll call you later on, is that okay?"

"Ohhhhkay." Talea giggled some more then said, "B-bye, ungh!"

"Okay bye," Natalia looked at Andre strangely. "What happened?" he asked.

"Either that girl was on drugs or she was having sex with someone while I was talking to her."

"Really?" Andre's ears perked up.

"Yes, she was just giggling away and sounding like she was trying not to moan."

"Humph, he must not have been really working her

out if she had time to answer the phone." Andre sucked his teeth.

"Andy, she sounded like she was getting a work out if you ask me and besides some people find that enticing while doing it. You know having the girl on the phone and trying to conceal the fact that she's getting her back banged out as my husband would say. Shawn's made me answer the phone like that before. I bet you didn't even know it when you spoke to me that he was punishing my coochie did ya?" she busted out laughing.

"Ugh, now I'm going to have that image in my head whenever I call you from now on." Andre chuckled.

"Hey, I can give you a preview..." she pulled off her shirt.

"Put those things away." He tried to cover her bare breasts with his hands.

"Now you know you're only getting me horny," she laughed and walked into the kitchen. She searched Andre's fridge for something edible. "Damn, Andy go food shopping why don't you," she sighed. "I suppose we're going out for dinner?"

"Actually honey bunny I'm going out with Adonis for dinner. I thought you were going out with Seth. And would you put something on over those bowling balls."

"Ha, ha. Anyway, I didn't tell him tonight. I planned to spend time with you. And why the hell don't you two just get married already?"

"Oh please girl. Adonis is hung up on keeping his space. If we did get married he'd still want to live in his own place. As for Seth, he's so hooked on you all you have to do is call him up and tell him you have no plans and I know he will rush to the rescue."

"I guess." She grabbed her cell phone and called Seth.

Just as Andre predicted Seth was all too happy to be her fill in date for the evening. She met him at a ritzy restaurant—late as usual. He hugged her tightly.

"You're a vision as always."

91

"Thank you."

They were escorted to their tables and ordered their entrees. Natalia even asked for a glass of red wine.

"Please don't tell me you've become an alcoholic," Seth teased.

"I have to explain to you about what you saw in Atlanta. I was angry at my husband and I drank a couple of glasses of champagne to spite him. I know it was stupid but I didn't think I'd get drunk so quickly." She sipped her wine.

"It takes no time at all lovely. So, you should be careful. Even with that wine. I don't want you getting drunk and forgetting all about me."

"I could never do that," she smiled.

"I have to ask, how is it that I'm always running into you? It's as if fate is trying to tell us something. Don't you think?"

"Well, I must confess it is uncanny. By the way, why were you in Atlanta?"

"My business is doing very well so I've expanded. I just set up an office out there. I built a house out there, too. I sublet my co-op in Brooklyn now. So I'm in between living spaces. I'm staying in a hotel while I'm here."

"Wow. I'm happy for your success. So you're making the move to Atlanta permanently?"

"Well, I won't say permanently, but I'll spend the majority of my time there because the office there needs a lot of attention. So what were *you* doing out there?"

"I'm living there...for now." Her mood transformed.

"Uh, if you don't want to talk about it you don't have to."

"No, that's not it. I'm just not too happy about living there. That's one of the reasons I jumped at the chance to come home. My husband built an entire community complex out there."

"That's right you have a husband..."

"Yes...but it's not—"

"You don't have to explain. I'm smart enough to know

92

if a woman is happy in her marriage she wouldn't find the time to go out on a date." He grinned then added, "Natalia you should really stop picking the wrong men and give me a chance."

"Hmmm, maybe you have to do a little more wooing. But women can be happy and still meet with a friend for dinner and it can strictly be platonic."

"And if you think any man on this planet will buy into that bullshit then you're crazy." Seth laughed loud.

She giggled, slapped his hand playfully and asked, "Never mind that just explain to me how you've managed to stay single?"

"Well, you know me I'm always on the go so whenever I try to get involved with someone they feel as though they're competing for my attention so they bail on me."

"They bail on you? I don't believe that."

"Okay, there were a couple of times that I did the bailing. But I had a good reason."

"So, you figured dealing with a married woman would be more convenient?"

"Honestly, I would rather you not be married. But you are like a rare diamond that I have to have."

"So, I'm a conquest to you. How many points am I worth?"

"I think you know better than that. I just keep hoping you'll see me as the special one and let me prove myself."

"Well here's your chance," she smiled coyly.

After dinner he took her to a jazz lounge and she was even bold enough to perform for open mic night. She sang so well she received a standing ovation. Seth was impressed. Natalia enjoyed her night out on the town with Seth. He made her laugh and they danced in the street on the way to the hotel that Seth was staying in. His room wasn't fancy but Natalia didn't mind.

"I'm sorry there's no where to sit except the bed." Seth looked apologetic.

"It's okay," she sat on the bed, took off her shoes and

scooted towards the middle of the bed. "I'm tired anyway. Would it be okay if I slept here?"

"Not at all." Seth took his shoes off. Natalia's skimpy mini dress rode up her thighs exposing more than she should have. Seth's eyes surveyed her body as she lay in the bed with her eyes closed. She wasn't wearing a bra so all night he fought the urges to stare at her supple breasts and protruding nipples. Then, as if he had willed it to, her dress neck line lost its battle with Natalia's abundant cleavage and a nipple peeked out. As hard as he was staring Seth swore that it winked at him. He went over to the bed and lay next to her. A murmur escaped her throat resembling a content sigh. She had him so turned on at this point that he wanted to bite her exposed nipple. He wanted to fuck her like she'd never been fucked before but he was a gentleman and if she wanted to sleep he would respect that. It pissed him off that she fell asleep so quickly but he just remembered the old adage, *good things come to those who wait*. She inadvertently slid her hand up his arm. He moved hair from her face and kissed her cheek gently and just watched her as she slept.

"Goodnight beautiful," he whispered.

Shawn was awakened by the doorbell. He looked around the room then down at himself. He was in bed. There was no sign of Talea. Then he remembered that he'd sent her home in the wee hours of the morning hoping no one saw her leave. He grabbed a pair of pants from his closet then yanked them on and rushed to the door. He looked through the peephole and saw Maleek.

"What's good Mal?"

Maleek had a disappointed look on his face as he walked in past Shawn. He handed Shawn a bag.

"I picked it up for you. But, them niggas ain't acting right. You gotta go lay down the law cause they busy picking up bitches instead of concentrating on their jobs. You gotta make them know this ain't a game. Your boys from New York aren't focused."

"Thanks for lookin' out and doing that for me man. I'ma go down there a little later. They acting a little crazy cause they in a different atmosphere right now, nahmean? They'll be aiight though."

"So, what you got into last night? why you ain't do the pick up?"

"I was sleeping."

Maleek wasn't stupid. He had already put two and two together. He suspected that Shawn had already fallen into Talea's trap. He remembered that he nearly fell at one time too. The girl was good. He wasn't Shawn's keeper so he had no right to chastise him. He went on to the real reason he came by.

"Tonight is the NBA party at the club. Are you coming?"

"What? You ain't got to ask a nigga that cause you know I'm in there." Shawn laughed.

"I need your help with something though,"

"What's that?"

"I've got to make an example out of that bitch ass nigga Smokey over in Decatur. I'm talking some serious shit. You got me on that?"

"Again with the stupid questions?" Shawn asked jokingly. "Where you want it head or gut nigga?"

Maleek laughed and said, "This niggaa has to be a serious commercial to them other muthafuckaz who got it twisted out here. They gonna know that I'm a serious nigga when I'm done."

Maleek rallied his troops and Shawn did the same and they rolled out to Decatur eleven deep. They were broken up into groups riding in untraceable loaners; a black Hummer, a navy Yukon and a black Denali. It was eleven o'clock at night and Maleek wanted to rush the ambush that he had planned because he had to establish his alibi. He was hosting one of the most anticipated and infamous parties thrown in Atlanta at his club. It had already begun. He made sure that he was there for twenty minutes so witnesses could confirm that he was at the party. He knew that he had to get back in time for the musical acts to perform since he was the designated M.C. who'd introduce them. Then his alibi would be airtight.

They pulled up in front of a club Maleek's former partner frequented. Tonight, there seemed to be less people than usual. They camped out across the street from the club on the lookout for Smokey. They knew that he came early to eat in the restaurant section of the club then went on to VIP right near the dance floor. Maleek had forewarned his ex-partner about his routine rut. Now, the very thing that he warned him about would be the very ammunition Maleek needed. His plan was to get Smokey and his right hand man outside. Maleek already set the plan in motion when he recruited one of Smokey's workers to defect to his side. The worker who was to betray Smokey thought after proving his loyalty to Maleek by luring Smokey and his right hand man outside that he would be handsomely rewarded. Maleek had other plans for him. But, for now he received Maleek's star treatment.

Shawn looked over at Maleek.

"You sure this nigga ain't double-crossing you?" Shawn questioned, adjusting his dark shades.

"If he is, it's aiight cause I got a plan B for his ass."

He looked out the window past Shawn and could see Smokey easing his way out the side door of the restaurant. He and two other men followed Maleek's informant right down the street away from passersbys and rounded the corner. That was Maleek's cue. He stepped on the gas and made a wide turn to follow them with the rest of his entourage in tow. They rounded the corner and could see Maleek's informant being draped up by Smokey. The informant was copping a plea as the other men looked on confused. The Hummer crept alongside them and the window went down then shots rang out. Smokey tried to dodge the bullets and in doing so he looked as if he were dancing.

The other two men went in separate directions. One guy ran down the deserted street and jumped over a fence. While, in mid air a bullet ripped through his thigh and he crashed to the ground. Unable to stand, he dragged himself to the front door of the house. One of Maleek's troops jumped out of the jeep, jumped the fence ran up on him and put a bullet in his neck. Just then the homeowner opened the door and released the collar on a pit bull and the dog rushed him. But the dog wasn't quick enough. He put a bullet right in its open mouth, just as the dog lunged forward.

The other man that was with Smokey ran back around the corner escaping the mayhem. Smokey got the worst of it along with his betraying employee. They were shot so many times that their blood formed what police described on the news later that night as a river.

The guy that got away happened to be Smokey's right hand man. He ran back to the club and got some of his men together and they ran back around the corner to find their leader dead. Maleek, Shawn and their men made a clean getaway. The vehicles were stashed and they all went to their respective homes to rid themselves of gunpowder evidence by showering and changing their clothes. Maleek had everything planned to a science that he had already bought a duplicate of the outfit he wore to the party earlier so that he could dispose of the one he wore to kill Smokey and he could return to his club without arousing suspicion.

They all met up at Maleek's club at different times. The club was packed and the party was well on its way to becoming the party of the year. Hip Hop and sports magazine photographers were taking pictures of all the famous people. Maleek and Shawn were purposefully caught in a lot of pictures with some of Maleek's old team mates and famous entertainers.

"I'm about to leave," Shawn whispered to Maleek who was sitting at a table being adored, laden by groupies. Faye had already left and Maleek had some drinks so he was feeling himself. If they were willing to cater to him he figured why not enjoy it. Besides, Faye had been through it all before with his fans so she'd already developed thick skin, rendering her immune. Either that or she just accepted it because she bore his children and owned his last name and she was living in the lap of luxury with him, so to her those women only had dreams while she lived out their fantasies.

Maleek gave Shawn a brotherly hug and whispered back.

"I owe you."

"Aiight man and listen I don't wanna see Faye on the news for killing your ass so make sure you go straight home and don't do no stupid shit." Shawn laughed knowing he was not the one to talk.

"I know you ain't talking. I saw you with that stupid ho Talea. I know why y'all leaving early." Maleek pointed a chastising finger.

Shawn laughed off what Maleek implied, even though Maleek was right. Talea staked out the party the whole night praying Shawn would take her home and do her like he'd done the night before. She watched and waited patiently. When he did show up, he was Mr. Popularity with all the ladies. But, when he saw Talea dressed to impress and remembered how she freaked him, he chose her for the night.

"Nigga I'm going home to my bed."

"Yeah, whatever you say." Maleek chuckled then turned his attention to the woman massaging his bulky bicep. Shawn left the club with Talea close on his heels. She kept trying to grab his hand and he kept snatching his hand from her. He finally acknowledged her in the parking lot.

"You drove right?"

"Yes," she answered.

"Meet me at the complex, but drive past the house and park in the cul de sac behind the house."

"Okay," she obediently agreed.

CHAPTER EIGHT

Natalia woke up in Seth's arms. His cologne's fresh scent rejuvenated her. She looked into his face and realized that Seth looked damn good, even while he slept. He had taken off his shirt. His Polo tank made his arms look huge not to mention the way he was laying had his peck bulging. She took in this sight and instantly she was sure that before she left New York she would sample Seth's fucking capabilities. She would make it her business to put him out of his misery and let him get what he'd been chasing for so long, just not this morning. She felt out of it and she was sure that her breath needed refreshing.

She eased out from under his outstretched arm and tiptoed into the bathroom. She brushed her teeth and came out to find her cell phone. She saw that she had a lot of messages on her cell phone's voicemail. She slipped back into the bathroom and called Andre's house because she knew that's who had to be calling her.

"Where've you been? I've been worried sick." He chastised her until she felt like a child.

"I'm sorry mother, but I fell asleep in Seth's hotel room."

"Say what? Girl, I'ma beat your ass!"

"But, mommy I didn't do anything. All we did was sleep." She laughed at how funny her explanation sounded.

"Get your ass home now! Sometimes I just don't know what to do with you, Missy," Andre sighed.

"Okay, okay I'm on my way." She hung up and opened the bathroom door and there was Seth greeting her with a bright-toothed smile.

"Good morning." She smiled.

"Good morning," he smiled and went in as she stepped out. He came out minutes later refreshed. She had her purse and was perched at the edge of the bed. He put on his shirt and his shoes.

"Ready?"

"Yes."

Seth dropped her off in front of Andre's building and he leaned over to kiss her cheek and she turned towards him so that their mouths collided. They kissed until their tongues became entangled.

"Can I see you tonight?"

"I don't know if Andre is going to let me out of his sight today but I'll call you later. If not tonight, then tomorrow night."

"Promise?"

"I promise." She smiled and opened the car door. He grabbed her arm and gently pulled her toward him. She turned to ask what was wrong but instead she got more tongue. Now that she was wet in between her thighs she wanted him to clean it up. But, knowing that she'd look too eager she decided against yelling, take me back to your hotel room now!

"Whoa!" she exclaimed and smiled seductively.

"Just one for the road, I hope I can see you again tonight. If not I'll be waiting to exhale until tomorrow."

"One way or another you'll exhale." She giggled and got out of the rental.

She floated into the elevator, down the hall and into Andre's apartment. He watched her suspiciously. He grabbed her and began sniffing her.

"Hmmm, I don't smell sex, but then again you could've taken a shower."

"Andy he is a gentleman. You know he could've taken advantage of me last night because I..." she didn't want to admit to drinking again so she didn't finish her sentence.

"Spit it out." Andre crossed his arms and tapped his feet.

"Alright, alright...I drank again but it was only table wine. I was a bit tipsy and he didn't take advantage of me. We slept with our clothes on in his hotel room. He's giving me butterflies and it's scary. It's the way that I felt with Shawn."

"Oh lord. Here we go. Honey bunny I hate to break it to you but Shawn is not going to deal with this the way Mark did. And since when have you started becoming a full blown slut?"

"Slut? Andy, how could you say that?"

"You're about to give Seth some fish and you was this close to giving Maleek some fish." He demonstrated with his fingers. "Hell, you gave him a lap dance."

Natalia listened thinking of how much Andre was right. What was she doing? She was a married woman and she had been through so much with Shawn that they were super bonded together. Nothing should come between them...right? But, if that was the case how was it so easy for Shawn to impregnate another woman? He cheated on her. He deserved payback. Whether it was with Maleek or Seth she owed him one or two or three.

"I'm far from a slut Andy. I hope that's not what you're thinking of me." If Andre thought she was a slut it would've killed her inside. He was the last person on earth she ever wanted to have any misconceptions of her. His opinions mattered above all others.

Andre walked over to her and looked deeply into her eyes.

"Nothing you do will ever make me think that of you. I know your heart. I will love you if you sold your ass on forty-second street right in front of the Toys-R-Us megastore! You will always be my honey bunny." He hugged her into his chest and kissed the top her head. "I love you girl."

"I love you too, girl." She giggled and Andre gave her a noogie on the top of her head with his knuckle. "So, we

101

straight?" she asked Andre with an innocent look on her face.

"Yeah son, we straight." Andy poked fun at her attempt at slang then sighed. "He done turned you into a ghetto girl."

"Nuh, uh."

"So, you're gonna fuck Seth aren't you?"

Natalia looked so guilty at that moment that she gave herself away. Andre shook his head.

on't even answer me. I don't want to be privy to that information just in case Shawn asks me."

Oh please! Shawn is too smug to ask you that. He thinks I'm Miss Goody Two Shoes with him. He thinks he's got me on lock."

"Well, in a way he does. He done whisked you away from New York and got you like some frumpy housewife and that's not you."

"I know Andy and part of me wants to stay here. I'm debating it. Besides, he can come visit me here. Since he trusts me so much he could agree to that don't you think?"

"What world are you living in? He wouldn't go for that. Especially the way y'all got together he knows better. Trust me he's going to say hell no."

"Well as soon as I get my money back things are going to change."

"When will that be?"

"I'm not sure. In fact let me call Susan right now." She called Susan and heard disappointing news. The FEDS still tightly gripped her accounts and claimed the audit hit a snag and would take longer than expected.

Andre took her to his salon so that she could say hello to everyone. Afterwards, they went to Adonis's Off-Broadway drag show. The day went by quickly and when evening fell Natalia was feenin' to see Seth. After the show they took Adonis out to celebrate his wonderful performance as a young Lena Horne. Natalia's cell phone rang and it was

Seth. She desperately wanted to see him so she asked Andre if he'd mind if Seth met her there at the restaurant. Andre gave her the okay.

When Seth arrived at the restaurant he looked *scrumptious* as Andre put it. They made small talk then left Andre and Adonis to celebrate together. Seth took her to one of his friend's Kung Fu tournaments and Natalia showed off her Tae Kwon Do skills. His friend was highly impressed as was Seth. After the tournament Seth suggested they go to a movie. Natalia didn't want to, so she figured on the way to the theater she'd convince him that the hotel room should be the next stop. She watched him as he drove and occasionally he'd glance over at her and smile his award-winning smile. He even put his hand on her thigh and gently rubbed. Natalia loosened the laces on her shirt and let her girls loose revealing her bountiful cleavage. When the light turned red and the car came to a stop she laid her head back and sighed loudly. Seth looked over and his dick had a spasm in his pants.

"Are you tired?"

"A little...maybe you can give me that massage you promised at the tournament."

"Yes, that's what I need to do. You look tense...very tense." He was so turned on that he prayed she couldn't see the lump that formed in his lap or the perspiration forming around his hairline.

He made it to his hotel in no time. Inside the room, Natalia peeled off her tight fitted clothing and lay on the bed in just her bra and thongs. She pulled all her hair up and lay flat on her stomach with her palms down and her arms outstretched above her head. Seth couldn't contain his excitement and tripped on his way over to the bed. Natalia wanted to laugh out loud, but she didn't. She found Seth's eagerness sweet. Seth took off his shirt and straddled her back. He applied pressure with his fingers at first then his palms. Natalia moaned delightfully as he massaged her into a state of relaxation. Her moans drove him crazy and her body movements under his warm hands made it hard for him to concentrate. He had to have her and he vowed to win at the manipulative game she so cunningly played. After he undid her bra and saw that she didn't protest he gently pulled her thongs down past her supple buttocks then he moved them down further past her thighs until they were off. She still hadn't protested and he knew that she was ripe for the plucking. He flipped her over with ease and she looked up at him longingly as if she'd been waiting for this moment, just as long as he'd been waiting. He practically ripped his clothes off. She sized him up once he was naked. He had a nice, well-proportioned physique but his penis looked quite small compared to Shawn's. She hoped that after having Shawn pounding her for so long that her walls would be able to grab a hold of Seth's smaller dick. Gradually his size faded from her thoughts as he tickled her clit with his tongue, expertly flicking it with enough pressure to make her beg for mercy. He obliged and moved up to her face, lingering. Seth wasn't really prepared for this moment. He had no idea that Natalia would let him get this far. He didn't have any condoms. At that very moment looking into her eyes he forgot all his senses and plunged into her, bare back. She wasn't thinking straight either so she didn't protest. Instead she reveled in the warm, moist friction between them. Seth stopped his long hard strokes and pulled out then went on to kiss and caress every part of her that yearned for it. He showered her breasts with attention, bathed her clit and tasted her moistness with his tongue. The amount of foreplay he gave her was extremely appreciated. Although Shawn had mastered her body he fell short on the amount of time he gave it during sex now that they were married. He was into punishing her vagina and although that was cool too she missed the sweet lovemaking he used to bombard her with in the beginning.

Seth made her come multiple times just as Shawn used to back in the days. With Seth she felt like a queen riding a float. He not only gave her orgasms, he tasted them, shared them with her, they even had them at the same time. He didn't force her to suck him. She actually jumped at the chance. She had to show him her appreciation for the wonderful *sexperience* he gave her. Afterwards, before they fell asleep Seth asked her, "When are you leaving New York?"

"I was supposed to leave in a couple of days... but..."

"Don't leave, can you stay another week? I mean I'll finish my business here and we can fly back to Atlanta together."

She was in no rush to get back to Atlanta and the prospect of spending another week in bliss with Seth didn't sound like a dilemma at all.

"I can do that."

"Good. So can you stay with me for the remainder of your trip instead of with you're friend?"

"Uh, I think he'd probably appreciate that more than you think."

She called Andre and pitched her plans to him. He could only sigh and agree to it. Her next call was the hardest and she had to leave the room to make it. She went into the bathroom and called her husband. He didn't answer. She got his voicemail and she let him have it.

"I can't believe that I've been in New York all this time and I haven't spoken to you once! Are you really that busy that you don't have time to answer your phone or call your wife? Shawn, I don't know what you're doing but I hope you realize what you're doing to this marriage. Well, I just called to tell you that I'm not coming home. Not yet, anyway. I'm taking another week to wait out this Federal hearing that Susan is trying to arrange for me. If you care, call me. If you don't, oh well, see ya when I see ya."

Shawn's snoring woke his own self up. He jumped up and saw the state his room was in. He and Talea went on a wild drinking spree before they sexed up a storm. Shawn looked around and realized that not only had he violated the sanctity of his marriage, but their bedroom as well. He had sex with a known whore in the very bed he made love to his wife in. He knew that alcohol was the culprit. It blurred his judgment and now he'd gone too far.

He jumped up and began yanking the sheets from the bed, yanking Talea right off the bed with them. She fell to the floor with a thud and woke up out of her inebriated stupor.

"What's wrong?"

"Get out," Shawn calmly said without looking at her.

"Shawn what's wrong baby? Why you trippin'?"

"Just go. I'll call you later."

"Is she here?" Talea became more alert now and tripped over sheets as she searched for her clothes. Shawn ignored her and after stripping the bed of all the sheets he bundled them up and went into the linen closet to find a new set of sheets. Talea grabbed her things and ran into the master bathroom. Shawn made the bed. Talea came out dressed.

"What's wrong baby?"

"Nothing." He walked past her into the bathroom and closed the door.

Shawn came out of the shower fully awake. Aware that he'd done a bad thing, a very bad thing. He came out of the bathroom and looked at the bed. It was weird how only now he regretted what he'd done. He picked up his cell phone and checked his voicemail. His wife had called, and called. Guilt ate him up and he didn't want to call her for fear that she would be able to tell that he'd just desecrated their bed. He paced the floor trying to figure out what to do. Should he call now or wait? He put the cell phone down and got dressed. He picked it up to call after he was dressed, but it rang right in his hand.

"Hello?"

"Sup lil' bro?"

"Sup?"

"Svel is gonna be there next week on Thursday. You gotta pick her up. She's coming in on American Airline flight

853. Check with the airline Wednesday night to confirm. So, is everything ready?"

"Yeah. You all set. But damn you could've given a nigga more notice than this."

"Yeah I know, but shit was hectic over here so I didn't get a chance to call you before. So you good?"

"Real good."

"How's enemy number one?" Tymeek laughed.

"You got jokes. Stop calling my wife that." Shawn laughed with him. "She aiight, she's getting on my damn nerves, but that's what a wife is for, right?"

"I wouldn't know about all that cause I ain't get caught out there."

"So, you're a comedian now, huh?" Shawn chuckled. "Get ready to make millions."

"We'll see. Holla at me later." Tymeek hung up. Shawn cleared the line then called Natalia's cell phone. He got her voicemail and he assumed she was pulling a tit for tat, ignoring his call. He called Andre's house and got his answering machine. He called Andre's cell phone and Andre told him that Natalia was out shopping. Shawn became suspicious because he couldn't picture Natalia shopping without Andre. His wheels were turning and he came up with his next move. He would go to New York and surprise his wife. He would make up with her. All the cheating he'd done would come to an end and he would focus on their marriage. First, he'd buy her something of significance to remind her of the way things used to be. Then, he'd take her someplace to force her to remember all of their times together in the beginning. He began plotting and planning until he managed to book a flight into New York, rented the same suite they shared at the Waldorf when they made up years earlier.

"I'll drop you off on my way to the meeting."

"Seth you don't have to worry about me. I can get to Andy's with no problem. I'll meet you back at the hotel later tonight. I'm supposed to go shopping with him. I know he's going to bite my head off for being this late." Natalia grabbed her purse and they left the hotel room together. Seth waited for her as she hailed a cab. He hugged and kissed her and went back to the hotel garage to get his rental.

Natalia met Andre at his salon and when he saw her strutting in with a feverish glow he grabbed her like an angry father would his newly deflowered daughter.

"Andy what's the problem?" she asked as they walked toward the sauna.

"You are clueless you know that? And that makes you dangerous."

"Whatever you're talking about can wait because I've got to give you the 411 on what went down. Oh, by the way I've got to get my things from your house to take them back to the hotel with me."

"You're not taking anything anywhere," Andre's face was so serious it worried her.

"What's wrong Andy?"

"First of all, I'm against what you're doing. Second of all, your husband, that's right your husband called the house and my cell looking for you."

"So? Big deal let him worry."

"That's just it. I think he was a little too worried. I have a bad feeling about this whole situation. You not staying with me while you're here is putting me in a bad spot. When he can't find you and calls me how am I expected to keep covering for you?"

"Andy I'll call him and tell him that I'll be in a conference with Susan and the FEDS or something. Don't worry about it. What's the worst he can think? He doesn't know what's going on. Besides, he's too busy out there having fun with those Georgia peaches. I don't think he cares what I'm doing anymore," she sighed and sat on a wooden bench.

"Y'all have been through too much to let little shit mess up what y'all have fought for. Who'd have thought y'all

108

would be married right now? Look at the odds y'all overcame. Look at the hurdles y'all jumped. Y'all would be so stupid to fuck it all up now over some nonsense."

"Andy, I love him. I just feel like he's falling out of love with me."

"Trust me, I don't think it's possible to fall out of love with you Miss Thang." Andre gave her a big smile and a big hug. She hugged back and thanked God that she had such a great friend.

"Andre, I love you like no other."

"This I know. So you call Seth and let him know you're not staying with him. In fact, you should go home to your husband now. I wanna know how you and that Seth person thought y'all were gonna catch a flight back together. Wasn't Shawn gonna be there?"

"Actually, Talea was supposed to pick me up but I don't think her seeing me and Seth together would've been such a bright idea either."

"Now you're coming to your senses. Well, I told Shawn you went shopping without me. So, we have to shop today like there's no tomorrow. And spend all his money girl."

"Haaay, you ain't said nothing but a word!" Natalia laughed.

The bags and boxes were so heavy that the taxi driver had to help them inside the building and the doorman helped them to the elevator. When they went shopping they hit every store imaginable until all the spending money Shawn gave her was gone. She couldn't wait to go back to Atlanta in the latest outfits that Andre helped her pick out. The shopping was therapeutic and with Andre selling her on getting her marriage back on track she totally pushed Seth to the back of her mind.

"I need a relaxing bath. Is it okay if I take one? Or do you want to go first?"

"Actually, honey bunny Adonis has another show tonight. I know you don't want to go again, right?"

"No thanks. So you're just gonna leave me, huh?"

"Well, yes. I'm spending the night by his house."

"It's okay. I just wish I'd known earlier. Can I just see Seth one last time before I go?"

"Nat you're a grown woman. If you wanna go ahead and cheat again on your husband that's up to you."

"Well, technically since I've already cheated and it's still the same person what will it hurt doing it one more time?" she winked.

"You have gotten so bad. Mmn, the devil done took over your soul."

"Aw, come on, if you could get away with it wouldn't you do it?"

"Girl, I can but I choose not to. Besides Adonis makes me not want anybody else!"

"Well damn it's like that?" Natalia laughed.

"Yes girl, you have no idea."

"Shawn used to do that for me too. He's changed so much."

"You've both changed. I've got to get freshened up to go meet my man." He switched hard past her and into the bathroom. Natalia sat in the living room and read one of Andre's magazines from his coffee table. Her cell phone rang. It was Seth. She explained her situation. He was very understanding and she felt compelled to give him one more bang before she left New York. She told him that Andre was leaving for the night and probably wouldn't be back until the next afternoon. She invited him over for dinner and...

Natalia practically rushed Andre out of his own home. She tidied up, cooked chicken parmesan, set Andre's contemporary iron and tempered glass dining table, chilled a bottle of red Zinfandel and took a relaxing bath. She put on a seductive lace and silk negligee. She swept her hair to one side and put on bubble gum MAC lip gloss. She played one of Andre's baby making CDs and swayed around the room to the music. The doorbell rang and she opened the door with a sexy smile.

"Welcome to La Palace de Natalia," she said in a

Spanish accent.

"Well damn," was all Seth could blurt out. He already knew what he wanted from the menu. She guided him to the dining room and he sat down. She poured him a glass of wine. She returned to the table with their food. Watching her glide to her seat made him incapable of waiting for desert. He couldn't wait. He had to have her so he got up and took her hand pulling her to stand.

"What's wrong?" she asked. Seth just grabbed her face and pulled it towards his. He kissed her and his hands roamed her silk and lace clad body. She loved the mere spontaneity of his attack. She didn't care if he took her right there. She'd worry about the mess and the guilt of doing it on Andre's table later. He must've had the same idea because he pushed her gently down on the table. He moved the plates and spread her legs. In the midst of slowly grinding into her, the doorbell rang. Natalia pretended not to hear it. Apparently the music made the person at the door diligent about getting in. The doorbell rang again and again and again until it messed up Seth's concentration and pissed Natalia off. He eased out of her and straightened himself out. She showed him into the guestroom that she never slept in whenever she came to Andre's condo. Natalia fixed her hair, pulled down her negligee and tied the robe closed.

"Who is it?"

The person just banged on the door hard.

"Oh for God's sake who the hell is it?" she asked, looking through the peephole. She saw nothing. Another bang then another followed. She put the door chain on and opened the door slowly.

"Yes?" she asked, nervously.

"Surprise!" Shawn's handsome face appeared. Natalia nearly fell over. Fortunately, she caught herself. She slammed the door shut and panicked. She ran into the guestroom where Seth was laying comfortably on the bed. He saw the wild look in her eyes.

"What's wrong?"

111

"My husband is here."

Seth popped up and looked around frantically. Natalia wracked her brain trying to figure out where she would hide him. Then it hit her. In Andre's huge kitchen he had a big pantry that Seth could fit in. There was just the matter of all the boxes and cans taking up most of the room. She prayed that Seth would fit regardless. She grabbed his hand and led him to it. He fit and he practically became as still as a statue. Natalia shut the door and ran back to the front door where Shawn was ringing the doorbell like a madman. She opened the door with the door chain in place once again.

"What?"

"Woman you better open this fuckin' door." Shawn was pissed now.

"Why should I? You were so busy before, now all of sudden you pop up and I'm supposed to jump?"

"Baby Girl, open the door please," he tried the sweet approach.

Natalia knew that if she didn't open the door she'd really cause suspicion so she opened it. Shawn dropped a huge shopping bag that was in his hand as soon as he got in. Then he grabbed her and kissed her so hard that he knocked the wind out of her.

"Whoa!" She pulled back. He squeezed her in his arms and looked around the condo.

"This place is just as weird as its owner."

Natalia pulled away from Shawn and walked towards the living room hoping to lure him away from the front door. She sat down on Andre's plush velvet chair that was shaped like a woman's pump. Shawn looked at her hard. He tried to figure out why she was dressed so provocatively.

"What's all this for?" he asked grabbing at her lacey robe.

"Don't worry about it. And why are you here?" she snapped.

Shawn looked at her suspiciously.

"If I didn't know any better I'd think Andre was faking

the faggot thing and giving you some dick."

"Don't be ridiculous." She dismissed his accusation with a nervous titter.

"Yeah? Well, why the hell are you walking around in his house looking all sexy?"

"I dress like this for bed a lot. Maybe if you paid closer attention to me you'd have known that."

"I do pay attention to you BG." He pulled her to her feet and rocked from side to side with her. He held her close. "It's like you knew I was coming cause you playing my song and looking all sexy."

She didn't answer him because her heart was beating so fast she couldn't breathe let alone speak. Then a noise sounded from the kitchen. She was sure that she was a dead woman now. Shawn stopped moving and listened. "What's that? Andre?"

"Maybe he came back," she said, praying that Shawn didn't investigate.

"Oh, he's not here?"

"No."

Shawn looked at her skeptically. She looked up at him smiling innocently.

"What?" Shawn ignored her question and left the living room. Natalia was too nervous to follow him right away. Then she gained enough courage, crossed her fingers and followed her husband into the kitchen. Shawn stopped to look at the table.

"Who was here?" he asked.

"I cooked for me and Andre but Adonis asked him to come to his show again. So he left me," she pressed her hand on her chest and tried to act hurt.

"Riiight," Shawn said with sarcasm. For some reason he felt compelled to search the house and started searching the other two bedrooms, both bathrooms, the closets then he came back to the kitchen. He eyed the huge door to the pantry. He looked at Natalia. She looked nervous, so he thought whatever or whoever was in the closet held the key to everything. He drew out the suspense by walking over to the pantry slowly and turning to look at her with each step.

Her chest felt like an earthquake was erupting inside it and she was sure that she would faint when he did open it. Shawn flung open the pantry door—nothing but boxes of cereal and canned goods. Natalia turned away so he couldn't see her exhale with relief. Shawn walked up behind her.

"Why did you look so nervous? You had me thinking you were hiding some nigga in here."

"Shawn just because you're fucking every bitch you see doesn't mean I'm whoring around like you. You're the one who got some hoochie mama pregnant! I should be checking up on *you*."

"See why you gotta go there? I didn't come to argue. I came to show you that I love you. I have something for you." He searched the shopping bag he brought. He pulled out a long gold box and a smaller gold box. He put them on the table and she opened the big box first. There were a dozen yellow roses like he'd given her the day she finally got to see his face after he had kidnapped her. She smiled to herself as memories flooded her head. She opened the small box and saw a diamond and platinum necklace with a diamond heart pendant.

"You have my heart now and forever." He caressed the side of her face. She looked up into his and smiled. "Get your things, I want you to come with me to your next surprise."

"Get my things?"

"Yes, everything cause you not coming back. We're gonna leave New York together." She didn't know how the hell Seth pulled the disappearing act but she was grateful that he did. She quickly packed up her things and got dressed. She left Andre a note and locked the door with the key he'd given her.

CHAPTER NINE

It was Friday night and Maleek's club was off the heezy fo' sheezy. It was packed and the bar overflowed with alcoholics, soon-to-be alcoholics and thirsty broke female vultures searching for a dummy to trick on drinks. Maleek made his way through the crowd to Shawn and gave him a bottle of Belvedere. An ungrateful looked at him.

"That's it?"

"Nigga, I'm lucky I got this shit." Maleek chuckled and swallowed some more of the alcohol concoction in his glass.

"Aiight, so when is Da Pitbullz gon' perform?"

"Midnight on the dot and them niggas look high already." Maleek laughed. They walked over to VIP where all of their friends were drinking, laughing and betting on which woman they were going to leave with.

Maleek sat his drink down and looked at his watch. He had to go to the stage to introduce the highly anticipated act that had his club so packed. He fought his way through the crowd and onto the stage.

"Niggas and Nigettes I got the hottest rappers out right now, just for y'all so y'all better appreciate this shit...these niggas came all the way from NYC. Make some noise for DA PITBULLZ!"

All the men shouted and barked, all the women screeched with delight and all the haters ice grilled. The group came on stage and booming beats blasted while the first of the crew began rapping. People jumped up and down with excitement. In the middle of the performance a group of men pushed their way past people until they got to the VIP section. They split up. A few remained close to the VIP

115

section, some went further towards the stage and others dispersed within the crowd. They pulled out guns and started blasting away at anyone in their way. It was pandemonium. People were screaming, diving and trying to hide.

One of the men shouted, "That's for Smokey muthafuckaz." Then he squeezed off more rounds into the club. The music was still playing in the background and two members from the rap group were shot and fell to the stage leaking blood over its edge. Shawn and Maleek lay next to each other on the floor under a table. Shawn saw blood and checked himself. It wasn't from him. He looked over at Maleek and saw that Maleek was hit in his hand. Shawn yanked the tablecloth off the table over them, glass shattered as tumblers and liquor bottles hit the floor. Shawn helped Maleek wrap the tablecloth around his hand.

"Thanks," Maleek said and used his good hand to push himself up. They cautiously stood up and looked around. A slew of bodies lay on the floor. It was hard to tell who was hit and who wasn't. The sirens sounded outside then police came running in with their guns drawn.

Shawn walked into the house and blew hard. It was happening all over again, the drawbacks of being a dealer. He had to watch over his shoulder at all times, lose more friends from silly retaliations and come home with blood splattered all over him. He was thankful that this time it wasn't his own, but nevertheless he shouldn't have any blood on him at all. He was sick and tired and he was sure that once he got Tymeek set up with a regular connect he would get out for good this time. No looking back. Natalia heard the door and came downstairs. She turned on the light and gasped. She ran to him and searched him for a wound.

"Oh God not again." She began sobbing. Shawn grabbed her hands and tried to calm her down. "Baby Girl be easy. It's not my blood."

"Not your blood? Then whose?"

"Maleek got shot in his hand. Some niggas came in

and shot the club up. They killed twenty people!" He sighed and pulled off his shirt and searched the kitchen pantry for a garbage bag. He took off the rest of his clothes and threw them in the bag.

"Oh, my God that's awful! Oh, no poor Maleek. Is he still in the hospital?"

"Nah, he's home. His hand is gonna be okay. It's a good thing Faye finally brought her ass home. He just needs some TLC."

Natalia felt so bad for Maleek that for a moment she forgot about her own husband's turmoil. He wanted to wash off the blood, the dirt from the club floor and the filthy feeling of hate. Hate for the game. It gave him a lot of things but it took away a lot from him as well. He ignored his wife who was trying to hug him. He pushed her away and went to the bathroom to shower. In the shower, he kept remembering when he was shot. He didn't want to remember but witnessing more bloodshed brought it all back.

He lay in the bed next to his wife and looked up at the ceiling. Natalia rested her head on his chest. He stroked her hair.

"I'm getting out. This time you won't have to worry. I just gotta stick out a few more months and then it's over. I'm tired of this shit." Natalia listened to his words. She tried to believe him. But for some reason she couldn't. If anything should have deterred him from getting back in the game it should've been when Junior died or when he was paralyzed or when the FEDs put a levy on her money. Why didn't he see that?

"Daddy, whatever you decide I've got your back." She gave him a noisy sherbet kiss on his six-pack. He laughed and pulled her on top of him and just held her there.

Natalia cooked a hearty meal Friday night for their international guest. Shawn told her about Svelanka and about Tymeek. He even explained certain aspects of the business he was in. He wanted her to be aware and to understand what was going on. This way if anything were to

117

happen she would know what to do. She listened and even accepted that he was a dealer and knew that her love for him would have to enable her to trust him. He went to pick up Svelanka and Natalia busied herself at home like Susie Homemaker making the house presentable. She changed the décor in the dining room and set the table for three.

The phone rang and Natalia answered it, winded.

"Hey, Natalia."

"Hi, Faye."

"Girl, I've got to leave again. You know what happened to my baby, right?"

"Yes, and I hope he gets better soon."

"Yeah, well I need a favor. If I don't leave in like five minutes I'm going to miss my flight. But, my sister can't come over here until after ten o'clock. So, I need someone to look in on Maleek and the kids until then. Can you please do that for me?"

"Well, I was supposed to be here for...never mind I'm on my way."

"Thank you girl, thank you."

Natalia hung up and pulled off her apron. She made sure everything looked perfect then she wrote a note for Shawn and left it on the table. She put on her shoes and left.

In Shawn's car Svelanka searched her bag for the gifts Tymeek sent for him. Shawn laughed when he saw the box of condoms, bottles of liquor and the huge sandwich bag of weed.

"You laugh, why?" Svelanka cocked her blonde head to the side like a confused puppy.

"Tymeek is a funny muthafuckah that's all."

"He iz." She smiled. Shawn loved her accent. He looked over at her and realized that he was instantly turned on. Maybe it was because to him white women were taboo. It used to be that white women turned him off. The paleness of their skin disgusted him but Svelanka was sexy as hell. She

118

had a bronze tan that would give Natalia a run for her money. She had a black girl's ass and to top it off she had breast implants and Shawn always wondered what they felt like. Plus, her collagen induced pout made him fantasize about her giving him head. Svelanka made a call on her cell phone and spoke in bad English. At the stop sign she put the phone to Shawn's ear. Tymeek was on the phone telling him how much money Svelanka was supposed to give him and the things he wanted her to bring back for him. Shawn listened until Tymeek requested Svelanka again. Shawn told Svelanka to take back the phone. He pulled up in his driveway and got Svelanka's hiker knapsack.

"Natalia!" he shouted from the bottom of the stairs. Svelanka waited nervously to meet her. Shawn ran upstairs to find his wife. He came back downstairs and went into the kitchen then the dining room. He found her note and turned to Svelanka.

"I'm sorry but my friend lives next door and his wife left him alone with the kids so Natalia is over there helping him out. I guess it's just us for dinner right now. Are you hungry?"

"Oh, Very," she giggled.

"Aiight lemme hook you up with some grub." Shawn shared out a plate of Natalia's jerked cornish hens and rice and peas.

"Let's drink the cream liquor I bring," Svelanka said as she sat at the table. Shawn poured them both glasses and he sat across from her. They ate, talked and laughed. She gave him insight on how Tymeek was now and he gave her insight on how Tymeek was back then. After dinner Shawn showed off his 60-inch plasma TV in the game room. He hooked up his PlayStation 2 game system and played games with Svelanka as well as drank more of the liquor Tymeek sent. Svelanka rolled a blunt so fat and with such skill that Shawn was impressed. They smoked and joked. With each laugh her cleavage jiggled causing his dick to wiggle. They played so long that his thumbs were hurting. He turned off the game then put in a DVD movie.

"You can understand English pretty good now right?" he slurred.

"Yah, but not good enough," she laughed again.

"Well, this movie is more action so you don't need to really hear what they're saying," Shawn said as he walked back over to her on the couch. "Damn I'm hotter than a muthafuckah in here."

Shawn took off his shirt then his wife beater. Svelanka's eyes bore right through his skin. Shawn caught her staring and slurred, "You like?"

"It's like Ty. What more you have like Ty?"

"He wish he got what I got."

Shawn laughed and nudged her with his elbow. Svelanka licked her lips.

"Show me, I show you."

Svelanka pulled her top down so that Shawn could see her plump pink nipples. Without thinking Shawn whipped out his semi-hard dick. Svelanka grinned.

"Taste it," Shawn prompted, pulling her head towards his crotch. Svelanka went to town on him and Shawn was turned on just watching her blonde head bob. He looked up and saw that the shades weren't closed. He watched the window and remembered that his wife was right next door. Strangely enough this excited him more, but he also knew that she was expected by ten o'clock. He checked his watch and it was only eight-thirty. He figured he should relieve himself quickly just in case she did come home unexpectedly, so he did.

"**G**oodnight Miss Natalia," little Maleek said as Natalia kissed his cheek.

"Goodnight sweetie."

She had already tucked Uneek and Fayette in. She was the perfect substitute mommy. She fed them, gave them desert played video games with Little Maleek, played dress up with Fayette and tickled Uneek mercilessly. She played with all of them and tired them out. Once they were all in their beds Natalia went to tend to Big Maleek who was just coming off of his painkiller high.

"Hey drug addict."

"I see you got jokes. Thanks for helping us out."

"Don't mention it. You guys are always helping me." She checked his bandage.

"Should I change the dressing now?"

"I think so."

Natalia opened a new box of gauze and tape and carefully removed the old dressing and gently wrapped his hand again.

Maleek watched her with adoration. Faye was such a woman on the go that he couldn't remember the last time she made him feel like the king of his castle. She wasn't very dainty or lady like when he really thought about it. She was rough and aggressive. It used to be the very thing that he loved about her. She could hold her own and she was down when he needed her to be. Now, he missed having a woman that would take time with him, cater to him.

"All done you poor baby."

Maleek smiled at her and Natalia wanted to kiss his sexy lips. *Damn he's fine.*

"You're gonna be a real good mommy," Maleek said unaware of what Natalia had gone through concerning motherhood. She felt a small pang in her stomach and her eyes glossed over. She jumped up and tried to wipe her eyes before they started tearing up.

"Do you need anything to drink?" she asked, turning her back to him.

"No thanks. Come sit with me and watch TV."

"Okay." She sat next to him on the sofa and they laughed at the comedian doing a booty shake on the screen. She felt so comfortable there on the sofa next to Maleek. Before she realized it, she was laying her head on his shoulder. When she realized what she'd done she jumped up embarrassed.

"What's wrong?" he asked.

"I'm sorry. I didn't mean to..."

"Why are you apologizing?" Maleek sweetly touched her chin with his thumb from his uninjured hand. "You are so pretty. I don't know how much longer I can hold out."

"What do you mean?" she asked innocently. Maleek moved in closer to kiss her.

"He's right next door...it's too risky." Her mouth protested but her hands were on his hard arms and she rubbed them instead of pushing them away. Maleek kissed her mouth and tasted her lip gloss. He sucked her tongue, then her neck. In between her excited moans and heaving breasts Maleek lost all his will power. He got up from the sofa and with his good hand, led her to an empty bedroom upstairs. He pushed her back on the bed and she kicked off her short shorts. She wasn't wearing any panties and Maleek's mouth watered at the sight of her clean shaven crotch. He had to taste it. He dove in with his tongue and savored her. Natalia couldn't believe what she was doing. What she found even stranger was that she didn't feel guilty. And the fact that her husband was right next door made her romp with Maleek even more delicious. Part of her mind was in ecstasy and the other drummed up images of Shawn watching her through the window. He was angry, but his dick was hard. The image made her drown Maleek's face in her juices. He seemed to be in hog heaven. Right before she was going to scream.

"I'm coming"...she could hear a faint voice off in the distance calling out.

"Daddy!"

"Oh God." she jumped up nearly knocking Maleek out with her knee. She felt around in the dark room for her shorts. Maleek got up fixed his clothes and wiped his mouth. He hurried out the room to his daughter. He met her right in front of the door. She was clutching her favorite doll baby.

"Daddy my belly hurts again."

"Awww, my poor baby. You need to go to the potty?" he rubbed her little tummy.

"I think so."

She rubbed her eyes with the back of her tiny hand. Maleek escorted her back upstairs to the bathroom and sat her on her Barbie potty. Natalia crept back into the family room and waited. She looked at her watch and saw that it was almost ten o'clock. She knew they wouldn't be able to finish what they started, once again. There was a knock at the door and seeing that Maleek was still with Fayette in the bathroom, Natalia answered the door. It was Faye's sister. Natalia let her in and went to the bathroom to tell Maleek she was leaving. He finished cleaning Fayette's little bottom.

"Okay, now you can go back to sleep."

"Okay." She got on her tippy toes to kiss her Daddy. He quickly turned his face so that her kiss landed on his cheek.

"Goodnight Fayette." Natalia smiled.

"Night." Fayette yawned. Maleek went to grab Natalia but she quickly pulled away and whispered, "Faye's sister is here."

Maleek sighed heavily, with a look of disappointment.

"So you're leaving?"

"Yes," Natalia answered regretfully. Faye's sister came into the hallway and Natalia took it as her cue. She bid them goodbye and left.

She could smell marijuana as soon as she stepped through the door. She wanted to scream at the top of her lungs. Then she found Svelanka on the couch and Shawn on the floor both of them were knocked out. Two empty liquor bottles and glasses lay on the ivory carpet in front of them. Now, she just wanted to hit someone. She picked up the empty liquor bottles, looked at it then at Svelanka whose head was buried in between the pillows on the couch. Her eyes rolled then found Shawn's body sprawled out on the carpet. She kicked his foot, but he didn't move. She wanted to kick him in the ass and crack Svelanka over the head with one of the empty bottles but she restrained herself. If it wasn't for the fact that she was next door giving Maleek more attention than her own husband she would've caused a scene. Instead, she just picked up the bottles and glasses and went into the kitchen where there was an even worse mess. She turned on the kitchen faucet and began washing dishes.

She cleaned up and was tired and ready for bed even if her husband wasn't going to be in it. She was about to go upstairs when Svelanka came into the hallway light from the shadows wreaking of alcohol and nearly gave Natalia a heart attack.

"I Sorry. Natalia?"

"Yes?"

"I'm so happy to meet you." She grabbed Natalia and hugged her. She caught Natalia off guard so she didn't hug Svelanka back, she just stepped back and looked at her.

"Hi," she finally said.

Svelanka yawned and said, "Oh thank you for the nice food. It was good. You have to teach me to make."

Natalia gave her a phony smile then said, "I'm glad you liked it. I'm sorry I wasn't here I had to help my neighbor out. But, tomorrow we'll make it a whole day of shopping and sightseeing, okay?"

"Oh, okay."

"Let me show you to the guestroom. So you guys drank yourselves to sleep, huh?"

"Oh yes. Ty send special cognac and herb for Shawn."

"Oh, I see," Natalia said, wishing she could not only smack Svelanka into speaking without the annoying accent but that Tymeek had fell into the canal instead of Nut.

She woke up to a kiss from Shawn.

"Good morning BG."

Natalia just gave him the evil eye. "I'ma call y'all later and see how everything is going. I'm sorry to leave you with her, but I got some things to take care of. But, y'all can do girlie things and go hang out in the mall or something. I left you some money on your dresser okay?" Again all he received was a glare. She turned her back to him and ignored his attempt to kiss her again. Shawn just chortled.

Shawn's cell phone rang continuously as many of his workers complained about being shortchanged by the man he left in charge. He summoned them all to meet him at one of the worker's house. When he got there only a few of them showed up and the man in question wasn't there yet. The first to speak was a short, stocky brown skinned nineteen-year old named Proof. His mouth was filled with platinum, diamond encrusted fangs. He sounded as if he had a lisp as he complained.

"That nigga, Niro, think we stupid and shit. He think we can't count. We all gotta eat nahmean? I ain't out here busting' my ass for no bird seed. I'm out here on the strength of you PB. I left New York and shit to make big cake like Betty Crocker not Little Debbie snacks."

Everyone else nodded along with him. Then another worker voiced his gripe. "Yeah and you could tell that this nigga is skimming something yo, cause he out here pushin' an X5 while we like two steps from the bus and shit! And he don't be hittin' me off wit work on da reg like when you was on top of things."

"Aiight, aiight. When he gets here we gon' squash this shit. I'ma make sure everybody eat. Everybody gon' get what they deserve. I know y'all been making those sales. I know y'all been beatin' the pavement so y'all gon' get what's due."

Just then Niro came in with his right hand man that was also complained about.

"What's good?" he asked with a cocky grin. Immediately Shawn realized that everything that was said had to be true. He could tell what happened to Niro. He'd seen it happen more times than he wanted to. He gave Niro a little power and he became money hungry and power drunk. Niro was letting his promotion turn him into a *dick-tator* not a team player. Shawn knew that if he didn't get Niro back on the team that either Niro would end up dead from one of the disgruntled workers or worse, he'd have an egomaniac on his hands and he'd eventually have to kill him himself.

"Listen, you're not distributing the wealth correctly. Plus, you gotta move more product than you've been moving. Explain this to me."

Shawn sat down in a leather chair and leaned forward with his hands folded. The rest of the workers poured into the house and joined in the meeting. Niro sucked his teeth and looked around at the sea of faces awaiting his response. He knew what he was doing wrong, but he thought that he was slick enough to get away with it. He didn't anticipate the workers getting together and conversing and comparing their pay. Now that he was busted and he could see that he was now suspect with all the workers he figured Shawn would demote him. This pissed him off, but he vowed one way or another that the workers would get paid back for this revolution. All in all, he knew he still had to deny the accusations.

"What? I divvy up everything fair and square. Y'all niggas gotta learn to stop spending y'all shit on bullshit. Plus, I can only give what y'all make. Y'all ain't out there slangin' no high numbers like y'all supposed to."

There was an uproar of shouting as all the workers started speaking simultaneously, trying to get their points across.

"Everybody shut the fuck up!" Shawn yelled then stood up. "This shit ends right fuckin' now. Ain't none of y'all out here acting like fam. This is a family right here. We can't have muthafuckaz tryna do they own shit. Now Niro you know your ass is wrong. This bullshit ends today. Now, you gon' report to me every fuckin' night. You come to me every night then I'ma send Quam with you to pay these niggas the amount I tell you."

Niro was heated at this point and he blew up at Proof because he knew that he was the one who instigated the whole thing.

"Yo, you bitch ass nigga! You fucked up."

"Fuck you muthafuckah!" Proof tried to attack Niro. Niro's right hand man jumped in his way and tried to part them. Some of the other workers cheered. Shawn grabbed Niro and forced him out of the house to scold him.

"You're a fuckin' grown ass man. I put you at the helm cause I thought you could handle this shit. I'm not gon' look like an asshole behind you're stupidity you understand?"

Niro nodded like a little boy being chastised by his father.

"You wanna go back to New York?"

"PB I'm saying' you know that short muhfuckah just hatin'. He mad that you ain't make him head soldier, nahmean. That little nigga can't say shit to me," Niro spoke through gritted teeth and paced angrily.

"What the fuck, are you in high school? This is a business. You do some stupid shit and fuck up my business that's your ass you feel me?"

Niro fixed his rumpled shirt and said, "That nigga better not say no stupid shit to me that's all I'm saying' cause I'm not no bitch."

"Just do your fuckin' job." Shawn emphasized and walked back into the house. He found Proof.

"You watch your mouth and do your job and trust me you'll get your money. The right money you understand? Don't go fuckin' with Niro and starting no shit that's gonna interfere with the business cause then me and you gon' have problems. You understand?"

"No problem P.B."

Shawn drove off with an unsettling feeling. It bothered him that his New York crew was messing up. He brought them out to Atlanta to school the Atlanta crew that he had assembled. With them at each other's throats, the Atlanta crew would see them slipping and act even more foolish and that would throw a monkey wrench in his plans. He couldn't have that. He wanted out and they weren't going to spoil it for him. All he needed to do was set up a solid connect for Tymeek. Get rid of the rest of the products his connection hooked him up with and finish out their agreed contract. He gave himself less than six months to accomplish that feat.

Shawn's supplier was highly connected. He wasn't willing to let Shawn go when it might shine a little light on himself. He didn't want to lose one of his major moneymakers. Just then his phone rang.

"What's really good?" Shawn answered.

"The powers that be requests that we come to the office."

"Why, what's wrong?"

"He ain't say, but he sound all nervous and high strung. I think I got an idea what's going on. Come get me from the gym. I got some shit to fill you in on."

"Aiight I'm on my way."

The gym was packed and he went into the back office and saw Maleek eating a container of vegetable fried rice.

"Where's mine at?"

"You want some?"

"Nah, I'm fuckin' with you. So talk to me?"

"Let's go for a walk." Maleek signaled with his eyes then winked. Shawn knew exactly what he was implying. The walls probably had ears so they went outside on the track where a few members were running laps. They walked in a lane where no one was running. Maleek looked around before speaking.

"First things first, Mr. X is on some shit cause he got wind of one of my customers." He took a pause to pluck a piece of broccoli from his teeth.

"And?" Shawn asked impatiently.

"Damn nigga can't I take a breath?" Maleek chuckled then continued. "Yeah, well there's something I didn't tell you about Mr. X...I told you he was a major player but I didn't say how. Well... he's the mayor's wife's brother."

"What? Get the fuck outta here."

"Yeah, so he's real petro about new contacts

nahmean? I vouched for you that's why he let you in. Now what he ain't know was that his niece who happens to be the mayor's daughter is one of my biggest customers. She's off the hook with her shit. So, now I think somebody ratted her out. That's the only reason he'd be calling me on some scary shit. Now, I told you all this so you could be prepared for what goes down next. I don't know what he's gonna do, but I'm just saying you need to be aware of what you might be walking into."

"So you fuck up and sell this nigga's product to his own niece and think he wouldn't find out?"

"Look the bitch is real slick. She threatened to lie to him anyway and tell him I sold her shit even if I didn't. So, I said fuck it."

"Damn Maleek." Shawn shook his head then sighed, "So you think this nigga gon' do something to you?"

"Nah, he ain't stupid. I'm making this nigga like close to a mil every couple of months, so he's probably gonna try and put his foot down where his niece is concerned. In any case, I don't give a fuck about her. I ain't gotta sell to her no more and that's fine with me."

"Shit that nigga is the mayor's brother in law so he can have any fuckin' body in his pocket. He can probably make a nigga disappear with no problem...damn that's some gully shit right there." Shawn grinned and rubbed his chin.

They drove out to Smyrna, Georgia to Mr. X's sprawling mansion. Maleek had been a loyal franchiser to him so he had no qualms with Shawn seeing one of his many homes. He trusted Maleek enough to bring someone who had sense not to get any ideas about visiting again without permission. Besides, his heavily guarded estates were a burglar's nightmare.

They pulled into a maze of winding roads and luscious green shrubbery. When they could see the mansion which looked like a castle set atop a moat of the clearest water, Shawn had ever seen. The mansion blew him away as he stole peeks in rooms as the butler escorted them to a huge marble encased office.

"Wait here please," the butler said then left.

Whenever Maleek met with Mr. X it was only for brief periods of time and Mr. X always wore dark shades and a hospital mask. Maleek usually dealt with Mr. X's middleman, Tenford. But, on rare occasions Mr. X would show up to emphasize an order or two. Maleek was notably nervous and that made Shawn nervous as well.

"Yo, you making me nervous. I'm starting to think this nigga about to kill us or some shit," Shawn whispered.

"Nah, it ain't that. I just know this is some serious shit cause he got us up in one of his houses. This must be important."

Shawn looked around the office. Its extravagance made him feel inadequate. With all the business he was doing and his custom built complex and townhouse he knew that what he had couldn't hold a candle to the mansion. The green-eyed monster, grabbed a hold of him as he enviously inspected Mr. X's office.

In walked a tall man dressed casually with dark shades on. He sat behind the behemoth desk and folded his hands.

"Big Mal, my main man. How've you been?"

"Aiight and you?"

"Chilling," Mr. X chuckled. "So, you're my number two franchiser." He turned to face Shawn.

"I guess," Shawn replied.

"Well, you both are valued by this enterprise. Now, there's a few miniscule incongruities that have come to my attention." He leaned back into his chair. "Shawn is it?"

"Yeah or PB"

"PB?"

"It's a long story," Shawn replied.

"I like PB. So, PB listen, I understand you're wanting to get out and I believe Tenford explained how that's going to work. But, I've changed my mind on that. Now, the change of plans consists of you appointing a replacement to continue where you will leave off. I will be willing to part with the three million as promised, but you will have to assure me that your replacement can handle the load that you use to handle. Now, as for your other situation... well I hope you've guessed by now that three is more than generous severance pay. I'm giving you that due to the introduction on your part with Amsterdam. I'm pretty stoked about this international deal. I'm taking considerable risks here in the off chance of this deal failing. So, I just wanted to put it out there that I'm a fair man. I'm not saying you should be on your knees right now kissing my ring or anything...although that would be a sight to see, huh?" He laughed then continued, "But seriously PB I'm all for what you're trying to do. You will be sorely missed, but a man's got to do what a man's got to do. Personally, I think you're crazy to give up on this being that you'll be missing out on nothing short of a fortune."

Shawn smiled and shrugged.

"Yeah, but I'm old now and I'm ready to retire."

"Old? Well if that's what old looks like then sign me up!" Mr. X laughed unnervingly. "Okay we're done PB, you and I. This will be the last we speak, unless you cross me. Now, if you'd excuse me and Big Mal here, we've got some perturbing issues that need ironing out. My butler will take you out to the pool. You can relax yourself, take in the sights, drink or eat whatever you wish."

Mr. X pressed a button and the butler appeared.

"Please escort Mr. PB here to the pool. Take good care of him."

"Yes sir." The butler nodded and Shawn followed him out of the office.

Out by the pool not only was the indigo blue water soothing to the eyes but the mellow breeze that swayed the palm trees back and forth made him feel as though he were on an island. Shawn figured the pool had to be about as big as a mall. The pool didn't even look like a pool. It looked like a tropical island. Then out of nowhere came four lanky model-type women with silicone boobies. They splashed

131

around in the pool and giggled. Shawn sat back and sipped the iced tea the butler offered him minutes before. He watched the women playfully dunk and splash one another. *So, this is what it's like being a billionaire.*

Shawn wasn't too happy to see Maleek. Now, his four woman massage therapy would have to cease. Maleek didn't look too happy himself. Shawn knew that whatever Mr. X talked to him about wasn't good. On the drive back Maleek was silent. He spoke briefly on his cell and barely mentioned Mr. X.

Back in Atlanta they decided to hit Glady's Knights restaurant. It was there that in between bites of seafood and soul food that Maleek filled Shawn in on the bad news.

"It was just like I thought."

Maleek put a forkful of food in his mouth and chewed slowly. Shawn swallowed his mouthful of catfish.

"What?"

"He found out about Tori. Now, he wants me to prove myself. He wants me to do something that will probably put me in debt to him, forever. I wanted out a long time ago, but this nigga kept drawing me back in. Now, he's bartering with me. I gotta do a couple of things before he'll let me go and to pay for selling to Tori."

"Fuck. What is it?"

"He wants me to murder this cat and some hooker bitch in Las Vegas. Then, he wants me to plant evidence...and get this...I'm doing this all to frame his brother-in-law."

"The MAYOR?" Shawn's voice was a little too loud for Maleek's taste.

"Shhh, keep your voice down muhfuckah."

"Get the fuck outta here."

"This nigga told me to recruit you in this mess. He's trying to cover all his tracks, nahmean."

"He wants me down with this shit?"

"Yeah, he's willing to throw in another half for you and he's gonna let me out and pay me the same he's giving you."

"Yeah right, nigga. You think I'm stupid?"

"What?"

"I know he's probably giving you more than he's giving me. Y'all go way back. I'm a new jack, but I'm not gon trip off that. So, all we gotta do is kill this nigga and a broad?"

"Plus, put some of this shit he gave me at the scene of the crime. That's it."

"So, when we gon' leave?"

"He wants this taken care of right away so I'm tryna leave by Friday. Can you manage it?"

"Yeah I can do that."

CHAPTER TEN

Natalia and Svelanka had been to every designer boutique in the mall. Natalia never thought she'd be so tired from shopping. Svelanka grabbed so much attention that Natalia became a bit jealous. Both women wore low rider jeans showing their belly buttons and tight baby tees that left nothing to the imagination. It was as if their bodies were in competition. Both were slender with shapely butts and racks boasting more than a mouthful. But Svelanka screamed exoticness with her intriguing accent. Her glazed, bronzed skin and cosmetically enhanced lips didn't hurt either. The Pamela Anderson resemblance made people do double takes.

Natalia gave her opinions on each garment that Svelanka picked up. Svelanka did the same. Natalia found her broken English and accent unbearable at times, but the woman was bubbly and funny so it sort of cancelled out the annoyance.

For lunch Natalia drove to Justin's, Diddy's Restaurant. They ate heartily because they both didn't eat the entire day.

"Is good," Svelanka said while chewing her food vigorously. She wiped her mouth with her napkin and took a sip of wine. Svelanka excused herself to go to the bathroom and Natalia's cell phone vibrated.

"Hello,"

"Hi, sexy."

The voice on the other end was jubilant. Natalia paused then figured out who the mystery caller was.

"Seth?"

134

"Who else would it be?"

"My God Seth, I didn't think I'd hear from you again."

"Why would you think that?"

"Well, when Shawn just showed up in New York I thought for sure you'd given up on me. Hey, how did you get out of there anyway?"

"Let's just say I have my ways. But, I'm not concerned about that. I'm back in Atlanta and I'm hoping that I can see you. I can't stop thinking of you so please tell me you'll bless me with your presence," he said in a sexy tone.

Natalia blushed and said, "Well I don't know how—"

"Just see if you can free up a few hours and I will treat you like the Queen that you are."

"But Seth I'm stuck babysitting this...uh guest. She's visiting from another country so I really can't leave her on her own."

"Damn. Well I'll take whatever time I can get. Please call me the minute you manage to free up your time."

"I'll see what I can do."

"I miss you, Natalia."

"I'll call you." She hung up just as Svelanka approached the table.

"So, we go home next?" Svelanka had reapplied her lipstick and her lips looked puffier than ever.

"Yes, unless you want to go somewhere else. We still didn't get to go sightseeing."

"I not really want to do that. You smoke?"

"No."

"Oh. I thought you smoke too like PB. I got natural weed that's good for you body." Natalia just looked at her as if she were speaking a foreign language. She couldn't care less about any drugs Svelanka brought over from The Netherlands. She wasn't a druggie and if that was what floated Svelanka's boat she knew they wouldn't be the best of pals.

"I don't smoke and I don't like it done in my house either. Shawn knows that, but the other night for some reason he did it anyway. I have nothing against people who do that, but I would rather it not be done in my house."

"I understand, " Svelanka grabbed her purse. "We go now?"

"Yes." Natalia sighed and mumbled under her breath, "We go now you plastic drug addict."

Back at home, Shawn packed a small gym bag. Natalia and Svelanka walked in just as he threw the bag by the front door. Natalia looked down at the bag.

"What's this?"

"Sup Svel?" Shawn smiled at Svelanka, ignoring Natalia's question. Svelanka gave him a bear hug.

"We buy so much today. I love your mall."

Natalia didn't like the hug nor did she appreciate how her husband ignored her question.

"Shawn, can I talk to you for a minute," she said coldly and went upstairs. Shawn stayed downstairs talking to Svelanka a couple more minutes before he went upstairs to his wife. She was sitting in her closet in a boudoir slipper chair with her arms folded, her legs crossed and an attitude written all over her face. Shawn came into the bedroom and called out to her. She cleared her throat alerting him to her whereabouts. He followed the sound of her voice.

"What's the problem?" he sighed knowing that when she crossed her leg and shook it that meant she wasn't a happy camper.

"First of all can you stop disrespecting me in my own house. It is *our* house isn't it?"

"Disrespecting you?"

"Yes. Last night you both left this place in a mess. Not only that but you smoked in here and left your booze all over the carpet. And she's your guest, but I'm stuck babysitting her. Then to top it off, I ask you a question and you plum out ignore me. You hug her hello, but you don't even greet me properly. I'm your wife." she pressed her fingers on her chest and paused for effect. "Doesn't that count for any thing?"

Shawn cocked his head to the side and rubbed his

hand across his chin and walked out of the closet.

"Oh great just walk away," Natalia barked as she heard him suck his teeth. She got up and followed him. He was rifling through his bureau. "Looking for some sexy boxers to take with you? So, you're still not going to tell me where you're going?"

"Listen, I'm not in the mood for no arguments. I've got to go out of town with Maleek and handle some important shit. I'ma leave tomorrow morning and I'll be gone for like a couple of days."

"What important shit?" Natalia asked, doubtfully.

"This is the one time I need you to hold me down BG. This shit I'm about to get into is deep and I won't involve you. I will tell you that I'm doing this for us."

He walked over to her and held her face in his masculine beige hands. "I want out BG. I'm gonna give you the life you deserve."

"Do what you've gotta do." She removed his hands from her face and walked out of the room.

Natalia barely hugged her husband goodbye. He was leaving on some unknown quest that sounded dangerous, yet she didn't act like a wife who was worried at all.

"Svel's flight is at two o'clock today so I got Niro coming over to get her and take her to the airport." As he walked out the front door he turned to look at her one last time. She stood there with a blank stare on her face. He couldn't figure her out or understand why she had the attitude. He could only hope that when he came back that she would be the old Natalia, the one that stole his heart from day one.

She closed the door and went back upstairs to her bedroom. She looked around the room at its disarray and sighed.

Just as Shawn told her, Niro was there before noon to pick up Svelanka. It was hard for her to pretend that she enjoyed Svelanka's company when she didn't. She hesitantly hugged her goodbye and helped her with some of her luggage

137

and shopping bags out to Niro's S.U.V. Now that Svelanka was gone she'd be free to get into all sorts of mischief. She called Seth and complained how things were deteriorating in her marriage. He of course offered her comfort. She accepted and ended up at his house. He didn't have much furniture but from what she did see, she was extremely impressed by his taste.

"So was this all your doing or some lucky lady's?"

"Oh sounds like jealousy to me...hmmm I think I like that. That would mean I'm more to you than a back up plan."

Natalia blushed and he walked over to her and put his hands on her hips, pulling her to him.

"I'm so glad to see you."

"As am I," she replied, her eyelashes fluttering.

His bright smile damn nearly blinded her as he grinned from ear to ear. Then he planted a kiss on her lips and she felt herself waver under his influence.

"You know what I want to do for these couple of days that I'm going to have you?" he asked still grinning. She assumed only one thing. And it was what she was hoping he'd want to do.

"I can only imagine."

"I'm going to take you golfing and fishing with me because you need to do things that you're not accustomed to doing. Shake up that mundane routine you've got going with him."

"Me golfing? Fishing? That's not my thing."

"Try it and see."

"I guess I could. I'll catch the fish but I'm not touching them. Ewww," she giggled.

CHAPTER ELEVEN

The Vegas heat was unbearable. Maleek and Shawn weren't used to the sun's torturous rays and felt like they would pass out. They hurried into the hotel which, interestingly enough was freezing. The contrasting temperature gave Maleek the sniffles. They reserved separate rooms using false names supplied by Mr. X. They made certain to wear baseball caps and shades to conceal their identities. They checked into rooms 500 and 504 using the false ID's as Mr. X had instructed. The mayor was booked in room 502.

Their first victim was a showgirl. It turned out that the mayor was not only cheating on Mr. X's sister, but he was in cahoots with a dealer who wanted to overtake Mr. X's position. Mr. X wanted the mayor to pay for betraying both his sister and him.

The hotel was out of the way from the glitzy glamour of the strip. It was extravagant nonetheless. Room 502 was quiet as Shawn and Maleek listened in from their rooms. They patiently waited to hear if the mayor and the showgirl finished having sex. Mr. X told Maleek that the mayor's sick sexual romps were like clockwork. The showgirl would tie him up, drip hot wax on him, spank his testicles and ass, then he'd worship her feet until she allowed him to gratify himself. This was all supposed to take only one hour. Then immediately after the mayor left the hotel room, the showgirl would shower then leave a half an hour later.

The showgirl was in on Mr. X's plot all except the part about her dying of course. Mr. X paid her more money than the mayor ever did and he made up a phony plot just for her. He told her that he was going to have a photographer burst in on them and snap pictures of them. He also convinced her that she'd become royalty on the talk show circuit after the affair was exposed. She saw dollar signs and did as he asked of her. She left tissue wedged in the card key slot of the hotel room door. The door was open the entire time. Maleek told Shawn that as soon as he heard the Mayor leave the room they would go in. Maleek was prepared to shoot her with a gun equipped with a silencer, another gift from Mr. X.

He also supplied them with evidence to plant. He gave them an engraved, eighteen karat gold cufflink that his sister had given the mayor on their tenth anniversary. He also gave them one of the mayor's designer dress shirts, an empty prescription bottle of Aciphex prescribed to the mayor for his acid reflux condition, two videotapes of the mayor with the showgirl and a computer CD filled with encrypted foreign account information from the mayor's secret overseas bank accounts. The mayor's accounts were funded by well-known white-collar criminals and dealers he accepted bribes from. Shawn's job was to strategically place the evidence in parts of the hotel room where Mr. X had instructed him to do earlier. Shawn also had to smear the showgirl's blood on the mayor's dress shirt.

It seemed like the mayor would never get off because the allotted hour had passed and Maleek and Shawn were still waiting for the peculiar groan Mr. X warned them about. Just as Shawn quietly rested the bag of evidence on the ground, something sounding like a cross between a wounded dog and a duck quacking could be heard coming from room 502. He nearly gave himself away as he burst out laughing. He stifled it by grabbing his mouth. He tiptoed to his room door to listen for the door to room 502 to open. The room knob's soft click was music to his ears. He slipped out of his room meeting up with Maleek in front of room 502. They pushed open the door slowly and saw the showgirl sitting upright on the bed with her back supported by the headboard. She was still naked and she didn't bother covering up when they approached the bed. She was smoking a cigarette and ran her fingers through her hair frustrated.

"You idiots are a little too late dontcha think? What in the hell took you so long? I tried dragging our session out until you could come in and start snapping away." She took another drag from her cigarette, twisted her lips to the side, blew smoke then sighed. "Now you're gonna have to wait a whole week for another opportunity. Shit!" She seemed really pissed off.

This made it much easier for Maleek because at first he felt bad about having to shoot a woman but she was just another slut. And he really hated calculating, money-hungry sluts so he raised his hand holding the gun and aimed the silencer at her head. By the time she looked up and realized that the men weren't photographers but assassins it was too late. Maleek shot her twice because his aim was off and his first attempt went straight into her open mouth as she intended to scream but never got the chance. He didn't see blood splatter on the headboard behind her so he assumed the bullet didn't do enough damage. So, to be safe, rather than sorry he walked right up to her, grabbed her frosted hair, yanked her head forward then put the gun to the back of her head and let off another round. Shawn had already sped into action. He finished most of his part and only had to soil the Mayor's shirt with the showgirl's blood. He rubbed the sleeve of the shirt against her bloody head. To make it authentic he held the top of the shirt under his chin and pulled the dead body up so she was back in the sitting position. He leaned forward over her so that her face pressed up against the front of the shirt. He stuffed the shirt in the now empty bag and they casually left the hotel room.

They were warned that victim number two would probably not be as easy. Their actions had to be well thought out and their escape route had to be a safe and fast one. This victim was an important man in Vegas. It was of great concern to Maleek when Mr. X gave victim number two's name, Mamoud. Mamoud was a billionaire rumored to be the nephew of the leader of a terrorist regime based in Cairo. He was guarded at all times and his home was like a fortress. Mr. X assured Maleek that there was one place where they'd have easier access to Mamoud. It was somewhere Mr. X knew a way in and out of without being detected. Maleek and Shawn would have to get there at four p.m. sharp. If they were a minute late the whole plan could be blown out of the water.

"**A**aaaaahhhh!" Natalia screamed and dropped her fishing rod. The fish on her rod's hook flopped about in the boat. Seth grabbed the fish and unhooked it. He threw it in a huge cooler full of ice.

"Damn girl!" he exclaimed then laughed. Natalia laughed too.

"It's so big and its eyes are scary. I can't believe I caught that big ol' fish."

"Well you did and on your first time out. I'm so proud of you." He chuckled and hugged her tight. He looked into her eyes and they kissed. Natalia looked out across the tranquil waters and up at the powder blue sky.

"I'm glad you dragged me out her Seth. It was different, but pretty peaceful."

"I'm glad you enjoyed yourself. We've been out here a while now. The sun will set soon. Are you ready to leave?"

"Yeah, I've had enough of Mother Nature."

On the drive back, Natalia noticed that living out of New York was doing great things for her health. Her skin had never looked better and she gained a few pounds in the right places. It seemed that the air was fresher and the sweet southern hospitality was rubbing off on her. She looked over at Seth and wondered what in the hell had she become. She didn't feel guilty about being with another man. The only explanation she could come up with was that she felt that she owed Shawn big time for not only impregnating another woman but giving her a sexually transmitted disease as well as being the catalyst for her stint in jail. In her mind what she did with Seth was far from the debt being paid.

She watched Seth de-scale and clean the fish they caught. Then she watched him impressively sauté them in olive oil with onions and herbs. The nasty odor went away and nothing but delicious seasonings filled the kitchen.

"Now that the cook has prepared the meal I think you should go shower and get ready for dinner," Seth told her as he pulled a casserole dish of scalloped potatoes from the oven.

Natalia was in awe watching him maneuver around the kitchen like a professional chef.

She was clean now and wrapped a plush chocolate brown towel around her moist body. She went into Seth's bedroom and found him on the bed under the sheets.

"What's wrong?" she asked crawling into bed with him. "Aren't you hungry? When will dinner be served?"

"I'm very hungry and I'm hoping you'll feed me right now."

She straddled his face and dropped the towel. He basked in her juices then maneuvered her body into a more accommodating position on top of him and she pushed herself up.

"We have to use something this time. I can't risk it." Natalia could tell that Seth was disappointed if not a bit annoyed by her announcement. She eased off of him and lay beside him on her back. Seth got up to get a condom. He came back to bed with it already on his semi-hard penis. He lay on top of her and kissed her long and hard. He reached down and Natalia felt his knuckles brush up against her inner thigh as he guided himself into her. After a while Natalia didn't feel the barrier of rubber as she anticipated. She was worried and she reached down and felt around until she was positive that he wasn't wearing a condom. He had slipped it off in the midst of their passion.

"Seth, please...put it back on..." she whispered in between pleasurable gasps.

Seth had other plans. He still didn't have the son he'd always dreamed of having and Natalia would be the perfect mother in his eyes. She was beautiful and smart and he believed that he could make her *his* wife with only a few more encounters.

"I promise I won't come in you," he lied.

"But...but..." Natalia couldn't help but enjoy the feeling that he was giving her and surrendered to the pleasure rippling throughout her entire body until Seth passionately declared that he was going to come.

"Don't come in me. Please Seth don't..."

Seth pulled out his dick from inside her a few seconds after her plea and emitted globs of semen on her pubic bone and thigh. She lay still as he wiped her clean with a towel.

"I'm sorry that I did that." Seth apologized and seemed embarrassed.

"Why'd you take the condom off?" Natalia asked, raising up on her elbows.

"You know how I feel about you don't you?"

"I guess." She shied away from his adoration.

"If I could steal you from your husband right now I would. Natalia I'm not going to lie to you...I wish that we could have a baby..."

It was the sweetest thing she'd heard thus far and it moved her.

"I'm so flattered Seth. You're so sweet. But I..." she searched her vocabulary for the right words to say but came up empty handed.

"I know you can't...it's okay. I understand. Are you ready to eat or should we work up more of an appetite?" He attempted resilience despite the rejection.

"I'm hungry." She got up and started getting dressed.

"I hope you don't want to stop now because you don't trust me."

"That's not it all. I'm really hungry."

144

CHAPTER TWELVE

Shawn's back hurt from being cramped up in an air shaft inside the Morocco Hotel and Casino. When Maleek first told him about the hotel he wondered what kind of plan Mr. X had come up with that would keep two big black men from standing out like sore thumbs in a lavish hotel rife with rich white people. Now, as he lay on his stomach slithering like a snake on his belly in a narrow metal vent with Maleek in front of him, he had to give Mr. X his props. They could hear voices and see the exclusive card game in progress right through the tiny slats in the vent grates. They crawled further along the shaft until they came upon the room where Mamoud was in a serious ménage a trois. They continued on with their confined journey until they were in the adjoining room that was empty just like Mr. X said it would be. They opened the grate and shimmied down into the room using a metallic cable.

The room was posh and if it weren't for the fact that they were on business they both wouldn't have minded taking a dip in the humongous pool right in the middle of the room. Mr. X told Maleek that Mamoud would be alone in the room. He didn't like having any males around when he did his thing with his women. He also advised them that there would be two bodyguards stationed outside the door the room Mamoud was in along with any adjacent rooms Mamoud had. The rooms were a playground for high rollers so they came equipped with almost everything including large terraces and jacuzzis. There was a lot of space in between terraces and Mamoud always took rooms on the top floor of the thirty story casino to ensure his safety. Shawn and Maleek carefully crept out onto the terrace. Maleek inched over to the terrace railing, looked down and got nervous.

"Yo, I can't climb this shit."

"Nigga, don't bitch up on me now."

"My big ass can't make it all the way over there."

"Yes you can cause the ledge is wide enough if you put your feet sideways."

"Man, that's a long fuckin' way down." Maleek looked over the terrace railing and shook his head disapprovingly.

"Fuck this shit, give me the gun." Shawn reached out his hand.

"Naw, I'm gonna do it just go first and help me across."

"We don't have time for all that. I got you on this. Gimme the gun."

"You sure?" Maleek hesitantly handed him the gun.

"Yeah nigga." Shawn stuck the gun inside his front pocket.

"I owe you big time."

Maleek tried to help Shawn over the terrace railing but Shawn swiftly swung his long legs over the ledge. Maleek watched Shawn scale the wall like Spiderman over to Mamoud's terrace.

Shawn took the gun from his pocket once his feet were safely planted on the terrace. He put his back to the wall and eased over to the glass doors. He peeked in and saw that Mamoud had one woman sitting on his face and another riding his lap. Shawn was sidetracked by the triple X show for a moment. Then he realized he had the perfect opportunity to kill Mamoud while he was pre-occupied. He quietly slid one of the glass doors open and tiptoed in. He immediately surveyed the room with his eyes then knelt down on the ground and crawled towards the bed. He crept near the woman riding Mamoud and kissing the other woman who rode Mamoud's face. She caught a glimpse of

Shawn form the corner of her eye, stopped kissing the other woman and gasped. The other woman cupped her own mouth in fear. Both women now watched Shawn's every move, their faces frozen in horror. Shawn switched the gun's direction from one to the other and quickly put his finger to his lips in order to hush them. They were nervous now and the woman on Mamoud's lap slowed her pace. Mamoud's eyes were closed until he noticed the change of pace in the woman's grinding pattern and he opened his eyes. Shawn already had the silencer's barrel at Mamoud's temple.

"What the..."

Before he could finish his sentence Shawn put a bullet in his brain. The women jumped off of Mamoud and tried to run to the door, but they never made it. Shawn shot them both in the back then walked up to them to check if they were alive. One of them coughed up blood and gasped for air. Shawn put her out of her misery with a bullet in the back right where her heart was. The other woman had no pulse and that was convincing enough for Shawn. Now, all he had left to do was plant his last piece of evidence. He stuck the CD in Mamoud's suit jacket pocket then he left the same way he came in.

On the flight home Shawn and Maleek surfed channels on the mini TV screens in the headrests of the seats in front of them on the airplane until they found Vegas news reports. Their handy work negated major coverage. They listened intently as a balloon head reporter eloquently gave a full account of their heinous deeds.

"Anonymous sources implicate the mayor from items allegedly found in the murdered woman's hotel room along with confirmation of the mayor's affiliation with the woman shot twice yesterday. She is believed to be a local showgirl. She is believed to have been a dominatrix. In a related incident on the other side of town last night three murder victims were discovered. The body of the infamous casino owner who was believed to have funded terrorists and also a suspected drug dealer, Mamoud Modanah was found dead

along with two women in the Morrocco Hotel and Casino penthouse. All of the murder victims were found naked and appeared to have been engaged in sexual acts. Investigators speculate that Mayor Hilforn is the number one suspect in both the showgirl murder and casino murders. So far the police chief neither confirms nor denies these allegations."
Then the program cut to a press conference where the police chief seemed stressed as he spoke warily.

"At this time we do not have any details to report. We ask the press to stop leaking unconfirmed reports to the public. We will release any information or confirm findings once we've finalized a thorough investigation. No more questions, thank you." He abruptly left the podium. Shawn and Maleek looked at each other and smiled.

Shawn called his house, then his wife's cell phone from the plane. She didn't answer either. It angered him that he couldn't even go home to his wife. Maleek was going home to his wife. Shawn thought of Talea who practically did anything he told her to do. He needed her tonight. He called her and she agreed to pick him up at the airport and take him to her house. Knowing that Maleek hated Talea, Shawn told Maleek that someone else would pick him up and he didn't need to ride with him and his wife. Maleek and Faye drove off leaving him behind at the airport.

Talea was angry at the fact that not only was Shawn some-timey, but she could definitely tell he was only using her for sex and she wasn't getting anything out of the deal, not even dinner or a movie. He never bought her gifts like she was used to nor did he take her out to expensive restaurants. He merely called her when he wanted sex. He'd tell her to come over and kick her out when he was done. Now, here he was calling her out of the blue asking for a favor after ignoring her phone calls for the past few weeks. The only reason she agreed to pick him up was because she had a special surprise planned for him. Well, that and the fact that he fucked her so well that she would always come so many times that she'd need a calculator to keep track.

But, she was going to fix him tonight and good.

Talea pulled up at the baggage claim area and looked out the passenger window. She spotted him and beeped her horn to get his attention. He rushed over to the car, threw his bag in the back seat and got in.

"What's good, Ma?"

"Me."

"True, true."

"So, you're going to my house?" she asked, easing her foot off the brake pedal.

"Yeah."

She glanced over at him quickly. "So you're not going to leave her are you? I mean I'm always there for you giving you whatever you want. But, you don't plan on making *me* wifey right?"

"What the fuck? Where's this coming from?" Shawn asked annoyed.

She turned to look at him. "Well, I'm asking because you've been fucking me for the past couple of months now and I'm always the one jumping when you call. But, you don't answer my calls and if you do you're too busy to talk."

"Come on with this soap opera shit. You act like this is some new shit to you, like you don't know."

"Know what? What does that mean?"

"It means let's not go through this shit. I'm mad tired and I don't wanna hear this shit."

She shot him an angry look then changed the subject. "Once again I cooked for you. This time I hope you'll actually thank me."

Shawn felt a little bad because he remembered when she made him a romantic dinner before and all he did was wolf it down then left. He never did act appreciative of any of the things she did like the massages, picking up certain things for him and of course the blow jobs in his car while he drove. He never once uttered the words, thank you.

"My bad, Ma I do appreciate you cooking for me. That shrimp scampi you made was real good, okay?"

Talea just kept her eyes ahead of her. She knew he was full of shit and she was going to leave him in a pile of shit, knee deep.

Talea had Shawn's plate of food sitting in the microwave. She pressed a couple of buttons and walked away from the microwave. Shawn was in her fridge getting a bottle of Pepsi. There wasn't much left in the bottle so he just opened the cap and guzzled until the bottle was empty. She watched him.

"Would it have killed you to pour it in a glass?"

"Wasn't shit in there. Yo, why you actin' up?"

"Whatever Shawn."

"Whatever? What the fuck is your problem?"

"Nothing...I'm just stressed out."

"Why?" He tried to offer her some comfort by rubbing her back while pulling her to him.

"It's just the whole entertainment biz. I'm just tired of dealing with phony, cheap-ass motherfuckers." She watched his eyes after finishing her sentence. She wondered if he knew that she was really referring to him.

"But that's the business you chose to be in." He squeezed her shoulders gently then dropped his hands. The microwave timer sounded and Talea took the plate out and passed it to him. He carried it into her living room and sat down in front of the TV. He went to eat and realized that he didn't have a fork.

"Can you bring me a fork?"

She sucked her teeth but brought it to him anyway. She ran upstairs to set up for her big surprise. She was going to make Shawn sorry that he didn't fall head over heels for her and even sorrier for not giving her anything in return for her services.

Shawn had filled his belly and he lay back on the couch watching CNN. He realized it had been a while since he'd seen Talea. She'd been MIA for quite some time.

"Talea!"

She didn't answer so he got up and went looking for

her in her bedroom. She was laid out on the bed in a rose colored corset with matching garter belt and stockings. She looked like a playboy playmate and Shawn couldn't wait to rip off the outfit. "So, this is what you've been doing?"

"Yes, baby."

He undressed so fast that she thought she was about to get pounded by Superman. Shawn was on top of her trying to unhook her corset within seconds. She gently pushed on his chest.

"I wanna ride you."

She grinned at him then licked her lips seductively. Shawn lay flat on his back and watched her grind down onto him until his dick disappeared in her. She took off the corset and leaned forward to feed him one of her taupe nipples. He eagerly sucked it with his eyes closed. This was the perfect opportunity for her so she reached over the edge of the bed and pressed a couple of buttons on her phone and strategically slid it off the nightstand onto the floor. Then she worked Shawn like she'd never worked him before. She looked deep into his eyes and whispered passionately.

"This pussy feels good don't it? Say my name. Say how good this pussy is. Tell me how good this pussy is to you, P.B."

Natalia's cell phone rang while she was walking into the house. She wasn't going to answer it because she thought it was Shawn again. She looked down at the blue screen and saw Talea's name and home phone number. She answered and her jaw dropped. She listened in horror as her husband calling out.

"Yeah, Talea work that shit! Take all this dick!"

She could hear Talea moaning louder and louder and she knew that could only mean one thing. Shawn was raising himself, driving deeper into Talea and causing that sweet friction that she missed from their lustful trysts in the beginning. The kind that always made her drown him when she climaxed. Now, she could hear Talea's screams of passion. Then Shawn growled and Natalia knew that it was a wrap, he had erupted. She could hear their heavy breathing and slapping noises which she recognized as Shawn's strong hands slapping Talea's ass just as he liked to do afterwards with her when she rode him. Her whole body trembled. She dropped the phone and her legs went rigid. She ended up on her knees. She looked down at the cell phone's illumination making a path in the darkness of the house. She picked it up and put it back to her ear. Now, she heard giggles and chuckles then a bed creaking then the line went dead.

"Damn girl, you went buck wild on a nigga!" Shawn chuckled.

"I'm glad you liked that."

She snidely replied, hopped off of him and the bed. She used her big toe to press the off button on her phone then kicked it under the bed. Shawn lay there in her bed and watched her take off the rest of the outfit.

"You asking for more doing that."

"I know how you do." She stepped out of her stockings and crawled back into bed with him. She laid her head on his chest.

"I want you to fuck me as many times as you can tonight...like it's the last time you'll ever be able to fuck me."

Natalia rose from the floor and trudged upstairs to her room. She fell back onto the bed and tried to figure out what just happened. Was that really who she thought it was? Her friend and boss fucking her husband? It was so crazy that she knew it had to be true. How could he do that? After he saw what she went through with Tracy's betrayal how could he do that to her? Then it dawned on her that he was back in Atlanta and Talea was the first person he went to see. *How could he?* It was bad enough that he went raw and got some diseased ho pregnant, but now he was doing it with her boss and the person she thought was a real friend. It didn't matter that she had just come from being with another man. She owed him. She owed him big time. Seth wasn't enough! She wanted revenge now more than ever. Shawn wanted to play this game, now she would beat him at it. But Talea was going to pay for the blatant disrespect. She knew that Shawn was her husband. She also had balls to do what she did to hip Natalia to the affair. Natalia surmised that Talea would pay first. And revenge is a dish best served cold.

CHAPTER THIRTEEN

"Good morning," Natalia said as Maleek opened the door. Maleek rubbed his eyes and smiled a big smile.

"Good morning beautiful."

"Maleek, I'm real sorry to bother you like this but I've got something that I need done and I don't know how to go about it...actually I do, but I need help. Can you help me?" Natalia rattled off.

"Whoa, slow down. Now what do you need done?"

"I don't want to get you involved so I don't want to tell you exactly what it is, but it's a little on the seedy side. You know thuggish kind of stuff. I really need one guy if possible." Maleek looked at her surprised.

"You wanna put a hit out on somebody?"

"Nothing permanent. I just want to...to hurt someone. Um, put them out of commission for a while. Do you know what I'm talking about?"

"I know that it still sounds like a hit. So, who's this unlucky guy?" Maleek chuckled.

"It's a girl...and you know who she is so I don't think I should get you in deeper than you have to be. Besides, if I tell you who it is you might try and talk me out of it. And I'm telling you this girl deserves it," Natalia said, angrily.

Maleek was extremely curious at this point. He grabbed her hand and led her inside the house. Let's go out back he said. She followed him out to the enclosed pool with an imitation waterfall. He placed a towel in a lounger by the pool and dragged another one over.

154

"Sit here." He smoothed out the towel with his hands for her.

"Thank you." She lay back into the lounger. He did the same.

"Aiight, you know I'm on your side? I don't give a shit who it is. I've got you on whatever you decide to do."

"See Maleek that's what I miss in Shawn. It's like he's not there for me anymore."

"Why you say that?"

"Well, for starters he didn't come home again and last night." She stopped herself. She didn't want Maleek to blab to Shawn that she knew. She wanted Shawn to be an unsuspecting mark. When she did her thing to get him back he would never know about it. He didn't deserve a heads up.

"Never mind all of that. I've got this problem that I definitely want to solve. Can you help me get a guy?"

"You're a funny girl. You say that like I can go to a store and pick somebody off a shelf."

"I know I must sound so un-hip right now. But Maleek I want someone to do this right away. Because when you sin as this person has you should pay a high cost," she said with a devilish look.

Maleek could see she was serious. "Okay, okay. I can get you that guy. But, I need details and what it is exactly that you need done. I can't set it up without knowing all of that. I know you don't want to involve me but I'm already involved just by this conversation alone, so talk to me."

"She's you're wife's friend. I thought she was my friend too but I was wrong." Natalia sighed and looked up at the dome net above them. Maleek sighed disappointingly. He didn't need to hear anymore he instantly knew exactly who Natalia was talking about. Natalia hadn't noticed the disgusted look on Maleek's face.

"It's Talea. She practically rubbed my face in the fact that she's fucking my husband. She called my cell phone while they were having sex. Can you believe this bitch?" She shook her head in disbelief then looked him in the eyes just as he finally found the words to speak.

"Shit, I told that nigga to leave that ho alone."

"What?"

"She's no damn good. She's a straight up ho. She tried to change her image with that acting shit, but she will always be a fuckin' slut! I told Shawn to watch out for her. I guess he ain't listen."

Maleek rubbed his head with both his hands. He looked disappointed. At that moment Natalia flashed back to what happened to her in junior high school when envious fake friends set her up to get robbed and raped, then her late best friend Tracy's betrayal with Mark hit her like a ton of bricks, again. She was supposed to swear off women friends forever. But, once again she allowed herself to be sucker punched by a woman.

"You mean she's one of those women who hunt married men?"

"She's a user and a nasty, grimey ho! I swear my wife only puts up with her because of the boutique and they promote each other's shit. Give each other customers nahmean?"

"So, Faye knew how she was too?"

"Not really. Faye don't know the half about that bitch. I couldn't tell Faye how many times that ho tried to get at me. But, see I already knew about her so I had an advantage. Most niggas out here wit' money know about her."

"She's gotta pay Maleek. I want her face slashed to shreds where no amount of plastic surgery can help her. Then I want her boutique shut down and her house burnt to the ground...ashes. I want her car smashed to smithereens!" Natalia's arms went all wild as she spoke and the far off look in her eyes made her appear demented.

"Ma, it's okay, it's okay." Maleek grabbed her flailing arms and gently held them down, "I got you. You want her out of commission for a minute. I got that. Now, the slashing and the smashing of the car sound good enough. Damn, remind me not to get on your bad side."

She looked at Maleek with a serious face.

"Maleek she crossed me. I'm sick of women doing this shit to me after I trust them. It's like I have a sign that says 'sucker' stamped on my forehead."

"Wow, women are really trifling." Maleek saw the look Natalia gave him and he tried to clean up his statement. "I mean some women...heh, heh," he chuckled.

"Heh, heh," she mocked him then burst out laughing.

Her next stop was to the boutique where she checked to make sure that Talea would be there. She hoped that Talea wouldn't hide from her because she didn't plan on confronting her about Shawn. In fact, she was going to pretend that she didn't even get the call. She wanted to see just how phony Talea really was. Would Talea try and explain everything to her? Or would she keep tight-lipped and be glad that her little secret didn't come out?

Natalia walked into the boutique with two outfits that Talea altered for a photo shoot. She walked straight to the back of the boutique and passed one of the sales associates.

"Talea," she called out meekly.

She saw Talea moving about behind a rack of sexy get-ups. "Talea?" Natalia walked behind the rack to see Talea pinning up the cuffs of a pair of chinos. "Hey girl." Natalia put on a happy face.

Talea looked up and realized who it was then sprung to her feet. She was sure that Natalia came to put her foot in her ass.

"Yeah, what's up?" she sounded nervous.

"Nothing, I just brought you these outfits from the last photo shoot. I remembered that you needed the others back so I knew you'd want these too."

Talea looked confused then she caught herself and put on one of her phony smiles. She figured that Natalia must not have gotten the phone call or she must not have heard Shawn's voice. Whatever the case, Natalia didn't look

157

like an angry wife out to kill her husband's mistress. Talea sighed with relief after Natalia hugged her then hung up the plastic covered outfits back on the rack.

"So, when's the next job boss?" Natalia asked in a bubbly tone.

"Oh, well there's a fashion show coming up in another week, but I'm tapped out on the magazine spots. I won't need to do anymore for at least a couple of months."

"That's great. So, are you busy today because I'm bored. I haven't got a thing to do. Plus, I don't know when my husband is coming back from his little trip," Natalia said sarcastically. "I don't know about that man. He's up to something though. Going away like that without me and then not calling me the whole time he's away. I don't know what I'm going to do with him."

Talea just listened with patient ears. She knew damn well where Natalia's husband was, right in her bed where she left him earlier that morning.

"Girl, please you know how men are. When I finish up here I've got a meeting with my agent. You should come with me because she could probably put you in a movie or get you a spot on a sitcom."

Talea knelt down again and finished pinning up the cuff on the pants. Natalia looked down at her head and wanted to kick her in it. She wanted to spit right in her lying, nasty, face. Instead she strained to smile.

"I would love to."

After hanging out at Talea's agent's office they went for lunch. Talea dropped Natalia off back at the mini mall so that she could get her car. Natalia made it a point to ask Talea where she was headed.

"I've gotta drop off some money for my sister then I'm going home to take a nap."

"Yes, girl, you do that because you're life is so busy. You do way too much you know that?" Natalia acted concerned.

"Yeah, you're right. You know what? Fuck that, I'm

going straight home. My sister can come get this money if she really needs it."

"That's right." Natalia chuckled as she got out of the car. "Okay girl I'll talk to you later and thanks again for today."

She waved goodbye and got into her car. She watched Talea make a broken U-turn in the parking lot then drive away. Natalia quickly called Maleek and told him the particulars that he so patiently awaited. Afterwards she smiled to herself and drove home, hoping to see her husband who was next on her list.

Talea drove into her garage and turned off her car. She pressed the button on the garage door remote. She went into her house and picked up her mail. She glanced at each envelope until she spotted a royalty check from a magazine advertisement that she'd done more than six months ago. She ripped the top open and slid her fingers in to grab the check and pull it out. She read the amount and her face lit up. She grinned and began singing happily. She dropped her purse on the hallway table and went into her bedroom. She checked her messages and kicked off her sandals when she heard a thump outside her window. She apprehensively walked over to it and looked out. She didn't see anything so she dismissed the noise with a wave. She undressed and grabbed her phone. She sat on her bed and called her sister's house.

"Tameeka, I was about to bring you the money but I thought about it and I'm loaning you money so why should I go all out of my way and bring it to you. Banks don't do that shit so why should I?"

"So, I gotta pack these damn kids up and come all the way over there when you could've just dropped it over here for me?"

"Do you want this three hundred or what? You're lucky my ass is even lending it to you after that shit you pulled last year."

"You got your money back though didn't you? Don't

start no shit. You know I'm going through something right now, but I will get you your damn money back okay? Don't try to play me like I'm some broke bitch off the street."

"Well you are! You need to get a nigga that's gonna pay like he weigh! That fat motherfucker you with now should have your ass in a mansion as big as he is. What the fuck does he do for you and your kids? I'm those kids' daddy. He ain't no real father. And you can tell that hippopotamus looking bastard that I said that!"

"Oooh, bitch you are evil you know that? That's alright though cause one day you gon' need me. I'm coming to get the money right now."

"I thought so."

Talea sucked her teeth and hung up. *Fucking bitch act like I fucked her and got her pregnant with all of her BeBe's kids!* She slammed the reciever back on its base and went into the bathroom. She turned the faucet on in the tub and poured bath beads in the water. She stood up after finding it and saw a figure wearing a white ghoul mask.

"Aaahhh!"

She screamed and tried to run away but the intruder grabbed her and she reached up with her hands and felt a stinging sensation. As she pulled her hands back she saw blood gushing out. She screamed louder this time. She became bombarded with flashes of silver and it felt like her face was on fire. Blood dripped all over her naked body. She stumbled over to the sink. When she saw herself in the mirrors along the wall she fainted.

Talea's sister pulled up in her mini van and saw that Talea's front door was cracked open.

"Stasha go get the money from Auntie Ta-Ta and hurry up." The eight-year old ran out of the car and into the house. "You kids better stop that fighting back there before I slap the..." Tameeka was cut off by the loud shrill coming from Talea's house. It was her daughter screaming her head off and she came running out of the house like a

160

mad dog.

"What's wrong Stasha? What's going on?"

The little girl was too busy shaking and muttering incoherently to reply. She was traumatized by what she'd seen. Tameeka practically forced her child inside the van then ran inside Talea's house. She followed the trail of red carpet stains and saw her sister's blood all over the bathroom. She screamed and tried to compose herself. She took a deep breath and ran off to find the phone, screaming out obscenities the entire time she dialed nine-one-one.

"Please, Oh God, come help my sister. There's blood everywhere!"

CHAPTER FOURTEEN

When Natalia got home she saw that the lights were on in the house. *Ahhh, my cheating bastard of a husband has finally made it home.* She walked in to hear him playing the song they first danced to when he took her out on their first date at the Stardome. K-Ci's raspy voice was breaking down the bridge of the song, *All My Life,* when she walked into the living room. It was empty. She walked back out and noticed that there were rose petals on the steps. She followed them straight into the master bathroom where Shawn apparently fell asleep in the jacuzzi waiting for her. His romantic ploy didn't mean a damn thing to her.

He thinks that he can just come home any time he wants, scatter dead, old-ass rose petals around the house and I'm supposed to swoon? she thought.

"Go fuck yourself," she mumbled before kicking the wine bottle that sat on the marbled platform next to the jacuzzi. It fell and landed on Shawn's knee. He jumped up.

"Oh, shit, what time is it?" he asked, rubbing his eyes. He looked at his Presidential Rolex then up at his wife who was leaving. "BG, where are you going? You not gonna get in?"

She ignored him and walked out of the bathroom. She went in her closet and grabbed a few things then she plopped down on a tufted bench. *What am I doing? Where am I going to go?* The money she made while working with Talea was enough to get her to New York and maybe hold her up in a cheap apartment for a couple of months, but then what?

She didn't want to burden Andre, so he was out of the question. She had no one else. She hated what Shawn did but God help her she still loved her husband. She was still in love with him. Yes, she fucked the hell out of Seth and she would do the same with Maleek if the opportunity ever arose, but Shawn was still the ultimate man in her eyes. He was still her action hero, eventhough he was a cheater and he neglected her more and more. The sweetness he used to show her now seemed like a cheater trying to mask the dirt he had done. It was so obvious that it disgusted her. He had changed too much for her tastes. She wanted the old Shawn back. But, for now revenge filled her thoughts. She knew that she would get her revenge on him soon enough. She wiped tears from her eyes and dropped the clothes on the floor. She walked out of the closet and into Shawn.

"What's you're problem now?" he stood there in the buff, his body glistening as if a million stars were pasted on him.

Damn him for being so sexy!

He pulled her chin up with his forefinger.

"Can I make love to my wife?" He almost had her when the phone call she got the night before was fresh in her mind at the moment. He gave away her stuff and he sounded like he enjoyed it more than he did when he was with her.

How could he fuck Talea then want to come and fuck me? It was unconscionable and he would not get his cake and eat it too!

"I'm tired," she rolled her eyes, pushed past him and walked out of the bedroom.

Maleek handed Shawn a huge duffel bag full of cash.

"I told you that nigga is a man of his word."

"That's what's really good! So, that's it? I'm done?" Shawn asked hopeful.

"You're done. And so am I." Maleek's smile grew a mile

163

wide.

"Say word? He let you out, too?"

"Yup. We did such a good job on that situation and he said one good turn deserves another. So that's that."

"Yo, Mal that's good to hear." Shawn slapped his hand into Maleek's and they pulled back their hands turned it into a ghetto shake then hugged each other in a brotherly manner.

"We gotta celebrate with the fam."

"Well, I can't cause Faye and the kids are gone again. Her moms is real sick. They say she don't have much longer. I feel bad for Faye cause she's trying so hard to be strong for her whole family you know?"

"Damn, I'm sorry to hear that. I guess it will just be me and you celebrating cause my wife ain't fuckin' speaking to me. So, you wanna celebrate tonight or what?"

"Nah, I'ma go check on the clubs then I gotta handle some business. I owe this nigga some paper so I wanna get that out the way."

"Aiight, well I'm going to celebrate nigga."

"Do you."

"I'ma definitely doin' me, I'm out," Shawn said as he patted Maleek's shoulder and left the gym.

Maleek looked down at his duffel bag. He heaved a sigh of relief. Happy couldn't describe how he was feeling at that moment. He was finally free. Free to just be an entrepreneur and not Mr. X's lackey anymore. He glanced out into the mall parking lot. He saw Natalia pull up in her Lexus. She stepped out in a pair of yoga pants and a midriff-bearing baby tee. He watched her walk straight towards the gym. She looked good enough for a work out, but not the kind that involved bar bells! He walked out into the customer area to meet her.

"Hey Xena," he affectionately called her. She laughed so hard she doubled over and hugged him.

"What's up, Big Mal?" She tried to give herself street credibility by putting her hands on her hips. Maleek laughed at her.

"So what are you doing here?"

"I'm bored out of my mind since my boss has met such an unfortunate, extenuating circumstance and I don't have a job. So, I figured why not work some of my stress out."

How about I work that stress out for you? Maleek wanted to say aloud but he didn't. "Oh aiight, I can be your trainer, but honestly you don't need to be here. You're naturally blessed." He smiled sweetly at her.

"Awww, how sweet? Thanks Big Mal. You know that went right to my head don't you?"

"Yeah, yeah now come on into my boot camp," he chuckled.

He took her over to equipment where she could sit down and do leg lifts, shoulder rolls and thigh squeezes. The whole time he instructed her, he watched her like one of the cartoon foxes with their tongues out. While she squeezed her thighs together then opened them again, he had to control his urges by squeezing his package every now and again. She never noticed because she was feeling the burn from all the exercising he imposed on her. It was exhilarating almost like sex, which she had held out on so she was long over due and her ulterior motive for coming to the gym was to seduce Maleek into finally helping her get the ultimate revenge against Shawn.

"You feel like you just ran a marathon don't you?"

"Hell yeah!" she blew hard. "Are you staying here?"

"Nah, I've got to drop this bag off home then I've got a meeting."

"Hmmm, a meeting?"

"It's not what you're thinking. I'm supposed to pay our associate for his services remember? I only gave him half to make sure he did it."

"Oh, really? Can I meet him? I need to thank him for a job well done."

"You're something else you know that? You're a thrill

165

seeker, huh. You think this is some Cloak and Dagger shit?"

"No I just really wanted to say thank you and see what kind of man takes money to do such a thing. I'm curious."

"Curious, huh? Well you know curiosity killed the pretty pussy cat?" He delicately rubbed the back of his hand along the side of her face as he stared into her innocent doe eyes. "Damn, you can make a nigga put on a dress and jump through hula hoops with those pretty eyes."

She made her eyelashes flutter as she batted her eyes. "You know I'd pay to see you do that," she tittered.

"I bet you would." They laughed and left the gym together.

Shawn didn't have a clue that Talea was cut up and in a hospital. So, he pulled up at her house after searching for her at the photo studio and boutique. He wanted to get some special celebratory head and her eager mouth was all he had on his mind. He stood there ringing her bell wondering if she went away for an audition or an acting gig. Usually she'd call him and tell him if she did, hoping that he'd ask to accompany her. He peeked in her window and turned around to see if any one saw him. It dawned on him just how much he was behaving like a fiend. Here he was out in the open sweating his wife's best friend. What if one of Faye's nosey friends saw him and relayed that information. It would just be a matter of time before Natalia was privy to that very same information. He gave up and went back to his car. Just then a neighbor approached his car.

"Are you looking for Talea?"

"Uh, yes." Shawn wasn't sure if he should've given that answer but it was already said.

"I guess you haven't heard."

"Heard what?"

"Oh, that poor girl. She was attacked right here in her own house just a few days ago. They sliced her up real bad...there was so much blood."

"What? She's dead?"

"No, no thank God, but she is never going to look the

same again that's for sure. The attacker saw to that. Cut her face to shreds I heard it's horrible." The woman shook her head and covered her mouth, visibly disturbed. Shawn was stunned by the news.

"Who in the hell did she piss off?" he asked the air since the woman had since walked off and went back to her vegetable garden.

Shawn called one of his workers that dated Talea's cousin and asked him if he knew anything. He told Shawn how someone set her up and Talea was in critical condition and was also on suicide watch. Shawn's worker explained how Talea attempted to jump out of a window in her hospital room after seeing her reflection in a compact mirror. Shawn felt so sorry for Talea. He assumed that she'd been with some psycho and played with his heart. In turn, he did major damage to her to keep anyone else from wanting her. Now that she was out of the picture he was forced to face the truth about his marriage. He needed to sit down and work out why he'd been cheating on Natalia in the first place. He loved her and they'd gone through so much. Why was he so willing to risk it all? It was her attitude lately. She seemed different to him and she still hadn't gotten pregnant yet and he wanted a son badly. He wanted to start early so that he'd be able to keep up with his little whippersnapper. He used to shoot in her until the cows' came home but for some strange reason, she still didn't end up pregnant. He was starting to suspect foul play on her part. He thought maybe she was secretly taking birth control. *She better not be getting those damn injections again,* he thought to himself. Then there was a bit of resentment left from her being the cause of his son's death. He would've had a son had she not beat Peaches to a bloody pulp.

He drove to Maleek's club Twisted to drink and clear his mind.

Maleek and Natalia pulled up into a dimly lit cul de

sac. They circled until they found the hit man's house.

"Wait here," Maleek told her as he got out the car. She watched him go in the modest looking house and she imagined how the hit man looked. *Maybe he's hefty with scars and ugly as hell.* A few minutes later Maleek came out with another man that could pass for his twin, except the man was a bit shy of Maleek's six foot six frame. It was apparent that either the hit man was kin to Maleek or they were separated at birth. They walked up to the passenger side and Maleek motioned for Natalia to get out of the car. She stepped out and the hit man's eyes smiled along with his mouth.

"Natalia, this is my cousin Malcolm. Malcolm this is Natalia." Malcolm reached for her hand and squeezed it gently.

"Nice to meet you. I heard you wanted to thank me."

"Um, yes." Natalia was a bit nervous having known what Malcolm had done for her. Granted, she asked him to do it, but now it dawned on her that this man was capable of doing massive bodily harm and to a defenseless woman at that. She kept looking into his face wondering how was it that this handsome man made being a hit man the way he made his living. She looked at Maleek then Malcolm.

"My goodness you two could pass for brothers," she giggled. Then looked at Malcolm. "I just wanted to thank you."

"Your welcome, ma. I hope to never get you angry in the future cuz you're vicious."

"That's weird because I was just thinking the same about you...it's just so hard to believe though...you know looking at you."

"Oh, yeah? Well, the same goes for you."

"Touché," she giggled then whispered, "I haven't seen her yet so I don't know how...uh...messed up she is. Is it really bad?"

"Trust me she won't pull no nigga ever again."

"Wow." The guilt creeping up on her was becoming a

nuisance so she shrugged it off. "I'm starving Maleek. Are you going home to cook?"

"This is a funny girl right here." Maleek chuckled pointing his thumb at her. Malcolm laughed hard at her.

"This nigga burns water!"

"That's sad Maleek. You can't cook? Tsk, tsk."

"That's what Faye is for," he laughed.

"So, what about days like today when she's not here to cook. What do you eat?"

"That's what restaurants are for!" Malcolm slapped his cousin's back. "Aiight yo, I'ma see you later. And it was nice meeting you Natalia."

"Same here." She watched Malcolm walk off then turned her attention to Maleek. "Where to now?"

"Either you're gonna cook for me or we gon' have to stop at Glady's restaurant for some grub."

"Well, I am starving," she said sarcastically.

"Yeah, aiight smart ass."

She downed her smothered chicken and greens in no time. Maleek's plate was overwhelmed by catfish and fried green tomatoes. Natalia watched him eat and thought how unfair it was that men could eat themselves silly and still manage to keep a lean body meanwhile women gained ten pounds just by looking at a cookie!

"Damn Maleek do you think you have enough food?"

"You got jokes, huh? Hey, I'm a big man. I gotta eat like this to sustain all of this." He pointed to himself with both hands. Natalia just laughed. "It don't matter no way cause I'm gonna work this off later anyway." He grinned at her mischievously. She caught on and secretly her vagina did a dance.

"We can go to a hotel if you want," Maleek suggested while shifting the gear into drive.

"Why? He's not home and he won't be hom. Besides, he wouldn't look for me at your house."

"I'm saying, it's mad risky with us living right next door to each other nahmean? He might stop by my house."

169

"I doubt it. He's probably at the hospital holding his mistress's hand in ICU." She grumbled then she frowned and her eyes became angry slits. Maleek looked over at her and knew she was in revenge mode again.

"So, are we really gonna do this? I mean if you changed your mind I'll understand." She watched him as he eased back in the driver's seat. He pressed his foot lightly on the brakes to stop for a red light. He looked over and their eyes locked. In his head a million warning signs went off. In her head a million ways to stick it to her man floated around. To him, she was sexy enough to betray his friend. In her mind, he was the perfect candidate to help her get revenge and then some.

"I want it," she finally whispered sexily. "Don't be using me to get back at Shawn. Do this because it's what you really want."

"Maleek even if that were the case you know I've wanted you way before I found out about Talea. So stop bitchin' up and show me what you're made of," she said trying to sound like a gangster.

"I'ma make you wish you didn't say that. I'ma show you what bitchin' up is, aiight?"

CHAPTER FIFTEEN

Shawn wasn't about to go to the hospital to see Talea. So, instead he decided to get his questions answered by the neighborhood's tongue everlasting, the authority on all street news. It was the owner of a soul food restaurant and she always knew everybody's business. She gave him the 411 on Talea and her condition. He felt bad, but not bad enough to visit her or even send her flowers. He hung out for a hot minute with some of his workers then decided to go home and try like hell to convince his wife that he was through with all the staying out and drinking. He was ready to change the game. She was angry and he partly understood her anger at him. He wanted to make it up to her and this time he was for real. He drove to the mall and bought his wife an adorable array of flowers arranged beautifully in a pink crystal vase being held by a white mink teddy bear. It took him more than ten minutes to come up with the sentiments for the card. Finally he found the right words: *You are my wife and I am your husband. Although they say nobody is perfect, you are as close as I've come to it. You have put up with me and stuck by me. You gave me the will to get over every obstacle thrown my way. It is you that makes my life more meaningful. I'm far from perfect but with your help I can come close to it. Don't give up on me now. I will never give up on you. Love infinitely, Your husband.*

Shawn drove home to find an empty house. He called his wife's cell phone but got her voicemail. He decided to clean up the house so when she did return home she'd not only be surprised but hopefully appreciative, enough so

171

where he'd get gratuitous sex. He finished vacuuming the entire house and plopped down in the game room. Through his window he could see the light was on in one of Maleek's windows.

Lemme go holla at my man, Shawn thought.

He put away the vacuum and went next door. One of Maleek's garbage cans was knocked over in the walkway. Shawn picked it up and wheeled it back towards Maleek's back yard. He rounded the corner and heard moans. They were loud. In fact, they sounded like his wife, the way she moaned when he tortured her pussy with vicious pounding. He just knew it couldn't be his wife, so he left the garbage can where he stood and turned to walk back to the front of the house. But, then there was a bloodcurdling scream that he knew oh, so well. If he didn't know his wife's screams of passion he would've thought Maleek was killing some poor little girl. He crept up towards the patio and listened. He could hear Maleek's authoritative voice spouting demands. Shawn crept back to his garage and got his ladder. He brought it back over to Maleek's house put it under the bedroom window and climbed up two stories. The window was halfway open and the sheer curtain panels couldn't shield his eyes from one of the most hurtful sights he had ever seen in his life. Maleek had his wife in the doggie style position, her hair was rapped around one of his fists and his other hand gripped her by the waist yanking her towards him. She screamed and screamed and he grunted and growled assertive statements and commands. It was more than Shawn could bear. Then she did the unthinkable, she screamed out, "Oh, yeah fuck me big daddy!"

Shawn couldn't believe his ears. She called his best friend by the name meant for only him. He felt as if he couldn't breathe and became enraged. On his way down the ladder he nearly fell, so he jumped down when he neared the third step. He rushed home and threw the ladder in the garage. He ran in the house and slammed the door so hard the crystal console in the hallway shook. He paced the floor like a deranged lunatic then sat down on the steps and fought back tears. The vision of his friend treating his wife like a common slut was too much for him to handle. He left the house in a huff and drove right to Maleek's club Twisted. He parked in front of it. He wanted to be bad. He wanted to blow the place up. Afterwards, to celebrate he'd fuck as many women as he could. Maybe even bring them home and fuck them in his bed. He wanted to beat the shit out of Natalia then shoot off Maleek's dick!

He'd already stocked up on his favorite poison before driving to Twisted. He alternated bottles of Hennessy and Belvedere and took them to the head. He wanted to be so blitzed that he didn't remember what he saw. The more he drank the more his blood boiled. He watched people laughing, going in and coming out of the club. He realized that they didn't deserve to die. But he knew who should. He was about to pull off when a familiar face ran up to the Escalade.

"Sup yo." Niro peered into the passenger window and grinned. Shawn wasn't in the mood for Niro's bullshit tonight.

"Sup." Shawn took another swig from one of his liquor bottles. "What you doing out here? Ain't you supposed to be over by Trenz and em' counting' my shit?"

"You forgot that I already did that? You drunk or what? Look at all those bottles." Niro stuck his head all the way in the window and looked around then pulled it back out.

"I'm out." Shawn threw the empty bottle out the window. It crashed onto the concrete and made a loud noise. People from across the street looked around nervously. Shawn laughed at them. Niro laughed too and said, "Yo, you shouldn't be driving nigga."

"Muhfuckah I'm the Andretti of the ghetto. Don't worry bout' me."

"Aiight nigga, later."

Shawn revved the gas pedal and sped off. Niro just

shook his head and went back across the street.

The red lights were blurring into green for Shawn. He started hallucinating. In his delusional state he thought he saw Maleek and Natalia in the middle of the street as he drove down it. He sped up just to hit them. All of his rationale left after he finished another bottle of Hennessy. Now, he was coming dangerously close to cars in front of him. He pulled into a gas station and swerved to avoid hitting a woman getting out of her car. He ended up driving right into the back wall of a WaWa smashing their garbage cans.

"Are you alright?" asked the woman as she ran up to the driver's side.

Shawn blinked then looked around. The last thing he needed was the police coming and locking him up for drunk driving. He had a score to settle so he had to make a clean get away. He backed up and sped out of the parking area. He ended up far from home and realized that he couldn't drive any further in his condition. So he drove into a mall parking lot and slept off his drunkenness.

Natalia woke up in Maleek's arms. She eased from under him and quickly dressed. She knew it was risky not showering and rushing home at eight in the morning but part of her wished Shawn would notice. Part of her wished Shawn would die inside after figuring out that his wife just cheated on him! She kissed Maleek tenderly on his cheek and looked down at his handsome face as he slept. Her mission was complete. As sexy as he was, along with the fact that he was great in bed she knew where she belonged. Even though Shawn would have to jump through hoops of fire to make it up to her she wanted to be with her husband. But, now it would be on her terms.

She needed to know about her money. Being broke was cramping her style and delaying her progress. She was bored not working and even more bored in Atlanta. She wanted out of what she referred to as Hicksville. It wasn't as New Yorkized as she hoped and New York was definitely calling out to her. She called Susan and found out that a conference pertaining to the audit with the FEDS was coming up. It was a week away, but knowing what she knew about Shawn and Talea prompted her to leave sooner. She decided that she would stay in a hotel using his money and maybe look into getting a job utilizing her degree in New York. Maybe even try going back to the clinic. And if she did find a job in New York, Shawn would have to move to be with her. She was going to make him sorry that he ever fucked Talea. She'd make him beg and plead and he'd have to come up with ways to make it up to her, over and over.

She walked into the house and looked around. It was spotless and smelled of the potpourri candles she bought last week. The wheels in her head were turning and she wondered what got into Shawn to make him clean up the way he did. She searched the entire first floor and couldn't find a spec of dust. She smiled to herself at the thought of her husband cleaning up to make amends. She went upstairs and saw more of the same. Then, she saw the mink teddy bear holding the pretty pink vase. Her eyes watered as she read the card. *He still really loves me.* And for the first time since finding out about Talea, she felt sorry for everything she'd done. Feelings of guilt overtook her as she thought about all she had set in motion. She slumped down to the floor at the foot of the bed and cried. It was too late now. She had crossed the line and she prayed that Maleek never slipped up and revealed their indiscretion. She prayed to God for forgiveness. She would hold this secret to her grave. Her husband loved her and their marriage still had a chance. She detached the vase from the teddy bear and she clutched him to her bossom. "I love you too Shawn...infinitely."

She showered and left the house to buy him something equally as sweet and meaningful. She went to the designer outlets to find something unique to show how much she appreciated him cleaning up the house, the teddy bear and flowers. She walked around in the outlets and found nothing. She stopped at a jewelry store and bought him a five-carat diamond earring. She used to poke fun at him on how his three-carat stud made him look like a *bitch* because he was such a pretty boy. He told her that he was going to get bigger ones but never got around to it. So she decided this would be the perfect make up gift, showing him that she did pay attention to him.

CHAPTER SIXTEEN

Shawn woke up and smelled vomit. He looked over at the passenger's seat and realized that either he threw up or a wino mistook his vehicle for a toilet bowl. His head pounded but he remembered everything from the night before. All that he remembered lead to his temples tensing up and more aggravation. His first order of business was to take care of his Escalade. He drove to an auto super mall where they fixed cars, washed, buffed, waxed and vacuumed them thoroughly. The three workers who had the unfortunate job of wiping up the vomit and deodorizing the inside of the jeep complained. But, Shawn hit them off with more than sufficient tips for their trouble.

His S.U.V. looked brand new when he came back from having breakfast. It smelled a helluva lot better than it did when he first pulled into the auto super mall.

He wanted to call Maleek's house to check if they were still there but he knew Maleek would get Natalia out if he did call. He didn't have his weapon of choice with him so he had to go home. After pulling the job for Mr. X they were supposed to give the guns equipped with silencers to a Welder at a metal plant for him to melt them down into obscurity. Shawn loved the idea of having a silencer, so he didn't turn his in. Now, it would definitely come in handy.

He ran upstairs and searched the secret compartment he had built in the bathroom wall. He pulled out the gun with the silencer still attached. He looked down at it, pausing before leaving to give his conscience a chance to talk him out of what he was about to do. He heard nothing, so he stuck the gun in the back of his waistband. He ran downstairs and out the front door. He looked around before going onto Maleek's property. His plan wouldn't work without the element of surprise. Just as he stepped up to the patio, he remembered seeing Natalia's things in the bedroom, which told him she'd already been home. With that knowledge, he assumed either Maleek was still home laughing his ass off at him because he'd just banged his wife or off to the gym where he usually went first thing in the morning during the week.

So, Shawn changed his plan. He decided to ring the bell and act as if everything was okay if Maleek was home. If not he would stake out the gym and follow Maleek to his next destination then knock him out and take him into the woods and make him one sorry son of a bitch!

As he suspected Maleek wasn't at home. Now more pissed than ever Shawn drove to Maleek's gym but couldn't locate Maleek's car. Now he was at a dead end trying to figure out where Maleek could be. He couldn't call Maleek and ask him where he was because it might tip him off. He couldn't ask around either because that would definitely be the cause for him to become the main suspect in the investigation of Maleek's death. Shawn sat in the parking lot hoping another one of Maleek's hangout spots would pop into his mind. He started wondering what other recourse he had besides murdering his best friend. How could he look at Maleek ever again? He could never trust him. It was final. Maleek had to go.

Niro called Maleek early in the morning with a bogus distress call. He lied and told Maleek that he couldn't get in touch with Shawn and asked if he would take him to get a larger supply of pills. Unbeknownst to Maleek, Niro was a stool pigeon now. One day after leaving his house Niro was pulled over by federal agents and taken to an unknown location. He nearly shit in his pants assuming the worst. He thought that he was about to be killed until the federal agents identified themselves. Then another load of shit flooded his rectum when they told him that either he became their spy or he'd be sent to regular state prison where they would purposefully brand him as an informant. He knew the consequences if that were to happen. He knew every contact that Maleek and Shawn had would shred him to pieces in prison. After asking the FEDS if they were sure that they could not only guarantee him immunity but protect him for life too, he agreed. They had Niro on a James Bond mission. They made him wear hi tech shades equipped with an audio and video device. This way he would never have to worry about being caught with wires taped to his chest or balls. Plus, they could get every move and condemning evidence on video. They made sure to give him extra shades. He was to plant one when he met with Maleek's middle contact. The other he was to plant somewhere in Shawn's house or jeep. He was supposed to get as close to Mr. X as possible. Then he was supposed to get Shawn and Maleek on film touching the X pills and distributing the money made from selling the pills along with any incriminating conversations like the mention of any murders they may have committed.

The FEDS gave Niro enough money to cover the amount of X pills Shawn had given him. Luckily, they didn't know Shawn's next move was to gradually hook Niro up with his middle contact to appease Mr. X. This way Mr. X would still have his steady flow of sales and Niro would be promoted into his old spot. Shawn saw Niro's greed as potential for his escape from his illegal life.

Maleek looked at Niro suspiciously.

"What the fuck are you talking about? We just stocked y'all wit shit."

"Nah, that shit is gone. See, I'm loaded down wit' cheese right now, I need to get rid of this shit," he showed Maleek a bag full of cash.

Maleek called Shawn's cell phone to verify his next move. Niro was sweating bullets praying that Shawn didn't answer because getting Maleek alone in this position again would've been damn near impossible. Shawn didn't answer. Maleek thought it was strange, but nevertheless he felt it was his duty to fix this problem for him, considering the guilt he felt about Natalia.

"Aiight come on," he said. Niro followed him to his truck.

The deed was done and Niro's spy shades captured Maleek discussing business with a supplier. After the deal was done Maleek dropped Niro off back at the block then drove to his gym. He pulled into the parking lot and saw Shawn who started walking up to his truck.

"Sup niggah?" he slapped his hand into Maleek's. "I just finished killing them machines, son," he flexed his biceps. He started getting out of his truck but Shawn stopped him.

"Yo, I need a big favor. Take me over to that spot where you got that food you had the other night."

"Oh, I see I got your ass hooked now."

"Yeah that shit was good." Shawn laughed and went around to the passenger side. He got in looked at the dashboard and noticed a pair of sunglasses. Whose fake ass Gucci shades?"

Maleek glanced over at the glasses in Shawn's hand.

"They Niro's. You'd think the nigga could afford some real shits by now. He got enough money," Maleek laughed.

Shawn sucked his teeth and dashed the shades out the window. "He don't need that fake shit."

Maleek rolled over them with his truck as he backed out of his parking space. Maleek remembered the favor he did for Niro and told Shawn what happened.

"I don't know how he sold all of that shit so fast." Shawn looked puzzled then grinned to himself.

"But that's good. Mr. X will be happy about that."

The restaurant looked like a log cabin and was surrounded by beautiful shrubbery. In the back of the parking lot were old train tracks hidden by clumps of trees. Shawn offered to order for Maleek but Maleek wanted to go in the restaurant. Shawn walked over to where the gate separating the woods and the train tracks had a hole. He scanned the area with his eyes.

"Come on nigga," Maleek called out to him. Shawn joined him at the restaurant's entrance.

As he sat across from the man who coveted his wife, Shawn's patience wore thin. He wasn't sure what he expected from Maleek. Maybe he needed to see signs of remorse on his face. Or maybe he wanted to hear an apology or a plea for forgiveness for stabbing him in the back. Shawn picked at his food while Maleek ate like a man without a conscience. He joked and laughed with Shawn. Anger built up in Shawn and the more Maleek laughed the more Shawn could envision silencing him. The only problem he had now was convincing Maleek not to go back to the gym. He figured his best chance was getting Maleek home. He wanted to torture Maleek at first. Tell him straight to his face that he knew everything and that's why he was going to die.

"Mal, I need a ride home cause I got some shit on me I need to drop off." Maleek looked up briefly from his plate.

"Aiight."

"So, where are you on your way to now?" Shawn asked, while getting out of Maleek's truck.

"I ain't really got shit to do. I was gon' work out but now I've got niggeritis," he chuckled then said, "I'ma go in the house and chill for a minute."

"True. I might stop by aiight?"

"Yeah, aiight."

Maleek drove into his garage. Shawn looked all around to see if anyone witnessed him talking to Maleek. He saw no one. He rushed into his house and peeked through his window. His blood was already boiling because of the effortless way Maleek disguised his loyalty. He was ready to spill his blood, but he wanted to give Maleek a chance to settle in and let his guard down, rendering him defenseless.

An hour had passed and Shawn observed that Maleek never left the house and he watched the last school bus leave the complex. Now was the time to strike. He threw away the bottle of liquor that he had just finished off then found the handcuffs that he bought years earlier when he held Natalia captive. Natalia thought it was sweet that he suggested they save them as souvenirs of their meeting. He shoved them in his pocket and headed next door.

Maleek opened the door and trudged back to his game room. Shawn watched him fiddling with the PlayStation 2 joystick for a few minutes. He slipped his hand into his waistband and grabbed the gun. He conked Maleek over the head with it. Not only was Maleek shocked but dazed. He fell out of his brand new leather game chair onto the floor. He tried to speak but by the time he regained his senses he was back in his game chair with his hands handcuffed to the metal bars of the armrests. He could barely see with everything moving in a blur of haziness. He opened his mouth and tried to put a sentence together.

"Wha-what the fuck are you doing?"

"Oh, you don't know what this is about?"

"No nigga! What the fuck is wrong with you?"

"So you just gonna keep lying to the very end huh?" Shawn paced back and forth in front of Maleek, shaking the gun in his face. Now Maleek knew the deal. Somehow Shawn had found out. The first thing he thought was that Natalia actually told Shawn what she'd done.

I can't believe that stupid bitch told him! That stupid, dumb ass fuckin' bitch!

"Listen PB, she was upset and you were out doing you, so she came to me. I didn't do it on some grimey bullshit. You know how she is, I couldn't help it. She came to me though."

Maleek's eyes were wild with desperation. Shawn sat across from him on the couch so hyped up on all the liquor he drank before coming over. It was coagulating his liver's blood supply, impairing his judgement. Shawn was disgusted as he spoke.

"So, because she came to you... I mean even if she came over here butt ass naked you should've sent her ass right back home. You don't violate like that you stupid

182

muthafuckah! I would've never did no shit like that to you. I would never push up on Faye, never! You supposed to be my man, I treated you like my brother. I can't believe you did some grimey shit like that." he shook his head. "Now look at what I gotta do."

Hearing those words set Maleek into pleading mode. "PB don't do this shit. You don't wanna do this. You still my nigga. Bro's before hoes."

"So, now you're calling my wife a ho right to my face?"

"Listen man, all I'm saying is I've been there for you nahmean? We like brothers...besides she still loves you. She was just mad and I was stupid. I wasn't thinking with the right head PB but I'm sorry man. Think of Faye and the kids...what they gon' do without me?" The high pitch in his voice told Shawn that tears would soon follow. Shawn didn't feel sorry for him. In fact, it made him sick to his stomach watching his statuesque friend who commanded respect in the streets now reduced to a cowering bitch.

"Fuck all of that bullshit you talking. You wasn't thinking about me when you was fucking my wife right? So why should I give a fuck about you or you're kids? Fuck them and fuck you."

He pointed the silencer's barrel directly at Maleek's forehead. Maleek squealed like a girl right before the bullet speeding through the silencer's barrel silenced him, for good.

CHAPTER SEVENTEEN

Natalia pampered herself at Faye's beauty salon after shopping up a storm. Her trunk and back seats were sailing with bags and she still had to stop at the supermarket. She planned on cooking her husband a delicious meal. She soaked in a mud bath, was soothed by a herbal body wrap, had a rejuvenating facial, pedicure, manicure and full body massage. As the masseuse finished kneading her calves like a clump of dough, she thought about where she was. She was in Faye's salon. She was supposed to be Faye's friend. At that moment she felt lower than dirt. She had done the very same thing to Faye that Talea did to her. Guilt and shame made her uneasy and she stopped the masseuse from finishing his job.

"Um, I'm done."

"I'm sorry did I do it too hard?"

"Oh, no not at all. It was wonderful. Thank you so much." she rummaged through her purse for his tip. She gave it to him and he thanked her then left the room. She got dressed and tried to come up with an idea for what to cook.

The door opened then slammed. Natalia pulled out a casserole dish filled with red potatoes. She took off her oven mitts and rushed out to greet her husband with a huge smile. Shawn shoved her away so hard she fell into the banister. He barely noticed her whimper and stormed upstairs.

"What the hell...?" she watched him in awe. She followed him into the bedroom and watched as he flung open a suitcase and furiously threw clothes into it. Natalia

184

watched in awe for a moment.

"Shawn what's going on?"

Shawn ignored her and continued throwing clothes in the suitcase.

"Shawn, what's wrong with you?" she asked then walked over to his suitcase and kicked the top of it until it closed. Out of nowhere Shawn rushed her and she toppled to the ground. He grabbed her neck and squeezed all while screaming.

"Why? Why?" He kept squeezing until her face was red and her eyes watered. Then it dawned on him she couldn't answer with his hand gripping her throat. He let her neck go and went back to packing as Natalia gasped for air, grabbing her throat and trying to speak.

"I don't understand...why, what? What's wrong?" Natalia coughed and sobbed. "Where are you going?"

"Don't worry about it."

Shawn closed his suitcase and went into the bathroom to go into his safe. Natalia stood in the doorway watching him confused and crying.

"Shawn? Where are you going?" Shawn didn't answer her he just pushed past her and grabbed his suitcase. She ran behind him, following him downstairs to the front door and before he could open it she jumped on his back. "Talk to me!" she screamed.

"Get off of me!" he shrugged her arms off of his shoulder. She slid down to his legs and held onto his leg, crying out.

"Pleassse don't leave! Talk to me! What's wrong with you? Why are you leaving?"

He looked down at her, shook his head then opened the door.

"Talk to me!" He left her right there on the floor.

She grabbed the phone in the kitchen and called Shawn's cell phone. He wouldn't answer. She left numerous messages on his voicemail in hopes that he would hear one and feel sorry for her, call back and explain everything. But he didn't. She cried and cried until she couldn't cry anymore. She didn't know what had gotten into him. She called Andre and told him what happened.

"What am I going to do with you two?" Andre sighed.

"I don't know...I don't know why he's acting like this."

"Keep calling him. He's bound to get annoyed and answer the phone."

"He can just turn off the ringer."

"I can't figure it out myself. What did you do?" Natalia was certain that Shawn couldn't have known about her and Maleek so she just assumed it had to do with the way she was treating him after she found out about Talea.

"I told you how I withheld sex from him and I was mean to him, but I felt he deserved it."

"Well, duh! That would make anybody with a brain leave!" Natalia knew she was wrong but so was he.

"But, Andy you know what he did."

"Well, that girl obviously did that shit spitefully. She probably seduced him and he's a man Nat, you know Miss Talea is almost as gorgeous as you."

"Gorgeous?" Natalia took offense. "She doesn't even come close," she sneered.

Andre laughed. "Well, you want me to fly out? I'm free until the weekend. I can hop a plane right now ."

"Would you? I need you here with me so bad."

"Super Gay is on the way to the rescue baby," he laughed and she actually laughed too.

Tymeek watched his brother's face as he sat wringing his hands together.

"You finally see what I was trying to tell you?" he chuckled and took a draw from his blunt. "I told you about her. You went and married her. Now what you gon' do?"

At that moment, Shawn regretted telling Tymeek anything. He knew that he was going to get an earful of Tymeek saying, I told you so. I was right and you should've listened to me. He really didn't need to hear that now. Plus, the weed smoke was irritating his tired eyes. So, when Svelanka offered to drive him to the store to get some toiletries he jumped at the chance to get out of the house.

Svelanka showed him the canal where Nut fell and died. She spoke of how she loved Nut's wittiness and his cavalier attitude. They laughed as they reminisced and Svelanka offered Shawn some liquor from a gold flask she claimed belonged to her father. They walked along the canal and Shawn complained about Natalia while Svelanka enlightened Shawn about Tymeek's activities.

"He say to me Svel I will make you my wife some time in the future. But, he is always in the red light district with his friends when he comes back from Paris. He stay so long in Paris too. I'm not stupid, I know what he do there."

"You don't know that, my brother is all business. He's about money, Svel. You should know by now that nigga is made up of greed." Shawn laughed but Svelanka's eyes saddened. She took a sip from the flask.

"My mother, everybody ask me what I'm doing with him, I say he will be my husband. I want a golden brown baby you know?" she giggled.

"I know they ain't wanna hear that shit."

"My father don't care anymore but my mother she say it's okay if he is good to me."

"Does he know all of this?"

"Yes, yes. But he just keep telling me some time soon."

Shawn looked at her sympathetically. He felt sorry for her because he knew his brother and Tymeek wasn't getting married, especially to a white woman.

"Well if that's what he tells you then you gotta just wait and see. I'm tired let's go back to the house." Svelanka's phone rang and she answered.

"Ya."

Shawn left her to go to the car. He opened the passenger door and got in and waited for her. She looked like she was having an argument then she hung up and stormed over to the car. She slammed the car door after getting in.

"What happened?" Shawn asked.

"He's gone again. He tell me to tell you he'll see us in the morning."

"What? Where the fuck is he going?"

"Again he say business. I'm tired of this."

Shawn just shook his head. He wasn't about to put his two cents in about their relationship when his was in shambles. What did he know about keeping a relationship solid? She sniffled and passed him the flask. He took a sip then patted her shoulder.

"Don't worry. You know you got him on lock," he laughed. Svelanka looked over at him worried then started the car.

The house stunk of weed. Svelanka opened all the windows and lit scented candles. She made some food for Shawn and served it to him in a fancy plate. Shawn loved the treatment. This was not treatment he was used to with Natalia. She hardly ever cooked. He was tired of eating out all the time or having to cook. He wondered if Tymeek did fall in love with Svelanka. It took all but five seconds before he came up with the answer, *hell nah!* If there was one thing under God's sun that Shawn was sure of, it was that Tymeek did not trust women. That being a given made it clear that Tymeek had his reasons for never being with a woman exclusively. He used them until their purpose wore out.

Svelanka was sweet and domestic and after dealing with his spoiled, too independent wife it was a welcomed change.

"Thanks Svel that hit the spot. You got good at cooking American food."

"Thank you." She blushed then scraped remnants from his plate into the garbage. Shawn watched her and thought how Natalia would never do that for him. She'd bitch about how she cooked so the least he could do was the dishes.

"Let's play that chess set I saw in the room."

"You can play?"

"Yeah, a lil' something," he laughed.

"Okay what we play for?" she looked at him mischievously. Shawn just laughed and they went to get the chess set. Svelanka set it up on the table in the kitchen and they began to play. Checkmate after checkmate by Svelanka made Shawn realize that his game was weak, weaker than a fifty pound crack head. After kicking his ass in chess she boasted.

"Okay now I beat you so you owe me something."

"Oh, here we go," he chuckled and began reaching into his pocket.

"Not that." She grabbed his hand to stop him from pulling out the bills in his pocket. Shawn could see that Svelanka was hitting on him.

"Svel I'm not gonna do that here. That's disrespectful, nahmean?"

"Why is disrespectful?"

"Cause this is my brother's house."

"No, this is my house."

She was standing in front of him now. She slid the chess game over with her hand. She lifted her dress and sat at the edge of the table, spreading her legs for Shawn. Her pretty yellow panties had him mesmerized. He knew it was wrong, but his hands were already trying to pull her panties down. She wiggled enough to help him get them off. He was aroused now which meant that Svelanka was definitely going to get fucked. She watched him open and unzip his jeans.

"No, you do me." She pointed to her crotch. Shawn looked at her dumbfounded.

"What?"

"I suck you in New York so now you suck me."

"Nah." He whipped Max out and stuck it in her so fast that all she could do was moan. "Oh, yeah baby."

It got so good to her that she pushed the chess game right off the table and it crashed to the floor while she gyrated under him wildly. Their animalistic grunts and moans were so loud that they didn't hear the turning of Tymeek's key in the door. Tymeek slipped to the side of the archway and listened to his brother's sounds of pleasure as he pounded his woman. He put on a good front for Shawn. He knew Shawn would never suspect that he did in fact care for Svelanka more than he let on. He was torn between his past though. He didn't trust women, but he'd come to trust Svelanka with his life. Many times she came through for him with flying colors. She was good to him and if it weren't for her color he would've probably married her a long time ago. He just never saw himself crossing the color barrier, selling out.

Watching the spectacle before him left him torn. It actually hurt him. At first he was surprised by how much it hurt. Then it shocked him that Shawn would even do anything like this and in his own house under the roof where he lay his head. Shawn should've known that Svelanka was special to him because she was the only one he had around for this long and the only one he trusted enough to handle his money. The fact that he trusted her to go thousands of miles to pick up his money should've been a dead give away to Shawn. Apparently, his brother didn't care. He just wanted to get his rocks off. Tymeek tiptoed back out of the house and got in his car. He drove off deep in thought.

CHAPTER EIGHTEEN

"Andy I'm not hungry," she pushed away Andre's hand. He kept trying to shove a piece of bagel into her mouth and she kept refusing it.

"Girl, if you don't eat this shit I'm gonna hurt you." Natalia just rolled over and buried her face in her pillow. "It's not the end of the world Nat. And you know damn well that Shawn is going to come back. All of this is his." He spread open his arms using them to illustrate. "Trust me he's angry not crazy! Sheiiit I wouldn't leave all of this cause my woman ain't giving me pussy!"

"Oh, please Andy you hate pussy so you can't talk!"

"You know I should beat your ass! You know what I mean." He whacked her on the behind with his free hand then shoved the piece of bagel in his mouth.

"Damn you Andy!"

She hopped up and rubbed her sore booty.

"That's right, get your ass up and let's get out of this house. You were fine when I first got here. All week we were having fun now all of sudden today is different?"

"I don't wanna go anywhere," she answered like a spoiled brat with folded arms and all.

"Well, I'll just leave your ass here all alone. I'm not throwing you any pity party. You keep fucking up and expecting shit to fall into place. You're both whores yet y'all don't want the other one to leave. Y'all are both crazy! Marriage means monogamy you idiot!" he poked her in the head with his finger as if he were trying to drill the statement into her head.

"Andy all you do is make a person feel worse than

191

they did before you cheered them up." She did imaginary quotation marks in the air then sucked her teeth.

"So I'm supposed to just take your side all the time? If you're wrong you're wrong. Besides you're both wrong."

"I know, I know we've already established that fact, duh!"

"Yeah, okay. So, then stop sitting in here sulking and let's get outta here. I wanna go to the designer mall and then visit Mama Bear. Oooh, she is gonna be so surprised to see me," he said full of excitement then got off the bed and headed for Natalia's closet.

"I'm going to pick out your outfit for today. You're going to look decent for once."

Natalia dragged herself towards the bathroom and the phone rang. It took the third ring to remind her that it could be her husband so she'd better answer it. This was a call she didn't want to miss. She dove onto the bed and grabbed the cordless phone off its base.

"Hello," she said winded.

"Listen, I know you don't like me and you know I don't like you but you need to come get your husband."

"Excuse me?" Natalia was shocked after recognizing the voice on the other end.

"Shawn is out here with me. I'm gonna give you all the info you need and you get on a plane and come get him before some shit go down that we'll all regret!"

"What are you talking about...I don't understand." She ran her fingers through her hair then grabbed a clump as if the confusion was making her insane.

"Get on a plane to Amsterdam today!" he said without emotion. She listened as he rambled off the flight information he set up for her. She didn't catch it the first go round and asked him to repeat it so that she could write it down. He did so with an attitude and keeping in tradition with the Wilson brother's rudeness, he hung up without saying goodbye. She knew now that they were related. They were both domineering and rude. But, Shawn was definitely the nice

192

one. She turned around and saw Andre holding up three outfits on hangers.

"Andy something has happened to Shawn and I have to go get him in Amsterdam," she said looking spaced out.

Andre dropped the clothes on the bed and came over to where she stood. He grabbed her arms.

"Come again?"

"That was...Tymeek...his brother." She looked worried as she finished. "He told me to come get Shawn."

"Huh?" Andre made a screw face.

"He sounded disturbed...like something was going to happen to Shawn. I have to go get him." She threw the phone down on the bed and walked into her closet in a zombie-like state. Like a robot, she took outfits off of hangers and brought them out to the bed where she dropped them and repeated her steps. Andre stood in a corner of the room watching her with one arm folded and his hand supporting the side of his face. He knew once she made up her mind there was no changing it. When she dragged her suitcase out and knelt down to pack the suitcase Andre saw tears falling into the suitcase. He rushed to her side.

"Why are you crying sweetie?" Natalia rolled up a pair of frayed bootie shorts and neatly placed it in the suitcase then looked at Andre. Her look scared him because her eyes seemed to look right through him. Her face was expressionless and her eyes were full of desperation. She didn't answer him, she only stared. Then he waved his hand in front of her face.

"Honey bunny you're scaring me."

She snapped back into reality and her mouth could barely curve enough to make the smile she so diligently attempted.

"Andy, I'll be fine. I'm going to get my man back. You'll see." She finished packing and stood up. She looked around the room as if she'd lost something.

"What is it you're looking for?"

"My purse."

Andre picked it up from the nightstand and handed it to her.

"Please don't space out while you're driving to the airport. In fact I'm going to take you. Now should I come back here and wait for you? When are you coming back anyways?"

"Oh, Andy, you're a God send." She hugged him, rubbing the side of her face on his chest. "But I think you should go on ahead to your Godmother's house and I'll call you when I get to Amsterdam. And thank you again...I don't know what I'd do without you."

"I'll always be here for you." He kissed the top of her head. "Come on I'll drop you off at the airport. Make sure you don't come back empty handed." He smiled affectionately at her and she back at him.

She followed Tymeek's instructions and called him when she reached the airport. As soon as she picked up her suitcase from the baggage claim carousel someone took it from her.

"Hey!" she yelled as she turned to curse out the culprit. Her heart skipped a beat and she instantly became nervous. Too nervous to speak.

"Come on," Tymeek commanded.

"What's...why did you call me?"

He was walking so fast, she felt as though she was chasing him as she tried to keep up with him.

"I'll talk to you in the car." He answered without turning in her direction.

She barely got a chance to look around at her surroundings the way he rushed to the car. He threw her suitcase in the back and got in. She watched him start the car all while she stood outside waiting on him to open the door for her. He finally looked over at the passenger side and realized she wasn't in the car.

"What are you standing out there for?" he asked as the window went down. She blew hard, shook her head, snatched open the car door and plopped down beside him. He looked over at her, really looked. Her head was filled with silky coils. She wore a tight baby tee with the words *KISS MY ASS* in clear rhinestones coming out of a mouth with big red lips. Tymeek thought her breasts were suffocating from the tightness of the shirt. He eyed her smooth honey glazed legs flowing from under her mini jean skirt as she crossed them. He had an ulterior motive for calling her. He planned on killing two birds with one stone. He knew that although Shawn witnessed Natalia cheat with his own two eyes that he'd still end up going back to her. So his plan was to not only avenge his own flesh and blood's betrayal but to get rid of Natalia as well.

"Can you tell me what's going on now?" she asked, trying to avoid his stare. He finished assessing her with his eyes and stepped on the gas. "Excuse me...hello?" she said with a hint of attitude.

"So, he finally found out that you're just a regular bitch, huh? Ain't nothing special about you."

It was a good thing that he saw her hand coming at his face from the corner of his eye so he could defend himself from her attempt to smack him. He slowed down and pulled the car over to the side of the road. He forcefully grabbed her arm and applied pressure.

"Bitch, don't try that shit with me you understand."

"You're hurting me," she whined.

"Shut up and listen." He shoved her arm away.

"Don't tell me to shut up. You have me fly half way across the world to insult me? You needed to call me names to my face? That's so mature Tymeek." She sucked her teeth, looked down at her bruised arm and rubbed it.

"Didn't I say shut the fuck up and listen?" This time his voice sounded so serious and his eyes looked so cold that it did shut her up. He could tell now she was back to being afraid of him and she gave him her undivided attention. Now he could spill the beans.

"You're the reason he came over here and did what he

did."

"What?"

"Which part of shut up and listen don't you understand?" She gulped and folded her arms to keep from responding. She wanted to haul off and punch him in the face, but she knew better. The way he looked at her alone sent chills through her. His light brown eyes were hypnotic but menacing when his thick brows angled. She looked at him as he began telling her his reason for calling her. His dark skin was unbelievably smooth except for the scar on his cheek. It was funny to her how the scar looked like it belonged there as if he were born with it. Her eyes moved down to his wide strong shoulders then down to his swollen arms. He had two enormous tattoos on each arm, one of a lion on the right arm with the words king of the jungle and a shark on the left with the words king of the ocean. They were so large they went from the top of each shoulder down each arm. His hand went to his smooth bald head as he rubbed it.

She came out of her trance in time to hear him say. "I couldn't believe that shit nahmean? My own brother fucking Svel in my house! He's like my son. I took care of him most of our lives, I can't believe he'd do some foul shit like that."

And for that brief moment Natalia saw Tymeek's vulnerability, his love for his little brother. Then what he said hit her in the head like a ton of bricks. Shawn fucked Svelanka? *That bitch!*

"He probably fucked her in my house too," she said out loud unaware that she'd said it. She was thinking it but didn't expect to say it.

"What?"

"The day she came to Atlanta I cooked food for them, but I had to go next door to help Maleek with the kids while Faye...," she realized now that while she had been close to cheating on her husband that night, he probably *was* cheating. They were both wrong. But, in her mind, Shawn didn't know about her and Maleek, so he cheated just for the hell of it. That made him more in the wrong than she was.

196

She looked at Tymeek to see if he could somehow read her thoughts. He was waiting for her to finish the story because this made a big difference. If Shawn betrayed him before he found out about Natalia's infidelity then the knife in his back would instantly become rusted, dig deeper in his back and twist.

Natalia exhaled and finished her story. "I came home later on that night to find Svelanka hanging halfway off the couch and Shawn sprawled out on the floor with no shirt on. Both of them were high and drunk. I was gone a long enough while, long enough for them to...to get it on."

She shook her head in disbelief. Tymeek just stared at her. She stared back. They were both deep in their own thoughts. Tymeek asking himself could it be possible? Could he be in love with Svelanka? Why else would it hurt this much?

Natalia was torn between guilt and anger. Shawn cheated on her, again. But she'd done the same. In fact, they were up to the same indiscretions at the same time. Should she really blame him? *Hell yeah! How dare him?* she thought. When all of her thoughts cleared she could see Tymeek. He could see her. Then, his ulterior motive came to her.

"You didn't call me because you wanted me and Shawn to make up. You called me because you want to get back at him, using me."

Tymeek turned back to the wheel and began driving again.

"Answer me Tymeek. Is that why you told me to come?"

"I called you to come and get him, before I did something I'd regret."

"You wouldn't hurt him would you?" she asked nervously. He glanced over at her as if she were crazy then he drove faster and faster. The narrow roads were scary enough without him putting the car in warped speed.

"Tymeek are you trying to kill us?" she shouted.

Tymeek slowed down then looked over at her.

"Don't you ever think no shit like that."

"What?"

"What you said about my brother. I'd never hurt him. Never."

"I'm sorry," she said in a whispered tone. He took out his cell phone and pressed a button.

"Ty, where are you?" Svelanka asked.

"Put Shawn on the phone." Svelanka sucked her teeth then passed the phone to Shawn.

"Sup yo?" Shawn asked, cheerfully.

"Where y'all at?"

"I'm in some store with Svel holding mad bags like I'm a bell boy and shit cause once again nigga you're missing in action. Where are you at?"

"I'm on my way home with a surprise for you."

Tymeek pulled into his garage and led Natalia into the house. He took her into the guestroom and dropped her suitcase on the floor. He was turned to leave.

"So what now?" she stood there in her tight little shirt and skirt looking oh, so sexy. He wouldn't be a man if he didn't notice that sexiness. But, two wrongs didn't make a right and after she asked him if he would hurt his own brother he knew that he couldn't go through with what he planned.

"Nothing."

"Nothing? So what are you going to do about Svelanka? You need to beat her ass!"

"That's for me to worry about. You just worry about taking Shawn home with you," he said matter-of-factly then mumbled. "I don't know why he married you're trifling ass anyway."

"Fuck you Tymeek! You've got a lot of nerve. You don't know me. Oh, but I know all about you, you murdering, drug peddling son of a bitch!" she yelled. Tymeek walked over to her and grabbed her face with his thick hand and squeezed.

"Don't fuckin' disrespect me."

198

"So don't disrespect me." She tried to pry his hand away from her face. Her next move was purely a reflex yet she regretted it. She dug her nails into his flesh as she tried to peel his hands away from her face. He shoved her down. She began kicking and screaming wildly. He tried to help her up but had to avoid her flailing arms so he grabbed her shirt and it ripped and her milk jugs spilled out of her demi cup bra. For a moment, Tymeek was set on getting her off the floor then opportunity and the fact that all the blood left his brain and went south stopped him. His light brown eyes softened in the light and his hands gently slid over her exposed breasts. All the fight she put up before his touch became intoxicating was gone. She knew what he wanted. In that moment, knowing what she knew and feeling the burn of revenge, mixed with the building lust in her loins, she wanted the same thing. She was still winded from fighting and her breathing seemed exaggerated but it turned Tymeek on more. She was under him defeated and vulnerable to his advances. He yanked her bra down further and her breasts popped all the way out. He squeezed her nipples, kneaded them until they were hard. She moaned softly and his dick poked her through his pants as he lay on top of her. He sucked on her nipples as he pulled her skirt up out of his way. He unzipped his pants and freed his massive penis. He pulled her panties off then his pants down and forced himself into her.

Oh God it runs in the family. She screamed with a mixture of pain and pleasure. She closed her eyes and thought of Shawn and how he made the pain disappear by moving slowly while comforting her by probing her mouth with his tongue. Tymeek seemed to be punishing her spitefully. When she opened her eyes, Tymeek was looking her dead in them. It was like he was savoring the moment. He looked driven. She couldn't tell if he was enjoying it or if this was just payback for him. Tymeek slowed his pace and she stopped screaming and whimpered instead so he drove it in harder to make her scream again. When she thought he

199

was done because he grunted a certain way as if he were ready to erupt, to her dismay she'd realize that he wasn't. He would stop for a moment to recuperate then start up again. She knew what he was doing, practicing Karma Sutra by withstanding the waves of pleasure that built up before an orgasm. He was holding back, preventing them from crashing ashore so that he wouldn't ejaculate therefore prolonging the sexual act as well as his pleasure. She'd had enough of his pounding and was ready for him to do his deed.

"Please...please," she managed to whisper in between whimpers and moans.

At that moment he grinned, realizing that he was wearing her out, but he wasn't about to stop. She saw this and had a trick up her sleeve too. She began gripping his penis with her vaginal muscles and working her pelvis under him, making it harder for him to hold back. She licked his nipples and worked under him ferociously until Tymeek couldn't and didn't want to hold out anymore. He tried to be nonchalant as he came but it was just too good to him. He practically howled. She let out a scream as she had an orgasm from the friction he caused as he hammered into her. He lay on top of her for a moment breathing heavily. She held onto his powerful arms and tried to catch her breath. Tymeek raised up.

"Now I see why."

"Why what?" She had an idea of what he meant but she wanted to hear him say it. Tymeek just looked into her eyes and she giggled then they both turned at the same time to find that they weren't alone.

"Was it good Ty Ty?" Svelanka was in the doorway with Shawn. Shawn's eyes were glossed over with pain. Natalia jumped up and stuck her breasts back into the bra's under wire lined cups. She pulled her skirt down, grabbed her panties from the floor and quickly pulled them on.

Shawn's teary eyes glared at Natalia then at Tymeek. Then without warning Shawn charged into Tymeek, knocking him to the ground.

"Be easy, be easy." Tymeek tried to hold Shawn's arms down. They tussled, Tymeek trying to avoid hitting Shawn and Shawn was trying to pulverize Tymeek. Svelanka stormed out of the room sniffling and pulling out a cigarette, ready to light it to calm her nerves. Natalia ran behind her shouting.

"You sneaky bitch!" she grabbed Svelanka's blonde ponytail. Svelanka turned around and tried to slap Natalia but got a knuckle sandwich and fell to the floor with a loud thud. Natalia stood over Svelanka gloating for a minute and spat at her.

"That's for fucking my husband you stupid white bitch!" she rolled her eyes, huffed and turned around to walk away when Shawn grabbed her and threw her against the wall. He stared into her eyes, seething.

"My brother? My fuckin' brother?" he grabbed her neck and squeezed. This time Natalia was sure that it was the end. She couldn't breathe and her heartbeat actually felt like it was slowing down, her head felt lighter than air. Tymeek rushed to her aid.

"Shawn don't do this. You don't want to kill her man. Let her go." Shawn kept squeezing. Tymeek wasted a minute or two thinking if Natalia died maybe everything would work itself out. Then he realized that his brother would regret it for the rest of his life. He loved his brother too much to let him go through that. Tymeek grabbed Shawn's hand with all his might, forcing Shawn to release Natalia's neck. She fell to the floor gasping and coughing. Shawn looked down at her then at Tymeek. He had to get out of there or he'd do something else that he'd surely regret. He got his suitcase then left.

CHAPTER NINETEEN

The plane was practically empty. Shawn was in first class enjoying the space he had to stretch out his long legs. He drank two glasses of champagne and a little bottle of vodka. He wanted to fall into a drunken stupor so that he didn't have to think about anything. He wasn't drunk, but all that drinking did make him have to pee badly. He was afraid to get up because although he wasn't drunk he was feeling tipsy. He didn't want to fall down and embarrass himself. He looked out the window into the darkness. That same darkness filled his heart. As much as he loved Natalia, if Tymeek didn't come to her rescue he would've killed her in his fit of rage. He felt guilty every time he remembered the look of fear on her face.

"Why Natalia?" he mumbled to himself. He couldn't hold it anymore so he braved the trip to the bathroom. It was occupied. He went around to the other first class bathroom and it too was occupied. He was frustrated and ready to whip it out and piss in a cup. Thankfully, a stewardess who had watched his dilemma came over and suggested he use a bathroom in coach. He hurried to the back of the plane and into the bathroom.

When he was done washing his hands he looked at himself in the mirror sighing at his bloodshot eyes. He opened the bathroom door and his heart nearly jumped out of his chest. Natalia pushed her way in the bathroom and locked the door. "I forgive you. I'm always forgiving you. Now we're even. I know about Svelanka and Talea and let's not forget Peaches. I've been in jail because of your

202

unfaithfulness. I know I've crossed the line, but somehow I felt vindicated doing what I did. It was like I owed you that for all the shit I've dealt with. But, I'm sorry Shawn. I really am. Please don't hate me, I love you more than you'll ever know." She grabbed him and tried to hug him. He backed away and just looked at her blankly. "Say something. Call me a slut, anything, hit me if you have to but please tell me we can work this out. Please Shawn." Tears fell down her cheeks. "Please Shawn," she whispered and pushed him down to sit on the toilet seat. He did so without protesting. "Talk to me please." She was in his face. She kissed his lips delicately and whispered, "You don't know how much I love you. I will do whatever you need me to do to prove it." She kissed him again and lowered herself onto his lap. She kissed his lips again and tried to wiggle her tongue into his mouth. He wrapped his arms around her this time and allowed her tongue to get in. They kissed feverishly then Shawn lifted her from his lap and gestured for her to get down on her knees. She did so and he fed her his penis. After being on her knees longer than she anticipated Shawn finally helped her up.

"Sit on it." He assisted her as she straddled him. He was ready to come after her slow grinding worked him up. He pulled her hair, yanking her head back as he exploded inside her.

"I love you," she whispered, resting her chin against his forehead.

"No bitch you love dick! You're a fuckin' nasty, grimey ho!" Shawn pushed her off his lap onto the floor.

"Sh-Shawn...what are you saying?"

"You heard me bitch. You think by you following me and sucking my dick that it's supposed to be all good? Is that all you can offer a nigga is pussy? That's all you're good for?" He stood up and zipped up his jeans. "Did you even wash your nasty pussy before coming in here to seduce me, bitch?"

"Why are you talking to me like this?" she palmed the

wall and slowly stood up, tears rolled down her cheeks.

There was a knock at the door. Shawn reached for the door and she grabbed his hand. He snatched his hand away from her and raised it readying to smack her with the back of his hand then realized what he was doing.

"You ain't even worth it." He dropped his hand. "I can't believe you did that shit, my fuckin' brother of all people." He shook his head, his eyes full of pain. "You crossed the point of no return. I can't even look at you." He shook his head again and left the bathroom. She wiped her eyes and splashed water on her face. She dried her face off before opening the door to an audience of nosey passengers. She lowered her head in shame and went back to her seat.

Shawn drove into the complex and saw Faye wandering around the front of her house in her robe and slippers. She looked lost and confused. He put the car in park and ran up to her.

"Faye what's wrong?" he gently took her by the arm and led her back into her house.

"Shawn?" she asked dazed.

"Faye are you alright?"

"I'm trying to find my car keys...I must've dropped them this morning." She looked all around the lawn.

"Where are you going dressed like that?" Faye looked down at herself then dropped to her knees and started crying.

"He's gone!" she screamed.

"Who?" Shawn had almost forgotten that he'd killed his best friend.

"Maleek...they killed him."

"What?" Shawn felt like the biggest heel in the world at that moment. He killed his best friend, a good husband, terrific father and all because his wife voluntarily opened her legs for him. Maleek had four damn good reasons to live, a wife and three kids. Shawn felt lower than dirt. How could he have been so heartless? He knew he must've been another person at the time because now he just couldn't fathom doing what he'd done. He lifted Faye from the ground and took her inside and up to her room. He helped her into bed.

"Where are the kids?"

"With my sister." She looked up into Shawn's eyes. "Why did they take him from me Shawn. His babies don't understand."

"I'm here for y'all." Guilt consumed him and a tear fell from his eye.

"Oh Shawn." She reached up and hugged him. "I know you miss him too. Y'all were like brothers." she started sobbing again. "I want to kill those motherfuckers, Shawn... help me find those bastards."

Shawn pulled back and looked at her surprised. His mind blanked out for a minute then he replied.

"I'll...I'ma find out who did it. Don't worry." He wiped his eye with the back of his hand. "Look do you need to come stay by me? I don't think you should be in here by yourself."

"I just needed to be alone without the kids seeing me like this you know? My family checks up on me but thank you for offering."

"Remember, I'm right next door so just call me or come by if you need anything."

"Okay."

"I'ma come check on you a little later, okay?"

"Okay." They hugged one last time and Shawn turned to leave.

"Where's Natalia?"

Shawn stopped, turned around and outright lied to her. "She went to New York."

"Oh, don't tell her while she's out there, it'll just ruin her trip." Shawn nodded and hurried out of the house.

His chest was heavy with guilt, regret and heartbreak. Natalia was the catalyst of all the things plaguing him. She caused him to kill his best friend, alienate his only brother who was more like a father to him and she ruined their marriage single-handedly.

The house was dark and empty and depression

205

loomed throughout. He ran upstairs into the bedroom. Anger gripped him as he looked around the room seeing reminders of Natalia. He went back downstairs and grabbed a box of garbage bags from the pantry. He stormed back upstairs and into her closet, ripped clothes from hangers and threw them into the garbage bags. When he was done, her closet was bare. He dragged the bags into the garage. He went back in the house and searched her dresser drawers and the bathroom cabinets. He threw all of her stuff into more garbage bags and put them in the garage also. When he was done he sat down in the kitchen and ate a hot pocket that he nuked in the microwave. His cell phone rang and he checked the screen.

"What's good, Niro?" he answered.

"Where you been?"

"Don't worry about that. What you want?"

"I tried getting in contact with Maleek so he could hook us up cause we ain't got shit. I gotta come through."

"I'll meet..."

"It's aiight cause I'm right down the street from you."

"Nigga, since when you just come over here? You know better. Let this be the last time."

"Aiight, " Niro replied.

The doorbell rang and Shawn sucked his teeth as he sprang up to go answer the door. He was pissed that he didn't hear Niro's car pull up as he thought he would. He wanted to meet Niro outside because he didn't want Niro in his house. His house was not a place to conduct business and he was so glad that soon he wouldn't have to deal with Niro or the business anymore. He was dressed and ready to go, yet as he tried to walk out the door Niro stopped him.

"Hold up PB I gotta take a leak."

"Nigga you waited until you got here before you figured that out?"

"I've been on the road all this time man. Please let a nigga get some relief," he insisted.

"Hurry up." Shawn went out to Niro's car and saw two

more of his workers in it. They greeted each other and the
one in the passenger seat got out and went to the back seat
so Shawn could sit in the front. Niro came out minutes later
with a grin.

"You feeling much lighter now nigga?" Shawn asked.

"Definitely," Niro smirked. "You gotta direct me."

"Just take this straight out to the highway."

"So, where were you?" Niro probed.

"Nigga, are you FBI and shit?" Shawn and the others
laughed. For a moment Niro saw his life flash before his eyes
then he realized that Shawn was joking. He nearly gave
himself away with the fresh glaze of sweat forming on his
forehead.

"Funny. But I'm just asking cause we been looking for
you from last Saturday."

"I was outta town. And can you watch the fuckin' road
and not me nigga!"

"Drop us back over at the shop," one of the workers
said. Niro glanced at him in the rearview mirror and nodded.

"Aiight."

"So, y'all be finishing shit quick out there, huh?"
Shawn asked.

The worker sitting behind Niro replied, "Always, yo.
We be doin' the damn thang! Hustlin' our asses off. I'm
serious son if you look up the word hustlin' you'll see me and
Wick's picture on there," he laughed.

"That's what's up. I like hard working muthafuckaz! I
see you schooling these niggas right Niro."

The workers sucked their teeth in unison and Niro
just chuckled nervously.

"What's wrong y'all?"

"Man this nigga be on some bullshit sometimes."

"What bullshit?" Shawn turned around in his seat.

"I don't feel like I'm getting paid my worth that's all I'm
saying," the worker glanced at the back of Niro's head then
fell back into the seat.

"Damn Niro I leave you in full command for a couple

of weeks and you back on that shit? Niggas are complaining again?"

"Fuck is wrong wit you Wick? You tryna say I'm not doing my job right?" Niro sped into the parking space in front of the barber shop where the workers wanted to go. He turned around and shot Wick an evil glare.

"Nigga you know you ain't hittin' us off right so don't even front. If it wasn't for us out there beating niggas in the head to get this shit off, nobody would eat. Am I right or am I right, PB?" Shawn stared at Niro.

Niro turned his head and looked out the windshield.

"Get the fuck out my car."

"Whateva nigga," Wick sneered then got out as did the other worker.

"I'm tryna make you the head nigga in charge and you out here losing your soldiers' respect?"

"Man, that nigga is on some greed shit. He don't know what the fuck he's talking about."

"Lemme tell you something that's gon' help your ass out in the long run." Shawn exhaled and shook his head disapprovingly. "You ain't out there on the risk tip like them lil' muhfuckaz. You gotta be fair or niggas will wanna kill you because they wanna be you. Learn from the Roman Empire nigga. Caesar was an unfair, fucked up individual so his soldiers down to his own sister hated his ass. You gotta make these niggas love you enough to wanna see you breathing. The day you lose their loyalty is the day you might as well kiss your ass goodbye pointblank. You understand me?"

"Yeah, yeah," Niro answered annoyed like a child who was reprimanded by his father.

"So, we going to see Mr. X now, right?"

Shawn looked over at Niro surprised.

"What make you ask me that dumb shit? When did I ever tell you I was gonna take you there? I told you that's a long ways off for you. You gotta prove yourself and right now son you failing like a muhfuckah!"

"So how we gon' get stocked now?"

"Through the middle man and why you so inquisitive all of a sudden? You're acting like a reporter for CNN and shit."

"I need to know these things for later don't I?" he asked nervously.

"Nigga, you'll know what I want you to know when I want you to know it. You feel me?"

"Yeah aiight."

Niro pulled out a pair of shades before putting the car in drive. As he placed them on his face Shawn remembered the shades in Maleek's car.

"Where did you and Maleek go the day you couldn't find me and he picked you up."

"When?" Niro tried to be elusive. It didn't work and his constant fidgeting with the shades prompted more questions in Shawn's head. Why was Niro acting so suspiciously? Ever since he came to pick him up he noticed his weird behavior.

"It was like two weeks ago, I think. Maleek told me how you ran out of product and he had to hit you off. He gave you some from his own or y'all had to buy?"

Now, Niro was really getting worried and he couldn't think straight. Why was Shawn bringing that up?

"Oh yeah we went to some spot downtown to get that."

"That's where we gotta go now."

Shawn's wheels were turning so fast he thought he smelled burnt rubber. It was official. Something was up with Niro and the shades were involved somehow. He threw them away how'd he get them back? Did the nigga buy a lifetime supply or something?

"Those are nice, lemme try those on," Shawn lied.

Niro looked anxious as he reluctantly took them off then handed them to Shawn. Shawn looked them over before putting them on his face. They looked like a regular pair of shades. He thought maybe he was being paranoid and he took them off and handed them back to Niro. He squashed the whole discussion and turned on the radio.

"Take them shits off. What you walking up in there looking like a cop for? You want them niggas to shoot us first and ask questions later?" Shawn asked annoyed.

"But I..."

"But nothing, take them off. You ain't gon' last too long in this game if you don't start listening and paying attention to shit."

Shawn shook his head and opened the door to a bakery. He walked in and a man with a Russian accent greeted him with a handshake.

"You go to back." He patted Shawn's shoulder then put up his hand to block Niro from passing.

"What?" Niro asked, ready to shit in his pants.

"I don't know this one."

"He came with Big Mal a couple of weeks ago. You don't remember?"

"No. I never see him."

"Oh, cause I had on sunglasses," Niro said then chuckled. "Oh and you weren't in the front when we came. I think it was that guy over there." He pointed to a man in a flour dusted apron wiping down a glass counter. The Russian looked at Niro disconcertingly then at Shawn.

"Only he goes. I don't know you. You wait outside." Shawn shrugged at Niro and followed the Russian man towards the back of the bakery. The man in the apron was now in Niro's face waiting for him to leave so Niro did.

The man offered Shawn a sample slice of chocolate layered cake.

"I'm good. How you been Romanoffsky?"

"Good, good. Unfortunately I heard about my poor friend."

Shawn's eyes grew sad and he looked down at the table.

"I feel so bad because he was good family man. He loved his kids. He always took them my black and white cookies. They so cute." He looked at Shawn and saw that Shawn was getting emotional. He put his hand on Shawn's shoulder. "I know he was like brother, it must be terrible for you. Today, I give you break in price."

"Thanks." Shawn tried holding back but sniffled anyway.

"I bake special cake for his wife and kids. You bring to them for me?"

"I will."

Niro drove Shawn home. Shawn took the cake next door and rang the bell. He didn't get an answer.

"Faye must be sleep." He mumbled then went into his house. He put the cake on the kitchen counter and got a drink of water. He went into the game room and sat across from the plasma television and leaned back into the sofa. He stared at the blank screen then at the line of arcade games against the wall. Then he noticed it, a pair of dark shades on top of one of his arcade games. He got up and walked over to the sun glasses. He picked them up. He looked them over then took them into the bathroom where he filled the sink with water and dropped the glasses in it. He put two and two together, the shades were bugs. All the times he worried about the FBI bugging him and now he finally found proof. He rubbed his hands over his head and sighed loudly. It was a fact. Niro was a snitch and he not only endangered himself but compromised Mr. X's whole operation, which spelled out trouble for Shawn, trouble he couldn't deal with right now.

He paced back and forth in the bathroom, occasionally looking in the sink at the glasses. He was tired of killing and after murdering his best friend he couldn't bring himself to do another person. But, if he didn't handle this situation now it would blow up in his face later. The only thing he could think of was to call Mr. X and explain the whole situation. He dialed the number slowly knowing that Mr. X would be angry on all sorts of levels. Not only would he have to break the news about Maleek, if he didn't already know, but he'd have to tell him about the FEDS heavy on their heels. Mr. X was going to be mad at him for handpicking Niro to replace him. This was a definite monkey wrench in his plans.

"Yeah it's PB."

"Hold on," the voice on the other end said then Mr. X was on the phone.

"Tomorrow, two o'clock, the gas station on route 80. Be prepared to leave your vehicle." Shawn understood. Mr. X had few places he felt safe discussing his business matters. One of them was in his listening, device-free and bullet-proof limousine.

"Aiight," he said and hung up. He took the glasses out of the sink and brought them out to the garage where he dropped them on the floor, stomped them, then wrapped them in an old rag he used to wipe down his tires. He threw the broken pieces in the garbage.

He lay in his bed tormenting himself by remembering all of the recent, horrible events in his life. Maleek giving his wife back shots, Maleek's head spewing blood, Tymeek having sex with Natalia, Natalia's wet face after he dissed her in the plane bathroom. He thought that he was strong, but with all the chips on his shoulder now, he was about to break. This latest development with Niro was the straw that broke the camel's back. He tossed and turned and couldn't get a minute of peace in his head. Every memory was flying at him from every which way.

CHAPTER TWENTY

Natalia couldn't find Shawn in the airport arrival area in Atlanta and she didn't think he wanted to be found. She didn't want to go straight home either because the way he treated her on the plane frightened her. She caught a cab and asked him to take her to a motel. He took her to one along the highway near the airport. They looked like bungalows.

In the motel room she cried and cried. She looked around the room and asked herself what was she to do next? She called the one person she believed could tell her...

"Honey bunny, what's wrong? Why are you crying?" Andre asked.

Natalia outright bawled and was incoherent when she tried to explain. He couldn't understand a word she was saying.

"Calm down mommita. Take your time and tell me what happened."

She inhaled then exhaled slowly. She told him all the sordid details of her drama. He let her take a breather then told her to go home and if they couldn't work things out that he would come get her and bring her back to his Godmother's house. Then, they would return to New York together.

She was so afraid that Shawn would slam the phone down on her if she called that she didn't bother calling him. She called the motel clerk and asked him for a car service number. He told her he'd call one up for her. Minutes later there was a minivan waiting outside for her. Her body was tired and her eyes burned from crying. The smooth ride in

213

the mini-van lulled her to sleep. When the driver nudged her awake, she jumped up. She looked out the window of the taxi at the house. It was dark. She paid the driver and he helped her to the front door with her luggage. She looked next door over at Maleek's jeep parked in the driveway. She wondered if Maleek could shed some light on Shawn's whereabouts. She left the bags and went next door. She rang the bell, nervously intertwining her fingers. After no one came to the door right away she looked up at a window in front of the house and saw a light on. She figured since the light was on someone had to be up. She rang the bell again. This time she gave up after no one came within a couple of minutes and began walking away.

"Natalia?"

"Hi Faye." Natalia turned around and walked towards her. "Oh you were sleeping...I'm sorry I woke you."

"It's okay. I've just been restless you know?"

"Why? What's wrong?" Natalia quizzed. Faye looked at her surprised then realized that she must not have known.

"You just got back?"

"Yes." Natalia could see that Faye had been crying her face was puffy and her eyes were bloodshot red. She looked worn out, the way Natalia felt. "What's wrong, Faye?"

"You better come in." Faye held the door open wide for her.

"Oh, wait let me get my bags from in front of the door before somebody snatches em' up... you never know."

"Oh, so you just got here? You didn't even go in the house?"

"No, I Just got here in a cab. I was coming to ask Maleek something about Shawn. We're going through some things." Natalia looked down. "I'll be right back."

She ran next door and picked up her luggage and brought it over.

"Here let me help you." Faye took a carry-on bag from Natalia, lightening her load.

"Thanks." Natalia placed her suitcase down on the

floor in the foyer. "I guess Maleek isn't home, huh?" They stepped into the living room. Faye wiped her left eye.

"You need to sit down." Natalia looked at her curiously then sat down as Faye suggested. Faye slowly sat down next to her, looked at her with tears in her eyes and began explaining.

"Maleek was murdered...about a couple of weeks ago. They found his body in the bushes near the old train tracks right by Mama's House. You know that restaurant he loved to go to all the time."

"Oh, my, God!" Natalia gasped and slapped her hand against her chest.

Murdered? Oh God what's going on? Why have you forsaken me? Everyone she loved or even remotely cared about seemed destined to be visited by death. She looked at Faye apathetically. How could she console Faye knowing that she betrayed their friendship. Her heart strings were tugged by the memory of Maleek with little Fayette. The poor thing was fatherless now. Who would teach his two bright, handsome sons how to be men? She felt disgusted deep down inside as Faye put her arms around her. She felt like a big fat fake. She was disgusted with herself for what she'd done and even more with the farce she put on for Faye right at that moment. Faye's grip was tight and she rocked back and forth forcing Natalia to rock with her. She laid her head on Natalia's shoulder and began bawling. Natalia stroked her silky weave.

"Oh Faye, I'm so sorry."

She was sorry, one sorry ass individual. Then she thought of Shawn and how devastated he would be from the news.

"Does Shawn know?"

"Yes, I saw him earlier. Poor guy was crying too. They were inseparable, like brothers."

What Faye said hit home in Natalia and made her cry. They cried together stopping occasionally to wipe their faces. After draining their tear ducts, Natalia realized that it was

215

very late and Faye needed some well deserved rest.

"Let me get you upstairs. You need to get some sleep. I can be over first thing in the morning if you need me, just say the word." Faye smiled and hugged Natalia again on their way upstairs. Natalia practically tucked her in, wished her good night then left.

Tired and sleepy she dragged herself and bags next door. She used her key and opened the door. She went upstairs into the bedroom and although she'd been out all day and truly wanted a shower she was too tired to be bothered. She crept into the bedroom's darkness and put her bags down at the foot of the bed. She could see Shawn's silhouette in the bed.

He is home, so where's the truck? She stripped down to her underwear and slipped under the covers. She carefully slid her arm around him, snuggled up to his back and closed her eyes.

In her mind, she prayed that tomorrow she'd awake to a brand new day filled with promise. The prayer turned into a dream deriving from wishful thinking. Maleek was outside playing ball with his son on the basketball court as he did almost every Sunday. She awoke to Shawn standing over her tickling her, trying to get her out of bed. He wanted to go out and play in the hot tub. She finally gave in and followed him out to the hot tub. They made fervent love until they were both starving for food. It felt so real that she could taste the juicy, ripe grapes that they lovingly fed each other. "I love you baby girl." Then he popped a grape in her mouth. She chewed the grape seductively, licked her lips and replied, "I love you more Big Daddy." They hugged and squeezed one another and when she looked up into the opaque baby blue sky over them, the sun sparkled as if it were winking. The warmth she felt was real. It was the radiance of her love for him coupled with the hot tubs massaging bubbles and the sun's soothing heat beaming down on them. As she looked at him she sighed with adoration. He looked his happiest, grinning from ear to ear and splashing her with water. Yes, all was right with the world.

Shawn woke up and felt an arm around him. He jumped up alarmed that he wasn't alone. He turned around to see Natalia asleep with a smile on her face. *Oh, fuck no bitch!* Shawn shook her hard. She jumped up.

"Wha-what...what's going on?"

"Get the fuck out of my house!" Shawn said with conviction, but he wasn't yelling. Natalia blinked and looked confused for a minute. Shawn snatched the covers off of her and began dragging her out of bed.

"You must be out your mind. I want you out of my house. All your shit is packed in the garage. You can have the car I bought you, but I want you and it gone, now!"

She held onto the bed with her right hand and tried to fight him off with her left. He was fed up of the whole situation and just yanked until she ended up on the floor.

"You want me to call the cops to get your ass out?" he asked, looking like a madman. He was very serious.

"Call them, so I can tell them all about the drug selling business that you're in. Go ahead you bastard!" she yelled.

"You better leave Natalia." His voice was threatening. She looked up at him with puppy dog eyes that instantly welled up with tears. She knew that she deserved all of his anger, but she hoped he would've had a smidgen of compassion.

"Shawn, please, don't throw us away. We've been through worse and made it. Please don't give up on me, please. I'm so sorry. We've both done bad things to one another. Let's talk or whatever we have to do, but please don't do this to me."

"You don't give a fuck about me!"

"How could you say that? I love you more than life itself! Look at all I've gone through because of my love for you."

"That's your favorite thing to throw in my face right? How I fucked up your life and made you lose Junior? I used to feel like I didn't deserve you. Little did I know, you ain't shit but a whore. But, that's my fault cause you did that shit to the white boy, so I should've known you would do it to me!" Natalia's jaw dropped and she stood up.

"You wanna take it there? Do you really want to take it there Shawn? Because I recall minding my own damn business until you kidnapped me, you fuckin' dick head! And don't try to pull that reverse psychology bullshit you trifling bastard! You cheated on me first. You gave me a fucking disease and I went to jail because of your cheating ass! If anyone has the right to be more than pissed it's me! You fucked a nasty ass teenager and got her pregnant!"

"So fuckin' what?!? Yeah I got her pregnant but you got me back for that already. Don't you remember? You killed my kid you stupid bitch!" This ripped right through Natalia's chest. She blew hard and tried to keep calm. She looked him square in the eyes.

"And you killed mine so now I guess we're even," she wiped away a tear from her cheek. "I'm leaving your house now. You don't have to worry about calling the cops."

She put on the clothes she wore earlier, grabbed her bags and left. She went into the garage and saw heaps of green garbage bags piled on top of each other. She looked at her small sports car then back at the bags. She knew there was no way she would be able to take all of her things with her. The garage door leading into the house opened and Shawn was standing there watching her. She ignored him, grabbed one bag and tried to stuff it in her tiny trunk. Frustrated she rammed it in the back seat. She got in the car and as she searched for the car key it hit her, where in the hell was she going? Andre popped into her head and she took out her cell phone and called his. She got his voicemail, which told her that he was sleeping. She dug into her purse and found the car key. She was about to stick it in the ignition when Shawn tapped on the driver's side window. She pressed the button and the window rolled down.

"Come back inside and sleep. You can leave

tomorrow." She rolled her eyes at him and against her better judgment.

"No thank you. I don't need your pity, I'll be fine. I'll call you to tell you where you can send my things." Seeing as how she shunned his act of kindness he couldn't resist but to curse her.

"Well, fuck you then." He turned to go back in the house. She hopped out of the car like a kangaroo, ran up on him and jumped on his back, screaming.

"No, fuck you!" She pounded his shoulder with a balled fist.

Shawn flipped her over onto a pile of garbage bags with her clothes and held her arms down as he spoke through gritted teeth.

"Listen you crazy ho, I'm not gonna let you make me do something stupid like kill your ass tonight. So, just leave my fuckin' house and don't look back aiight?" he waited for her to say yes, instead she pounded her foot on the back of his leg. He started to slap her but decided against it.

"You're not worth it you stupid bitch!"

"I've got your bitch." She tried to knee him in his crotch, but he pressed his left knee down on her thighs. She screamed out of pain and frustration. "You've got a lot of nerve. You fuck all the women you want, give me a STD and you're calling me the ho? And I know all about Talea. After what I went through with Tracy fucking Mark I can't believe you'd do that to me. I let you slide, Shawn but I stooped to a low level and hired someone to hurt that girl all because of you. You say I keep throwing it up in your face but it's true that ever since I've been with you I've had nothing but chaos in my life! You fucked Talea and Svelanka and God only knows who else and you're talking about me like you're so fucking innocent?!?"

"You did that to Talea?"

"Yes," her voice trailed off.

"Fuck Talea! She's not your sister and she ain't your best friend. But, Tymeek is my brother and Maleek was my

219

best friend. Because of you I did some real dumb shit that I can never take back. Why Natalia? Why you fuck Maleek? And right next door to us y'all ain't even take it to a hotel." His voice wavered and his eyes watered. She looked into his eyes and could see how deep the pain went. It took over him at that moment. For the first time she watched him cry. Tears fell and he released her arms and wiped his face, turning his back to her. The picture became clearer now. Shawn found out about her and Maleek. Now she understood why he acted so weird and left for Amsterdam. How could he love her anymore? Then she threw salt in his wound by having sex with Tymeek. She remembered when he told her that she had crossed the point of no return. Now she knew what he meant. Revenge killed her marriage and Shawn's love. He looked back at her for a brief moment.

"Just leave, please." He sighed and went back into the house.

She got up and fixed her clothes. She watched the door slam. She wanted to go after him, tell him how sorry she was but she knew this was the wrong time. She got back in the car and opened the garage door with the remote clipped on the sun visor. She sped out of the garage without putting the garage door back down.

She drove for miles when she got an idea. She'd go to the airport, stay at a nearby hotel then board a plane to New York in the morning. Although it sounded good in theory, logically she would be close to broke, having to depend on Andre unless the FBI came up off of her money like they'd been promising to do for the longest. She'd have to actually find a job until then. The future didn't look so bright and her dismal outlook only made her fret more. Before she knew it she was back at the airport. She sat in her car in the parking lot and wondered about the car. If she could at least take it back to New York maybe she could sell it and have money to live off for a while until she got on her feet. She could have it shipped over or driven in a truck, but it would cost her a pretty penny. She was running out of the money she had

220

stashed for a rainy day. *Why don't I just go back to Shawn and beg him to let me spend the night?* Pride is a motherfucker, it'll make you do stupid things. On this clear, sunny morning it made Natalia sleep in her car at the airport parking lot.

CHAPTER TWENTY ONE

Two o'clock was steadily approaching and Shawn sped down Route 80 towards the gas station. Mr. X was not a patient man. Shawn knew that he'd be better off being early than late. The Niro predicament was a thorn in his side. It was bad enough that he had to deal with his other pressing issues but now this. The gas station looked busy when he drove up to a pump. He actually needed gas so he bought some. As he stood there holding the pump, filling his gas tank, Mr. X's unmistakable limo pulled up. Shawn nodded at the driver as he rolled down his window.

"Park the car around the back and get in."

"Aiight."

Shawn did as he was told. He came back around and got in the back of the limo. Mr. X was sipping what looked like water from a tumbler. His eyes were hidden behind his dark sunglasses, as usual. He put the tumbler down on the bar.

"PB, PB, PB."

Shawn could tell right away that Mr. X was perturbed and blamed him for the whole ordeal.

"I know what you're thinking, but I've already figured out how to..."

"Shhh," Mr. X said and put his finger to his lips. "Maestro."

Instantly, the limo was filled by the sound of a full symphony. Oddly enough the music lightened the tension in the limo. Mr. X smiled and waved his forefinger to the sounds of violins mixed with piano and flutes.

"Now I will talk and you will listen."

Shawn paid close attention as Mr. X's right hand man pulled out a handkerchief and opened it up to reveal a Desert Eagle point fifty. To Shawn's surprise it looked just like the gun he used to kill Maleek. If he weren't sure about the fact that he threw it in the Chattahoochee River after hiding Maleek's body, he'd swear that it was the very same one.

"You did a very stupid thing. I can't even imagine what Mal did to you for you to take him out the way you did. I'm quite sure that whatever it was it could not have possilby warranted his untimely demise. But your biggest mistake was using a weapon such as the one I so kindly provided. I distinctly recall instructing you to dispose of that weapon after the job I commissioned you for was done."

He picked up the tumbler and took a gulp. He shook his head disapprovingly.

"You disobeyed me. Now, the police have bullets matching the murders in Las Vegas. I'm sure you can see why this is disturbing to me."

Shawn rubbed his hand over his face and felt uneasy about being in the limo now. Not only did Mr. X know that he killed Maleek, whom Mr. X admitted liking more than most of his business associates, but he now felt that Shawn compromised his plans. It did not look good for him. It was at that moment that Shawn realized this might turn out to be his last ride. He looked over at Mr. X's right hand man who was a big no-neck, dead ringer for the wrestler, Big Show. He refused to show fear so he confidently responded.

"Look, Maleek did some real foul shit. I fucked up with keeping the gun. I didn't handle that situation right but I will handle this Niro situation correctly. That's why I called you. However you want it dealt with that's how it'll be done."

"I'm not concerned with that simpleton. You see he poses no real threat. What does is the fact that not only do you have the FEDS sniffing your ass, but you're leaving them bits of a trail, a trail that leads to me." He reached inside his jacket pocket and pulled out a cigar case. He flipped it open, pulled out a cigar then a clipper and clipped the end. His right hand man lit it for him then went back to eyeing Shawn.

"You see Niro is an integral part of the dilemma but getting the evidence back from the FEDS was a magical feat. But, as you should know, I'm the David Copperfield of the drug trade. So, you can breathe easier knowing I took care of that but I need you to take care of a few things for me."

He took a puff of the cigar and blew the smoke upwards then looked Shawn square in the eyes.

"I'm not about to go down because of some macho bullshit that you two ghetto boys got yourselves into. So, you're going to torture that asshole until he coughs up every bit of information that he gave them along with all the names and dates of the agents. After you've pumped him for the info...pump him with lead and this time you are to call my friend here to help you dispose of everything when you're done."

Shawn's cell phone rang and Mr. X watched him to see if he was going to answer it. Shawn put the phone on vibrate. "Pardon me."

Mr. X smiled and continued. "You will unload this last batch of product that was intended for Mal. I don't care how you do it but you'd better be smart about it. The last thing I need for you to do is leave Atlanta once our business is complete. You can visit but you may never conduct business here again, ever. Am I understood?"

"Yeah," Shawn nodded.

Shawn waited for the wee hours of the morning to find Niro. He knew that if he called Niro and told him to meet him that Niro would figure out what was about to go down and he'd either run to the FEDS or leave town. Shawn knew the one place Niro would be. Niro always slept at his baby's mother's house. Shawn kept telling him he should get his own place, but Niro was too busy wasting his money on diamond jewelry and cars. So, instead of investing in a house he went from his mother's house to his daughter's mother's house.

Shawn crept past the front of the house and clipped the metal lock on the gate leading to the backyard. He was grateful that she didn't have dogs. He tiptoed through the lush green grass and drilled the door's lock with a whisper quiet electric drill. He opened the door and carefully crept inside. He opened the door to a room but saw pink walls and knew that it had to be Niro's daughter's room. The moonlight shining through the soft pink petal curtains spotlighted her little head on a Power Puff Girls pillow. After seeing her he closed the door and wandered down the hall to find Niro. This time he opened a closet and saw towels. Now he was not only pissed off but full of anxiety. He wondered if this plan was a good one. What if his girlfriend woke up? Then he might have to kill her too. He decided the only thing that could save her is if he hid his face. He opened up the closet and took out a hand towel. He loosely tied it around his nose and mouth and pulled out his gun. The next door looked like it would be the right one. If it wasn't, Shawn was going to go insane. He reached for the door knob, but it turned as if a genie heard his wish and granted it. Niro came right out into the hallway. Shawn knocked him in the back of the head with his gun repeatedly until blood leaked out. The towel fell from Shawn's face onto the floor. He picked it up and wiped off his hand and put it on the back of Niro's head. He looked around to make sure there wasn't any blood on the floor or anywhere else that would indicate foul play. He picked up Niro and took him outside to the car. He was glad the car wasn't his as Niro's bloody head seeped into the gray fabric. This car was dispensable and he would have it junked right after he finished his mission. He took Niro to an empty boarded up house deep into woods territory. He lay Niro down on the floor then poured a bucket of ice water from a cooler in his face.

Niro sputtered, gurgled and jumped up. "What the fuck?" he asked in shock. He looked up and saw Shawn standing there pointing a big gun at him. He looked closer and saw that a silencer was attached to it. Unconsciously, he peed on himself. Shawn looked down at the wet spot on Niro's boxer shorts growing by the second.

"Yeah nigga you better be scared cause you done fucked up." Shawn's face was twisted into a look of disgust. "I try to help you're ass and this is the shit you do?"

"Whatchu talkin' about, PB? I didn't do nothing I swear man."

"Nigga, don't fuckin' lie in my face! I know all about you and the FEDS. Now you gonna tell me everything that you told them and everything they know. Then I wanna know who's your contact and the dates you met with em', everything. You better not leave anything out."

"PB, I swear I had no choice man. They were gonna kill me."

"Kill you? Nigga, are you stupid or fuckin' retarded? You should've been worried about me killing you and your fuckin' family. You know how I do. Why would you fuck yourself like that for the FEDS? Them niggas can't do shit to you. They're bound by the law stupid ass. Now me, I don't have rules to abide by. Why didn't you think about that? Now you're fucked!"

"Come on PB please cut a nigga some slack." Niro broke down and started sobbing.

"That bitch shit don't phase me. This shit is outta my hands. You can talk and make it easier on yourself." Niro stopped sobbing, wiped his face clean.

"Easy how?"

Shawn was appalled by his desperation. Niro looked pitiful sitting in his own piss with snot smeared all over his face.

"Tell me what I need to know and I'll shoot you

somewhere where you'll live. Cause as long as your ass disappear I won't have to kill you. Understand?" Niro sniffled, put his head in his hands and started crying again. "Shut the fuck up and talk Niro. I ain't got all day...neither do you. Make it easy on yourself, yo. Now tell me what you gave em'."

Niro wiped his nose with the back of his hand and looked up at Shawn,

"Honestly all they got was the video of me and Maleek when we went to get that X, just that one time. But, most of it was too dark, plus I ain't get to stand over by them when Maleek got the shit so they was mad and told me to get you on tape. But, I ain't get nothing. All I know is they went up in the bakery but ain't get nothing cause someone tipped the Russian off." He began to shiver.

"Move away from the ice dumb ass. Damn, how the fuck did I ever think your ass could step in for me?" he shook his head.

"So, who's your contact?" his arm was tired so he lowered it with the gun pointing at the ground.

"This white dude named Vixon. I meet him at the Downtown Brown Cleaners. It's right behind the copy center. I meet him every Friday night at 10:30. And, if I'm not gon' make it in time or anything happens I gotta call his cell."

"So you was gon' meet him this Friday?"

"Yeah, but like I said I ain't get nothing so this Friday he supposed to give me something to help me get more info."

"Like what?"

"I don't know what it is. He just told me to be there Friday and he said once I did this it would be the last time we had to meet cause they'd get what they want. That's it."

Shawn looked at him suspiciously. "Niro, don't fuckin' play with me. You better be telling me everything."

"I am man, I swear. Look, if I don't show up Friday they gon' know something went down. They gon' come for you cause Maleek is dead."

Shawn shifted his weight and raised his arm holding

the gun again. "Trust me they won't."

"Wait man, wait. So, you just gon' wound me right? Can I get it in the arm?"

"Sure." He shot Niro in the arm as if it were nothing to him.

Niro grabbed his arm and yelped. "Aarrrgh this shit burns man. Oh shit, oh shit." He rocked back and forth. "Take me to the hospital please man. Just throw me out the car like a block away. Come on PB please. This shit ain't no joke," he whined and tried to stand up.

"Where you going?" Shawn asked him still pointing the gun in his direction.

"Come on I gotta get this taken care of," he stumbled to his feet then realized the gun was still pointing at him. "You said you was only gon' wound me PB. Why you still pointing that shit at me? I can't do nothing to you, I'm shot!"

"I know nigga, I shot you." Shawn shook his head and laughed. Niro was really dumb and now he could see how he was slipping himself by choosing Niro as his successor. It bothered him that his judgment was so off. Niro didn't have heart like he did. Niro wasn't a gangster when necessary nor was he business minded even with all of Shawn's tutoring. Niro was a waste of time. Knowing this only made Shawn angry. He wouldn't have had to been up all this time dealing with Niro's pissy ass if he'd chosen a better candidate to take his place in the game.

"PB, please I'm bleeding man," Niro whined interrupting Shawn's self-critical moment. Niro inched closer to Shawn dramatically reaching out as if he were too woozy to be on his feet. "Help me PB,"

"Aw, shut up!" Shawn shot him at point blank range in the chest. Niro stumbled and fell back. Shawn pulled out his cell phone to call Mr. X's right hand man.

The wrestler look alike was there within an hour. Shawn was pissed off for having to sit with Niro's carcass for an hour plus his stomach was growling from hunger.

The man brought the biggest roll of bubble wrap

Shawn had ever seen.

"Give me your gun," the man said with his hand out.

"What you gon' do with that?" Shawn asked pointing at the bubble wrap with a chortle. The man ignored him and started unraveling the wrap.

"Roll him onto it." Shawn did as he was told and watched as the man expertly wrapped Niro's body and the gun up like a Christmas gift. He was so strong that he didn't even need Shawn's help with carrying Niro's body out to his van. Shawn watched him lock up the back of the van. The man pulled out his cell phone and dialed. "I'm here and the deed is done. Okay hold on," he handed Shawn the phone.

"Very good PB now what news do you have for me?"

"You want me to talk on here?"

"All I want to hear is if you have news."

"Well, yeah."

"Good. Get rid of what you have to and meet Mr. Chevy back in that same spot in two hours. And when I say two hours I mean two hours. Understood?"

"Yeah."

CHAPTER TWENTY TWO

A policeman tapped on the car window and Natalia jumped up. She pressed opened the window.

"Miss, you have to move your vehicle." He handed her a ticket.

Natalia looked around and it all came back to her. She was in the airport parking lot. But, she was parked in a handicapped space. It was the only one available last night. She sighed and realized that she was practically homeless. She was ashamed of herself, but she had no choice. She had to save the money she had for her plane ticket as well as getting her car into New York one way or another so a hotel was out of the question.

"I'm sorry officer I must've blacked out."

"Ma'am are you intoxicated?"

"No officer."

"Are you on any controlling substances right now?"

"Not at all. I would never," Natalia became indignant.

"Step out of the car ma'am."

The officer stepped back to enable her to get out. She sucked her teeth and got out of the car. He pointed a small flashlight directly into her eyes checking her pupils response then asked her to blow air. He sniffed close by her mouth.

"Okay ma'am, I'm sorry to trouble you but it just doesn't seem right for you to be asleep out here in the parking lot and in a handicapped space."

"I understand, but this is all because of an extenuating circumstance. I have to catch a flight today and well..."

The cop wasn't really interested in her explanation and had a job to do so in order to get rid of he simply cut her off.

"It's okay. I just suggest that next time you check into a hotel."

"Duly noted," she answered sarcastically and plopped down into her car. She started it and drove off as he watched her.

She called Andre's cell phone hoping that he'd already left and was at the airport.

"Hello," Andre answered. "Andy please tell me you're at the airport."

"Ummm, okay I'm at the airport."

"Thank God! Which terminal?"

"Girl I'm just messing with you. I'm on the road in a cab. But, I am on my way to the airport. What's going on?"

"Shawn put me out so I slept in my car. I'm going to New York with you, if I can get on the same flight."

"Oh honey bunny. When I didn't hear from you last night I figured everything worked out."

"It didn't. I know why he's so upset. I understand why he never wants to see me again."

"Wait a minute, he told you that?"

"Not in those words but close to it. I'll explain all of this to you when you get here. Where should I meet you?"

"The double A terminal 165 in like another fifteen minutes okay?"

"Okay." *Now all I have to do is figure out what to do with this car.*

She decided that she'd ask Andre to buy her plane ticket and she could pay to have the car delivered to New York. After paying for the ticket and the car transport service, she was left with only sixty-seven dollars. She was starving and went to the food court and bought a cup of tea and a bagel. She sat in the food court and ate. She wondered what Shawn was doing at that very moment. Was he thinking of her? How would she go on without him? Her mind was filled with questions and her demons tried to make her insane by answering them with all the wrong answers. She glanced at her watch and noticed that fifteen minutes had come and gone. She hurried to terminal 165. There was a long line at the check-in counter. She scanned the line for signs of her savior, Andre. She didn't see him and became discouraged. She was about to walk outside to see if he was getting out of a cab then she heard Andre's loud voice calling her name. She turned around excited, her eyes searching for him. She spotted him in a black T-shirt in the middle of the line.

"Andy, how did I miss you before? I searched the line."

"Well, obviously not hard enough." She slapped his arm. "I need a favor," she gave him her puppy dog look.

"Spit it out."

"Can you pay for my ticket?"

"Of course silly. I can only hope they have a seat on this plane for you."

"Oh, God, please let there be one."

God answered her prayers. There was a seat on the plane and even though it wasn't anywhere near Andre, Natalia was happy to be headed back to New York. She wished that they were seated together so that she could tell him what happened between her and Shawn. Since she couldn't tell him on the plane she gave him an earful in the cab on the way to his house, on the way into Andre's building, on the elevator even when they got inside his condo....

"Girl do you see how life can be one way one day and another way the next?"

"Yes, unfortunately I do," she sighed and flopped down on Andre's bed. He threw his bag down.

"Mmn, mmn, mmn and all of your clothes is back in Atlanta. I gotta take you shopping."

"Andy, I feel like a moocher...I'm a bum. I hate having to put you out like this." Andre's jaw dropped and he cocked his head.

"I know you don't think that's how I see you. You're not a burden to me."

"Well, aren't I with all my drama? It seems as though I need your help every five minutes." She buried her face in her hands. Andre tipped her chin so that she looked up into his face.

"Don't you ever think that. That's what friends do. They're there for each other whenever they're needed. Point blank. I keep telling you that I'll always be here for you and I mean it. Look how many times you were there for me in college. Shit, I practically lived off of you for like two years. You're like the sister I never had."

"Hee, hee. You're so funny I forgot to laugh."

They laughed.

CHAPTER TWENTY THREE

Mr. Chevy was five minutes late pulling up in a G-wagon instead of the black van he put Niro's body in. Shawn got in the back seat since Mr. Chevy had company in the front. The man sitting in the front was wearing glasses and looked like a nerd. The nerd turned around and held out his hand to Shawn.

"You must me PB. I'm called Professor." Shawn shook his hand and nodded. "Well, part two of your mission will commence Friday night at precisely 10:30."

"Part two?"

"Yes, you have to replace the deceased at his meeting with agent Vixon. You show up, take him out, call Mr. Chevy here and that will be the last time you'll have to play The Reaper."

Shawn sighed heavily and sucked his teeth. Not only was he tired of killing people but he had his own shit to deal with that he didn't even get a chance to mull over. It still weighed heavy on his heart. To top it off, he had no one to console him, no one to talk out his issues with. He had no best friend, no wife, not even a brother right now.

"Is there a problem?" Professor asked, adjusting his glasses on his nose. Shawn knew he couldn't very well answer yes so he shook his head no. Professor pulled out a small black bag and handed it to Shawn. "Here's your Reaper kit. As you did earlier, you will turn it over to Mr. Chevy. Also, you will be sure to approach agent Vixon with caution. I can't stress the importance of this one going smoothly. No loose ends." He reached down under his seat and pulled out

234

a large duffel bag then handed it to Shawn. "This is the product promised to you and you know what to do with it. That's part three and I understand that you comprehend part four and will comply, correct?"

"What?" Shawn asked agitated.

"Oh, do forgive me, I forgot who I was talking to." Shawn not only took offense to this but was ready to knock the nerd out...if only big ol' Mr. Chevy weren't there. So, before he went ballistic on the Nutty Professor he just laughed it off.

"What I said was you've agreed to leave after you've squared off your debt, right?"

"Yeah, yeah."

"Good then we're all done here." He smirked then turned around. Shawn looked at the back of his head for a moment and wondered could he get away with snuffing the Professor. *Nah,* he thought to himself and got out of the jeep.

He got back into his car and drove home. He took a long shower hoping it would cleanse the filthy stench of death from his body. He'd been on the go ever since he ended Niro's life. He had to get rid of the car he drove earlier, find a second in command on short notice, make sure everything was straight amongst his workers, re-count and divvy up the proceeds from the day before. By the time he'd done all of that it was almost time to go back to the scene of his crime.

He lay on the bed looking up at the ceiling with his cell phone glued to his ear as he listened to his voice mail.

Message no. 1 *Ay, yo, this is Wick and that nigga Niro ain't show up and niggas is mad aggie right now. Holla back!*

Message no. 2 *Now baby I know you think I'm going to give you advice until the cows come home and you know what? You damn right! Stretch, you better bring those long legs over here as soon as you get this message. I need to talk to my baby. Okay, I know you too far to just drop on by but call me sweetie. But, if you can come home to New York baby, come* on home. *Oh, by the way if you didn't know that this is your second Momma, Auntie Freda then you gon' get an ass whuppin' when I do see you! Now get on the horn and call yo mama!"*

Message no. 3 *I need to talk to you Shawn. I just wish that we could...Sorry isn't enough but I have to say it, I'm sorry. I love you so much and always will. Even with every hurtful thing you've done and said. I still love you. I forgive you Shawn because I can't be without you. Please forgive me, please.*

Message no. 3   *It's your mother. The mother whom you haven't called in how many months? I wasn't going to call you but Freda told me what happened with you and Tymeek. I know all about you getting married without my blessing. God cannot bestow his light upon a union that did not take place in his house of worship. So, I'm not surprised that it's over now. Call me and maybe we can pray together and ask his forgiveness. Maybe he can help you through your confusion and pain. Call me for once.*

Shawn hung up on that note. His mother always managed to piss him off by spouting scripture or some sort of self-righteous blather.

There she go with that religious bull. His thoughts were cut off by the vibration of his cell phone in his hand. He looked at the screen and saw that it was his Aunt Freda's phone number. His voice weakened when he answered.

"Hey aunt Free."

"Don't you hey me. Where've you been?"

"Well I was work—"

"Never mind that. You just tell me your side of the story let me figure out which one of you is getting the spanking."

She always made him smile.

"Aunt Free, I don't even want to talk about it."

"No, baby, you have to. Even though y'all are brothers you know Ty Ty loves you like a son. You don't know how bad your brother is hurting right now do you?" Shawn hadn't given it much thought. But, he was hurting too.

"He called you?"

"Of course he did. How do you think I found out about what happened?"

"Well, he knows he was wrong—"

"You're right. He does know and he feels terrible about it. He felt so bad he was about to do something really stupid."

"Like what?"

"Like bring his dumb ass back into the U.S. and get captured! All because of some white woman who probably don't give a shit about his black ass no way!" Shawn chuckled on his end.

He noticed that she didn't mention anything about Natalia. *I wonder why?*

"Aunt Free, Svel ain't nothing to him that's why I don't know how he could compare her to my wife. Why would he do that to my wife? I could see if he loved Svel, but he don't. You know how he is. He knew how much I loved Natalia, he knew."

"Stretch, I'm about to give you an earful but dammit it's for a good cause. Your brother has always had to be the strong one for the both of you. He could never let you see him sweat because he wanted you to grow up strong for yourself. So, all that hard rock show he puts on for you is half ass. Yeah he's tough as nails but he's still human and he has a heart. I think Ty Ty is in love with that damn piece of white bread, but he's entitled to it. To you, she was some chick he was using, but to him she was as close to being in love as he was gonna get. So, he did something a little crazy behind seeing his brother betray him in his own home. Do you understand now?"

Shawn did understand. His aunt opened his eyes. Tymeek must've felt for Svelanka what he was still feeling for

237

Natalia, love. But, two wrongs don't make a right.

"But, Aunt Free two wrongs don't make a right. Plus, how was I supposed to know he loved her?"

"Aaah, Stretch you men are so blind sometimes I don't know how y'all make it around in the world."

"Why I can't find a good woman like you Aunt Free?"

"When God made this fine thing right here, he threw away the mold!" Shawn laughed hard. So did Freda then she got serious on him.

"Shawn you call Tymeek and apologize and he will do the same. Don't call him going over what happened just start out with I'm sorry and I love you and we're family and that's all that matters."

Shawn thought about what she said. He wasn't too good with apologizing, but he would do the best he could. He hoped that Tymeek was as apologetic as he planned on being.

"I'ma do that just for you Aunt Free."

"Oh, please, you're gonna do it cause it's the right thing to do. And another thing—"

"Oh boy...what now Aunt Free?"

"Don't you gimme no lip cause I'll whip you with this phone. Now, as I was starting to say, you need to forgive that half breed that you married. You can't fault her cause the poor thing was confused from birth."

Shawn laughed and laughed.

"Seriously though sweetie I think she was only trying to get back at you, but she didn't think of the consequences or the level of the damage she'd do. All I know is from what I've seen and y'all have the rarest kind of love... unconditional. That thicker than mud kind of love. Y'all have been through hell and high water and kept it together. Somehow, I think y'all can make it through this too."

Shawn wished that were true. His brother was a different story from Natalia. His blood came first. Natalia was a woman, the kind that couldn't be trusted. How could he overlook that?

"Stretch?" Aunt Freda cut through his thoughts.

"Yeah?"

"You heard me?"

"Yes, Aunt Free, I hear you. I don't know. I love her to death, but she was with Ty. I saw them with my own two eyes. It's hard you know?"

"I know, baby. But, in time you're gonna miss her and none of that is gonna make a bit of a difference then you're gonna end up calling her and begging her to come back."

Shawn could feel his Aunt's condescending stare right through the phone and he knew it was accompanied by the infamous smirk she usually had after saying something that she was certain was on point.

"You think you're psychic don't you?" Shawn chuckled.

"When you're right you're right." She chuckled back. "Get your wife back, she's the only fool that will put up with your ass!"

CHAPTER TWENTY FOUR

"Well how do I look?" Natalia asked Andre and spun around.

"Like a teacher for sure."

"No, no, no. That's not the look I was going for." She began unbuttoning the princess seamed suit jacket.

"I'm kidding you girl." Andre slapped her hands away from the buttons and buttoned it back up. "You look like a psychologist. Is that better?"

"You're just saying that."

"No really, you look very professional. I just hope those little boys don't jump your bones. Oh I forgot who I'm talking to wacko jacko's little sister cause you love sleeping with little boys too," Andre cackled.

Natalia laughed and shook her head. "Andy that's sick." She picked up the brand new briefcase that Andre bought her for her brand new job. Weeks earlier she sweet talked an old principal from one of the schools where she used to sponsor programs into hiring her as the school psychologist. After losing his previous psychologist to a private practice he agreed that with her credentials she was naturally a shoe in. Luckily for her, Susan managed to get her conviction expunged from her record so that she could take the job.

She was nervous about this position. It had been a while since she spoke to a child let alone sat one on one with a child in crisis. She hoped that she would do well and truly be of help to the children, but she also hoped they weren't as mischievous as the principal warned.

She opened the doors to PS 893 and a rush of

screams, laughter and indecipherable noise engulfed her as she walked in. There were little kids, big kids even kids that looked about as old as she was. She squeezed past a crowd of little boys trading cards on the steps. She went into the administrative office and found a time card with her name on it next to the time clock. After reading Natalia Wilson on the top of the card she sighed and wondered if she'd have to go through the whole ordeal of changing all of her I.D. back to her maiden name. She wished in her heart that Shawn wouldn't ask for a divorce even though she expected him to. She called him repeatedly, but after not hearing from him she assumed that the hate he had for her, had not yet subsided.

She punched in and opened her office door using the key the Principal had given her.

She spent most of the day re-arranging files, moving the office furniture to suit her tastes, reading through current cases left behinf by the old psychologist and observing the special education students on her case list. By 2:45 her work was done. Principal Abners commended her first day on the job. She grabbed her briefcase and walked out of her office. On her way to punch out, a child from one of the kindergarten classes on the first floor ran up to her and gave her a big ol' bear hug. She gasped from surprise. She looked down at his little head full of soft loopy curls, his face buried in her lap.

"Hello sweetie." She smiled down at him, trying to lift his chin so that she could get a better view of his face. " "What's your name cutie?"

"Elijah," he replied, looking up at her adoringly. "You look like my mommy." Natalia was so touched by this. She wanted to snatch him up and twirl him around. It was then she could've sworn that she could see Junior in Elijah's face. He was just as pale with a cute-as-a-button nose and a head full of curly hair just like her deceased son. She stared at him for a moment, thinking that God must be showing her what junior looked like now in heaven. He was still adorable.

241

She wanted Elijah to be Junior right at that moment and as she went to hug him a teacher came over and snatched him away.

"I'm sorry was he bothering you?"

"No, not at all," Natalia smiled at little Elijah.

"Oh good." She smiled at Natalia then frowned at Elijah and scolded him. "Don't you ever run away from me like that again do you understand. We have to go out into the yard for dismissal so that you're mother can find you. Okay?"

"Okay. Bye, bye." Elijah waved to Natalia.

How odd, Natalia said to herself as she went to punch out.

"How was your first day?" Andre asked as soon as she stepped foot into the house.

"It was great." She dropped the briefcase and got herself a glass of cranberry juice. Andre walked up behind her and rubbed her shoulders.

"So, did those little monsters give you a run for your money?"

"Nope. They were all sweet. You know what happened?" she said with a far off look in her eyes.

"What?" Andre kept right on rubbing.

"There was a little boy there, Elijah and he ran up to me and hugged me so tight. It was the sweetest thing. Then he told me I looked like his mother and please don't think I'm crazy Andy but he looked like Junior, like how Junior would look at his age." Natalia turned around to face Andre. His eyes widened. "I know you must think I'm overly dramatic or it was wishful thinking."

"No, honey bunny. I read up on this. You know what that could've been?"

"What?" she keenly listened.

"Well, children are drawn to maternal women, you know? Women who have many children or are..." Andre's eyes really widened now and he looked down at Natalia's stomach.

242

"What Andy? Women who are what? Tell me, tell me."

"Girl, you told me that your period is late so I don't think it was from stress like you said. I think you're pregnant!"

"Oh, God! You think so?"

"Yup. Children can sense pregnancy."

"Oh, Andy you really think so? We were trying for so long, but I didn't get pregnant..." her eyes brightened.

"Let's go get a pregnancy test." he grabbed her hand then his keys from the counter and rushed her out the door.

The drug store pregnancy test tested positive, but Natalia insisted that she take a blood test. She called up Dr. Summers and went to see her. Andre waited patiently in the waiting room as Dr. Summers relayed the news.

"You're pregnant," she said with a grin.

"I am? Oh my God, Oh my God!"

"I love it when a mother is as excited and as happy as you are when I give them positive results."

"I'm just so happy. How soon can I get a sonogram?"

"Well, I won't be in tomorrow so how about Thursday?"

"That will be fine. It will have to be in the evening, is that possible?"

"That's okay because the technician leaves at six." Natalia glided out to the waiting room and grabbed Andre's hands, yanking him out of the chair. She squeezed him so hard he could hardly breathe.

"Girl, let me go before I pass out," he laughed.

"I'm pregnant, I'm pregnant."

"See, father knows best," he chuckled then sang. "I'm gonna be a God Daddy, I'm gonna be a God Daddy."

Andre was walking out of his salon and forgot his car keys. He doubled back to his office and found them right where he left them on top of a paper bag with a half eaten wheat and salami wrap still in it.

Ewww, Mickey Mouse would have definitely came out to play up in here if I would've left that out, he thought aloud. He crumpled up the bag and threw it in his waste basket. He shoved his keys in his pocket and left the office. Before he made it outside some one grabbed his arm. He turned to see Shawn. Andre turned pale and his eyes popped out of his head, he gulped from surprise then he caught his breath.

"Shawn! Wow!" He couldn't think straight and it wasn't just from the shock of seeing Shawn. It was also from how handsome he looked with his macho, tattooed arms showing in all their glory.

"I know you know what went down. I don't know if she told you all truth or her version of the truth, but I need to see her. We've got some things to discuss. So, tell me where she is because she's not at your house. Where does she stay now?"

Andre blinked trying to figure out whether or not he should meddle and give Shawn the 411 on Natalia. So much had changed, especially since her pregnancy was now showing. He felt it wasn't his place to tell Shawn the news about the baby, but he deserved to know so he sent Shawn to her. This way she'd have no choice but to tell him.

"She has a job now. She works as a psychologist at a public school." Shawn smiled to himself. She was so resourceful and it still boggled him that such an intelligent woman with so much going for her would've thrown it all away just for him.

"Is that where she is right now?"

"Yes, PS 893 over on Chambers near ground zero. She gets out at 2:45 so you'd better hurry if you're going to catch her."

"Thanks," Shawn smiled gratefully. Andre smiled back. He hoped they would just get it together.

"**D**arius please stop kicking the table."

"No."

"You had a good day yesterday. What's wrong today, Darius?"

"Ms. Justine won't give me my scissors."

"But Darius they're not your scissors and you don't need them for class work today. Their dangerous and you don't want to get hurt right?" Darius kicked Natalia's desk then hopped out of the chair.

"We done? I'm hungry."

"Darius you've just come from having lunch. Didn't you eat all of your lunch?"

"I don't like that nasty stuff. I ate the yogurt."

"Well, it's no wonder you're hungry." She shook her head and opened her draw. This pregnancy made her crave all sorts of junk. She looked down into her goodie draw and pulled out a bag of pretzels and a juice box. "Here you go. Hope this can tide you over until you get home." She passed them to him.

"Thanks." He looked at the stuff then at her. He walked out of her office and bumped into a man who was eavesdropping.

"Here you go, shorty. Get yourself something to eat after school, aiight?"

"Thanks." The kid took the ten dollar bill glanced at it to make out the amount then stuffed it in his pocket.

"Mister, why you giving me this?"

"You hungry right?"

"Yeah?"

"Aiight then get something to eat. No toys and nothing other than food, aiight?"

"Okay." Darius skipped down the hall happier than an Ethiopian with a juicy steak.

Shawn pushed in the office door and Natalia looked up from her desk in time to see him strutting in.

"What are you doing here?" she asked in astonishment.

"I'm here for you. Can I take you out so we can talk?"

"Sure."

She wanted to do cartwheels but her condition wouldn't allow it, well that and her pride. She reached down to unlock her draw to get her purse and her round tummy reminded her that there was still the matter of her being pregnant and him not knowing. She sat in the chair debating whether to get up and let him find out by seeing for himself or should she prepare him with words. She looked up at him and he looked at her.

"Oh, don't tell me you're gonna make a nigga beg?"

"No it's not that."

"Then what is it?"

"Well can we talk here?"

"Come on, this is where you work. Plus, you leave in like ten minutes right?"

"How did you know that? Oh never mind I know how. That Andy couldn't keep a secret to save his life."

Shawn came over to her desk to get a better look at her. He hadn't seen her in almost six months. Even still, he would look at their vacation videos and pictures over and over while listening to the messages she left him. He wasn't ready back then, but now as he stared in her sweet face he realized that they did belong together. He missed the hell out of her and he moved back to New York hoping they could start over.

"I missed you...a lot," he said in almost a whisper.

She smiled as tears welled up in her eyes, tears of joy. She didn't want to cry but her heart overflowed with happiness at that very moment.

"I missed you more."

"I'm such an idiot. I don't know what I was thinking, daddy. I'm so sorry."

"You're not the only one who did dumb shit. I don't even want to talk about that shit. I just wanted to see where your head is. Do you think you can overlook all the shit I did and not feel like you gotta get back at me?"

"Yes." She rubbed the side of her face in his hand like a purring kitty.

"Do you believe that I'm not going to fuck around on you no more?"

"Is that what you're telling me? Can you be faithful, daddy?"

Shawn removed his hand from her face. "There you go starting. I'm asking you do you believe me when I say that. I love you like I've never loved any other woman on this fuckin' planet. You see it. If you don't see it then you're blind. You fucked my brother and I'm still willing to be with you."

"You're still willing to be with me? Oh, that's just great Shawn. So I see that you're going to throw that in my face every day all day." She sighed and shook her head disappointingly. "So, you coming here is like a charity run? You feel sorry for me so you've come to rescue me? I don't need you to do that. So, you can stop feeling bad. You've made you're honorable gesture and now you may go."

She grabbed a case folder from her desk opened her top drawer and slammed it in it. It didn't matter that the folder didn't belong in that drawer. Then as if she didn't have enough to deal with the baby karate kicked her bladder, making her have to pee.

"Damn it!" she slammed her hand down on the table. Hormones and reeling emotions were surging through her, making it hard for her to think clearly.

"I didn't come here to argue or bring up shit from the past. I'm here because I want you home where you belong. Don't take it there on me and start up some shit that will fuck everything up."

"Well, excuse me for feeling like you're dumping on me."

"I'm not BG. Come here and give Big Daddy a hug." He walked around the desk and tried to pull her up from the chair.

Natalia hesitantly allowed him to. He gently slipped his arms around her neck and pulled her into him.

"Damn, BG you got fatter than a mutha."

Shawn looked down and backed away from her. "Surprise!" she exclaimed with a nervous grin. "I'm pregnant."

"What?"

"I said I'm pregnant."

"Were you gonna tell me?"

"Well, yeah. I just had to um..."

"You weren't going to tell me at all were you?" his hand went to the top of his head. "I don't believe this shit." He shook his head in bewilderment. Natalia tried to hold his hand as she explained herself.

"Well, I'm sure you understand why it was so hard for me to find a way to tell you. Don't you?"

"No, maybe you can understand why I'm mad right now."

"Yes, Shawn I do. But, you never answered you're phone and you didn't even call me to find out if I was alive or dead."

"Look, I knew Andre would take good care of you. I knew that's where you had to be."

"How could you be so sure of that? What if I was homeless?"

"That would never happen."

Natalia didn't show any emotion and Shawn saw that she was serious. The situation itself was serious.

"Wait a minute, that baby could be my brother's right? Y'all ain't use nothing. SHIT!" he growled. "Fuck no. I can't deal with this shit." He paced like a mad man.

"Shawn, we don't know anything yet, please calm down, sit here." She tried to pull him towards the chair at the side of her desk. He pulled his arm away.

"That baby could be my nephew. How the hell do you expect me to raise that child when he will remind me of what y'all did?"

"I will have an abortion Shawn. That will be my sacrifice, so that we can stay together. I love you that much."

"Oh so you killing my nephew will make it alright for me and you to work things out?"

"Yes, no, I don't know. I only did it to hurt you. I wasn't thinking straight. This wasn't supposed to happen. I-I don't know how or what you want me to say."

"There's no excuse for what you did. You done fucked up my family with this shit. Now there's a baby involved. What the fuck?"

"Please just tell me how we can go on from here?" she said, wiping away a tear.

"We don't," he spat and walked out of her office.

"Shawn don't go." She followed him down the hall, wiping away the wetness from her face. She grabbed his arm and he yanked it away.

"I can't talk to you right now." He was still walking with her right on his heels openly crying in front of the children leaving their classrooms for the yard.

"Please wait. Stop walking, please." Shawn stopped looked around and noticed that people were staring.

"Look this is your work place and they're gonna talk about you and this ain't good for the kids to see so just stop following me. I can't deal with you right now aiight?"

"But, I need to know what to do. I love you and I don't want to lose you. Please Shawn don't leave me."

Shawn looked away from her teary eyes. "I can't even look at you right now. I don't know." He turned and walked away. She stood there a while longer because it felt like she was in a hallway full of molasses and her feet were sticking to the ground. Her world had come crashing down and there was no knight in shining armor to save her this time. He was fed up and when a man is fed up all hell breaks loose.

She finally realized that she could pick her feet up. She went back to her office and got her purse. She left her office and was about to lock the door with her key when her body felt like a bolt of electricity shot through it.

"Aaaarggggh!" she screamed a loud shrill that echoed throughout the hall. A teacher ran to her aid.

"What happened?"

Natalia couldn't answer because another bolt went through her.

"Hospital, please!"

She woke up in a hospital bed with her feet raised above her heart on a stack of pillows.

"What in the world?"

"Hi honey bunny." Andre smiled at her and moved a curl from her face.

"Andy the baby, the baby." She sprang up frantic.
"No, no, calm down. Lay back down. You have to relax with your feet up. The baby will be okay. They're keeping you on bed rest for a few days while they run more tests."

She sighed a heavy sigh of relief then looked around the room at all the cards and balloons.

"Oh, no not again, don't tell me I've been out for a long time."

"No silly, I bought all of that because this dreary ass hospital room looked so pitiful. I couldn't have my honey bunny waking up in Drearyville, USA." Natalia laughed.

"So, you want to tell me how this happened?"

"Shawn came to the school. I told him about the baby and we argued then he left. I chased him but he practically told me to go to hell. I've lost him Andy."

"Nat you're losing sight of what is important. My Godchild is important. As much as I like that hunk of a man you married, you need to remember that men come and go but that baby is your responsibility for life. I don't care who the daddy is you're the mother who is most important to that child's upbringing. He needs your total devotion and attention. Don't go all postal worrying over Shawn. All you need to do is let him go and if it was meant to be then he will come back to you. No man wants a needy, low, self-esteemed, begging, clingy ass fi..."

"I get it, I get it."

Andre's lecture made her feel like those women she watched on Jerry Springer. They all seemed to define their worth by the men in their lives. That was not a complementary comparison. She was strong and survived more than some would ever encounter in their lifetime. She didn't have time for self-pity with her baby in jeopardy.

"Andy I know what I must do. Thanks for putting things in perspective for me." She reached for his hand. He squeezed it lovingly.

"You lost your way just a tad bit but I knew you'd find it again."

Calling Shawn wasn't a pathetic attempt to get him back, but to inform him of her hospitalization. She wanted to let him know about the baby since he was a possible father. The phone rang twice and for some strange reason she was nervous. On the third ring she heard his smooth hello and exhaled.

"Hello?" he asked again waiting for someone to respond.

"Shawn I'm in..."

"Look, I told you I couldn't deal with you right? So don't call me with this bullshit!"

"But, I was only calling to tell you..."

"To tell me that you're sorry? You're sorry for fuckin' my brother and getting pregnant!"

"But, it could be your baby too!"

"I can't talk to you. I can't deal with this." He hung up.

Natalia looked at the phone in disbelief. "Did he just hang up on me?" She asked the air then dialed him back.

This time she got his voicemail. She had reached her boiling point and if she were a kettle she'd be whistling with steam shooting out of her ears. She slammed down the phone and let out a frustrated sigh. He really let her down. He wouldn't even let her reason with him. To make matters worse she looked down and saw blood on her hospital gown.

"NO!" she screamed. "The baby, the baby, someone help me!"

A nurse ran in and tried to calm her down. "Okay,

okay. The doctor will be in soon."

"I'm bleeding, please, get the doctor, please save my baby."

The doctor came in and told her to lay back and let him do his job. He warned her that her panic would create more havoc. That being said she did as she was told from that point on. With all the fuss going on around her she still managed to tune them out. She zoned right into her belly and kissed her baby's tiny forehead.

"Mommy's sorry. I'm gonna be strong for us now. You have to help Mommy okay?" The tiny baby was sucking on his thumb and just smiled. Natalia winked at the baby and blew a kiss.

"Count backwards from one hundred Ms. Wilson."

"Ninety-nine, ninety-eight, ninety-seven...seventy-free."

The room was blurred, faces were swirling, her body was lighter than air.

"Wait, Junior," she blurted then she faded to black.

When she opened her eyes the first thing she saw was a nurse wheeling in a see through bassinet.

"Oh," she gushed as she tried to get a better look. "My baby."

She smiled adoringly at the white and blue bundle in the bassinet. The nurse looked at her as if she were really in the loony bin.

"No Ms. Wilson." She didn't even follow that up with anything else. She just wheeled the baby right over to the woman in the next bed.

Natalia watched the new mother as she fed her baby a tiny bottle of milk. The woman looked so happy. Then Natalia noticed how pretty the woman was. For a white woman she had color to her skin and her face gave off a glow that highlighted her green eyes. Natalia admired her with her baby.

"Where's my baby?" Natalia asked as the nurse was walking out the door.

"The doctor will be in to talk to you in a few minutes." She walked out of the room. Natalia's heart began to race. *What kind of answer is that? Where's my baby?*

Her body hurt, her heart hurt and she felt like she had been dragged all over New York's pot hole ridden streets then used for a punching bag. She lay in the bed and wondered what happened to her. She didn't feel like this when she had Junior. She was only tired and sleepy. Her stomach felt tight like someone was yanking at her skin. She started pulling up her gown.

"Are you okay?"

"Yes, thank you." Natalia smiled. "What's you're son's name?"

"Mark, well actually it's Marco but we'll call him just Mark. Oh I'm Caroline Delucchio." Natalia couldn't believe her ears. What were the odds that she would end up in the same hospital with a woman who named her child after Mark and had his last name. This can't be happening, she thought to herself.

"What did you have?"

Natalia was still trying to decipher the whole coincidence thing so she couldn't answer. "Are you sure you're alright?" Caroline asked, looking more concerned now that Natalia's eyes seemed vacant.

"Oh, I'm sorry...I um don't know. I can't remember much...I..."

"Hey sweetheart," said a man whose identity was concealed by the loads of balloons and flowers he carried. Natalia watched the balloons tenaciously to see if the mystery man was Mark. She waited for the balloons to shift and reveal him. The balloons and flowers were placed on the night stand and in the chair next to it.

Geesh he's kind of old for you girl. I bet he's got money though.

The man kissed Caroline's cheek and carefully rubbed the baby's tiny bald head. He looked over at Natalia and smiled.

"Hello, where's your little tyke?"

"They haven't brought him to me yet." Natalia was jealous now and becoming more depressed by the minute. *Where is my baby?*

"Oh," the old man said, realizing that something must've went wrong if she didn't see her baby yet. He watched Caroline as she doted over her baby.

"He's beautiful honey. I'm so proud of you."

Proud? He acts as though she just got accepted into Harvard. She had a baby that's a miracle of nature not some academic achievement you old fool.

"Can I hold him?" he asked.

This just keeps getting weirder by the minute, Natalia thought. *Why would the father of the child ask to hold him?*

As Natalia was busy being nosey watching the Delucchios with their son she thought of her dilemma. Her husband wasn't there with her because there was a chance that he wasn't the child's father. He might be the uncle. She heard the word echo in her head...uncle. It sounded so sick and twisted. How could she blame Shawn for not wanting her back? Out of nowhere a revelation came. She slept with Maleek without a condom before the Tymeek disaster. *I am a Jerry Springer Show. I don't even know who the father of my child is. Better yet, Maury. I need Maury. What the hell was I thinking. Shawn is right. How can I ever explain to him?*

Finally, her doctor came in looking disheveled and worn out.

"Where's my baby?" she asked and tried to push herself up into a sitting position. He ignored her for a moment while he glanced over her chart.

"Okay...okay...alrighty then we're in business," he smiled at her.

"Excuse me doctor, but where's my baby?"

"Oh, he's in intensive care. In fact, a nurse will be taking you to him shortly. There was a risk factor so everything was done STAT. I had to do an emergency C-section."

"What?" Natalia's voice rose as well as her brow and she reached down to her stomach and felt the dressing.

"Yes, your baby was in distress and had to be delivered right away so I induced labor but I still ended up having to do the surgery. But everything is fine. Eventhough, he was weeks premature, he doing quite well. He's a fighter." Natalia was still in shock concerning the surgery part. All she could imagine was a big ugly scar on her stomach. It would take a lot of time for her to get over that. She had so much to deal with. The doctor patted her hand.

"You'll be with your baby soon."

He switched the position of the charts in his hand to where hers was now underneath Caroline's.

"Hi Caroline, I see mother and baby are doing fine."

"Yes we are." Caroline smiled at him then at her baby. The old man reached out his hand to shake the doctor's hand and the doctor shook his.

"Thank you for this healthy boy," the old man beamed.

"Don't thank me, thank this lovely lady right here." He patted her arm. Just then a man rushed in with a teddy bear and balloon.

"Oh baby he's beautiful."

Now, Natalia wanted to die. She watched Mark as Caroline passed him his son. He looked ecstatic as he rocked the baby in his arms. Natalia wanted to shrivel up and disappear, but no can do. Then it happened. He saw her. The lump in her throat would've killed her had she not swallowed hard. It was obvious that when it rained it poured.

Now, she had to deal with the embarrassment of having had a baby all on her own with her husband nowhere in sight while Mark's wife was surrounded not only by men but flowers, balloons and a freakin' teddy bear too!

Mark handed the baby back to Caroline.

"Thank you for giving me a son."

Natalia wanted to puke. She knew his adoration was real and not just for her benefit but she still wanted to regurgitate even though her stomach was empty. He bonded with his son while Caroline held him for a few minutes more. The old man hugged him then Caroline

"Thanks for stopping by Dad," Caroline told her father as they said their goodbyes.

Mark walked over to Natalia. She blew hard and expected the worst.

"Nat, I wouldn't dream of seeing you here."

"Ditto," she replied weakly.

"Well, what happened?"

"I had a baby Mark. What do you think happened?"

"Where's your baby? What did you have?"

"He was premature, but he's okay."

"A boy, huh? Well congratulations to you and Shawn?"

"Thank you?" she smiled nervously.

"Well you guys are lucky. As am I."

"Yes, congratulations to you and Caroline, we met already. She's sweet and I wish you guys the best."

"Thanks Nat," he smiled and held her hand briefly, patted it, looked into her eyes as if he could read her soul then went back to his little family closing the curtain to give himself privacy.

Natalia lay back into the pillow and listened as they shared the joy of their newborn. They reminded her of what she lost, a chance at a family.

CHAPTER TWENTY FIVE

There was nothing that she could do to prepare herself for the postpartum depression she was hit with after giving birth to Everton Gary Foles Wilson. She named him after her father. When she saw him for the first time all she could think was how adorable he was. But, after a couple of weeks passed, a resentment she'd never known built up inside her. There were days that the visiting nurse had to take over caring for Everton because Natalia was too withdrawn, even too belligerent to handle Everton.

At first, she thought it was either the pain from healing from surgery or the medications her doctor had prescribed. But, then she noticed how angry she'd get when she saw her naked reflection in a mirror. The scars made her feel ugly, undesirable, and reminisce over all her demonic battles. Everton represented a lot of pain to her.

When she was diagnosed with postpartum depression she thought her world had really come to an end. How could she not love this baby with all her heart? Was it because there stood a chance that he wasn't from the one true love of her life? The psychiatrist told her that was a definite possibility. Every day was a struggle for her. The psychiatrist prescribed her more medication but the pills sedated her into a zombie state that scared Andre and scared her even more. Week after week she prayed that her feelings would change towards little Everton.

Then one day it happened. The visiting nurse had a family emergency of her own and couldn't wait for her substitute to arrive, so she left Natalia alone with Everton. Natalia panicked and called Andre hoping that she wouldn't hurt her own child. Andre spoke to her on his cell phone the entire time while he was on his way to her new apartment. He was delicate with her feelings as he tried desperately to remind her of how much love she contained, reiterating how happy she was when she found out that she was pregnant. He even managed to coax her into bathing the baby. He remained on the phone to give her the moral support she needed while she bathed Everton. Andy was scared she might drown the poor baby, but instead she was gentle with him, loving like a mother should be.

While looking into his cute little face she realized that Everton was made out of love no matter who his father was. God had blessed her with enough love and trust to allow her to become pregnant after losing Junior. With a blessing like that how could she not appreciate her son or love him wholeheartedly? She took him out of his bathtub and wrapped him securely in a soft warm towel. She cuddled him close to her bosom and kissed his forehead then she stared into his tiny bright eyes for a moment. It was then that Everton met his mother.

She was all packed and ready to leave for the airport. Andy lugged her bags to the door of the hotel room. She was staying there for the past month due to subletting her apartment.

"You ready?" he asked before he opened the door.

She rushed out with Everton strapped to her chest.

"Ready."

She took a deep breath and blew it out. She wasn't really ready to leave New York and move all the way to St. Croix where she would have to reacquaint herself with their way of living. But, she knew that living in the states would only make her want to stalk Shawn. She loved him that much. She'd have to move far away and try to forget him, maybe even swear off men completely at least for a year or two.

It was lucky for her that Susan had called her with good news just a couple of weeks earlier. She finally got her money and all of her assets back. It couldn't have come at a better time.

Now that she was rich again she could provide Everton with the life she knew he deserved. She set up a trust fund in his name and liquidated all of her assets so that she had no more ties to New York. She would be free to travel without worrying about running any businesses.

The money saved her from a lot of humiliation. She resigned from PS893 as their psychologist. She sold the car Shawn bought her and decided to purchase a new vehicle in St. Croix.

Andre opened the door and dragged her luggage down the hall to the elevator.

"Oh, darn I forgot the baby's diaper bag."

She rushed back into the room to get it and the door slammed itself shut.

"Sorry, Andy, I'm coming."

She opened the door and Andre stood there grinning.

"What are you grinning about?" she asked suspiciously.

Andre tugged on what looked like an arm until the whole body appeared in the doorway.

"Shawn?" she asked in a mix of confusion and happiness.

She forgot about Everton and tried to hug him. When they both realized they would squish the baby if they kept trying to hug they stopped abruptly. Shawn delicately kissed her on the cheek.

"Oooh, I love it when a plan comes together," Andre said with a satisfied grin then he left the lovebirds alone.

Shawn watched Andre sprint down the hall then he took Natalia's hand.

"Listen I love you, but I don't know how to deal with this. I was talking to Ty and he suggested a paternity test.

And, if he's the father he said he'd give up his rights and let me raise him if I want to. I still don't know how to handle this, but I'm willing to try. You gotta understand though this is gonna be real hard for me."

"I know I'll try my best to make it up to you."

Her mind was going a mile a minute as she thought about what Tymeek suggested. He was right about getting a test done. She remembered when she had sex with Maleek. She couldn't remember if both times that they had sex if pulled out ahead of time or maybe she only thought he did. Even still this would be yet another heart breaking secret she'd have to reveal.

"Shawn, we need to talk but I'm supposed to be on a flight to St. Croix in two hours."

"What? You're leaving without knowing if that's my baby or not?"

"I thought you didn't care about us so I made the decision to leave. You wouldn't answer my calls or return them. When we last spoke you practically told me to get lost! You haven't seen me since God knows when. You didn't even try to contact me or anything. I can't take being here without you, so I decided to leave."

"You're kidding me right? You telling me that you were gonna move thousands of fuckin' miles away with our kid and not say shit to nobody?"

"Shawn, please, you haven't been here. Stop blaming me for every little thing. Besides you thought it wasn't yours and we don't know if it is, look Shawn you don't understand what I'm dealing with. I know I fucked up and I did something disgusting and horrible that I will have to live with for the rest of my life. Everyday I look at my son and I will remember my mistake if he is Tymeek's or..."

She decided it best not to even mention Maleek. God knows he'd definitely storm away from her and she didn't want that.

"Get the fuck outta here. I don't believe this shit. It wouldn't be a mistake if it was mine, so you saying there's another nigga involved?"

It clicked in his head at that moment that the baby might be Maleek's. He killed Maleek and now there was a chance that he would be raising his kid while forcing him to relive his regretful mistake. He couldn't explain how angry he was to hear that Maleek was a possible father to her child.

"Shawn, I told you I wanted to talk to you but you blew me off so many times and I never got the chance to explain."

"Damn BG it's like that? You turned into a real fuckin' ho, huh? Damn girl."

"I did my dirt and shit but, you doing that to your body BG, that's nasty. So how many other niggas have to get tested? Ten more?" he asked sarcastically.

"Fuck you Shawn! I'm not going to stand here and let you turn this around on me when you're the one who did foul shit too! Everything in my life turned to shit when I met you. You know what? I'm not wasting my breath or my love on you anymore. Fuck it all and most of all fuck you!"

She stomped past him, sobbing. For a moment Shawn didn't feel like stopping her but then flashes of everything they had ever gone through or shared compelled him to chase her. He caught up to her and grabbed her by the arm.

"We're both in the wrong but no matter what we always find our way back to each other. I can't explain why I love you like this Nay-Nay."

"You called me Nay-Nay."

She smiled as tears slid down her cheeks. He hadn't called her that nickname in so long. She remembered the day he gave her that nickname. She remembered how no matter how many times their relationship went awry somehow just as he said they found their way home to each other and healed together. There had to be something to their love that kept them together through it all.

"You're still my Nay-Nay and you always will be." He caressed the side of her face lovingly. She returned the adoration. He didn't want to argue. He just wanted her to stay. "All I know is that I miss you so much and now I'm not even mad at you like I used to be. I just needed time, don't leave me Nay, I don't know if I'll be able to handle that. Besides we're starting with a clean slate now, OK?"

She didn't want to leave. She just wanted to forget all of the anger and pain and the past. She wanted to start over and make it work this time. She wanted their lives to go back to the way it was the day she first knew deep down that she loved him. She wished she could erase the shame she felt. She hoped that Shawn could somehow get past what she'd done. She was positive that she could get past his indiscretions and love him as she always had, unconditionally.

"Okay, then I have no choice but to stay. I can't leave my daddy hanging."

He kissed her forehead then looked at baby Everton who slept quietly against his mother's lulling chest. He gently rubbed Everton's small head then kissed it and slipped his arm around Natalia's back.

"He's got to be mine. He looks just like my baby pictures."

Natalia smiled up at him as they left the building and asked

"So what's the destination this time Daddy?"

"Home, baby girl, home. Just you, me and our baby. I don't even want that test. It doesn't matter to me anymore. I've had enough of all this crazy shit. We're going home to be some regular folks from now on you understand? All that extra shit is over with you hear me?"

"I hear you Mr. Wilson."

"Good, cause we're gonna start over and we're going to start acting proper, join the P.T.A. and shit, ya feel me?"

"I feel you son, nahmean?" Natalia laughed so hard, the laughter echoed in her chest and woke up the baby.

Andre threw Natalia's bags into the trunk of Shawn's truck. As they all got in Andre pointed towards the windshield.

"Look at that! The sun is setting, look at the colors. How nice? It's just perfect for this occasion."

With that said, just like the ending of any sweet fairy tale they drove off into the sunset, in a sparkling money green Escalade sittin' on dubs.

THE END.

IN STORES NOW

True to the Game;

B-More Careful;

The Adventures of Ghetto Sam;

Dutch;

Triangle of Sins;

Tell Me Your Name;

Dutch II;

Deadly Reigns; and

Double Dose.

265

ORDER FORM
TERI WOODS PUBLISHING
P.O. BOX 20069
NEW YORK, NY 10001
(212) 252-8445
www.teriwoodspublishing.com

RECTANGLE OF SINS $14.95	
Shipping /Handling (Via U.S. Priority Mail)	3.85
TOTAL	$18.80

PURCHASER INFORMATION

Name: _____

Reg. #: _____
(Applies if incarcerated)

Address:_____

_____

City: _____ State: ___

Zip Code: _____

HOW MANY BOOKS? _____

For orders being shipped directly to inmates the costs are as follows:

RECTANGLE OF SINS:	$ 11.21
Shipping and Handling	$ 3.85
TOTAL :	$15.06

True to the Game, B-More Careful, Dutch, Deadly Reigns, Dutch II, Triangle of Sins, Tell Me Your Name, Adventures of Ghetto Sam, and Double Dose are all the same price.